THE GIRL WHO STOPPED WEARING CLOTHES

D.H. Jonathan

Naturale Publishing
Fort Worth, TX

Front cover: "Persistence" Oil on canvas, 60" x 48" by Jess Tedder, 2022

Cover design by M.H.Pasindu Lakshan

Visit the author's website at www.dhjonathan.com

First Edition

ISBN: 978-1-7330908-1-0

For Jake Drake who was a huge fan of *The "Volunteer"* and was a big help in getting *Life Models* ready for publication. His untimely passing makes me wish I had finished *The Girl Who Stopped Wearing Clothes* sooner. Rest In Peace, Jake.

1

Adam

Los Angeles is full of girls willing to take their clothes off on camera for a part in a movie or television show, hoping it would lead to a shot at fame and fortune, but Adam Munch drove out to Palm Desert just to meet a particular naked girl anyway. She was known as Naked Dani, and he had, of course, seen the news reports about her over the past few months and had watched her live appearance on *Stossel* when it aired. But he had been in the film and television production business long enough to know how staged even the news could be. Sure, they had gotten footage of her walking naked through the campus, and she had been naked for the *Stossel* show. But was that much different than the nude-in-public videos that were shot in Europe and marketed as soft porn on the web? Surely, she wasn't naked twenty-four hours a day seven days a week as was being claimed. First of all, how could she legally get away with it? And wasn't she leaving herself vulnerable to all kinds of attacks: verbal, physical, and sexual?

By chance, Adam had found an advance reader copy of her upcoming memoir *The "Volunteer"* at a book festival in LA. He read the entire book in one day, and her story resonated with him. Adam was especially intrigued by her philosophy of combating sexualization of the body in pornography and mainstream media by going about casually nude. He was also fascinated by her religious upbringing and her desire to go to church services even in her undressed state. The ideas started turning, so the first thing he did was contact the girl's literary agent, Audrey Lambert, to inquire about film and television rights. Those had not been optioned yet, but two other producers had inquired about them. Adam had asked for a meeting with both Audrey and the girl. Audrey had referred him to a publicist at the girl's school, Coachella Valley University, since any such meeting would have to take place on campus due to her constant state of nudity.

The meeting was to take place on the fourth floor of the main administration building which Adam found with minimal difficulty after the security officer at the campus entrance gave him a map and directions along with the visitor parking pass. Adam rode the elevator to the fourth floor and found the room number he had been given, a conference room with a clear glass wall facing the corridor and large window overlooking most of the campus. The room was empty since Adam was almost twenty minutes early. He set his briefcase down on the table and stood at the window watching the foot traffic below. Seeing Naked Dani down there without a stitch of clothing in the middle of everybody was jarring even after seeing the news reports and reading her book. Two women in business attire walked on either side of her. Adam recognized Audrey Lambert, the agent. He had met her before and, remembering the name, had researched her before calling her to ask about the film rights to *The "Volunteer"*. The other woman had to be Sylvia Smith, the university's publicist. The three of them were heading toward the administration building, each with a Starbucks cup in hand.

Adam watched the rest of the people walking to and fro. Those walking the opposite direction seemed to be nodding or saying something in greeting to the naked girl, but only one or two of them took a look back at her once they had passed. Adam was surprised to see how many people seemed to take no note of Naked Dani at all. Had seeing her naked and out and about on campus really become so commonplace? According to her book, she had started going naked right after spring break. It was now early October. She'd been doing this for seven months, minus the time spent back home away from campus.

Adam watched the three women until they disappeared from sight at the foot of the building below him. He turned away from the window and opened his briefcase to make sure his written questions were still there on top of everything else. They were, so he closed the briefcase without latching it shut. He sat down and tried to look casually comfortable as they came into view in the hallway next to the conference room's glass wall. The three of them walked in talking and laughing but quieted when they saw Adam stand to his feet.

"Hello, I'm Adam Munch from Munchie Productions."

"Oh my gosh, I'm so sorry we weren't here to greet you," said the woman he didn't recognize. She stepped forward and offered her hand. "I'm Sylvia Smith with Coachella Valley University."

Adam shook her hand. "Pleased to meet you."

The other dressed woman offered her hand and said, "Audrey Lambert. We spoke on the phone."

"Yes, we've met before. About two years ago, I think. You were representing Claudia Coker."

"Ah yes. I remember you now. I'm sorry that project didn't work out for you."

Adam shrugged. "She seems to have found something better."

"Yes, she did."

"Hopefully, we can work out something here."

"I hope so," Audrey said.

The nude girl stepped forward, about twenty-one years old and darkly tanned from a summer in the desert sun. Adam reminded himself to maintain eye contact no matter how much the shapely bare breasts hovered just at the edge of his field of vision.

"I'm Dani Keaton," she said, smiling.

"Adam. Please, call me Adam."

The four of them stood beside the table for an awkward moment, as Adam marveled at how poised Dani seemed. She didn't appear to be in the least self-conscious about her nudity.

"Thank you for meeting with me today," he said to try to break the ice.

"Thank you for coming all this way," Sylvia offered.

Audrey was already walking around the table to take a seat on the other side, and Dani followed her.

"Why don't we all sit down, and I'll go over my proposal," Adam suggested.

They all sat, and Adam couldn't help but notice that Dani's bare breasts were visible through the glass wall to anyone who happened to walk by in the corridor. Her brown hair was long enough to touch her shoulders but not long enough to cover anything below that. Adam pulled the worn copy of *The "Volunteer"* from his briefcase and set it on the table.

"Let's talk about your book first," he said.

"OK," Dani said before either of the other two women could respond.

"It ends in June, and we've only gotten to October. That's a really fast turnaround."

"Yeah," Dani replied. "I wrote almost all of the first two-thirds when I was at home between the spring semester and summer session. And it didn't take long to write the stuff that happened in May and June."

"And it's a true memoir? You didn't make any of it up?"

"No, everything in the book is true. I had to leave a lot of stuff out of course. That project did run two months, and I didn't want to give a day-by-day account of all sixty days."

"Well sure," Adam replied. "No one could have included everything." He checked the questions he wrote on his notepad. "Is there anything you left out that you wish you had included?"

"Oh yeah," Dani said. "When I got home, my friend Samantha and I had a long talk about the project."

"The nudity project?" Adam interrupted.

"Yes. I told her that I was glad it had ended, but not. If you know what I mean. She really is my best friend, so she agreed to arrange a few scenarios where I could be naked. I even wrote it that way the first time."

"Her editor thought the scenes back in Texas might read better if there was someone to root against," Audrey said.

"Yeah," Dani agreed. "I rewrote them and kind of made Samantha look like a bad guy. But really, the swim party and everything was pre-arranged. She wasn't being mean; she was doing what I wanted her to. I did put in the book that she agreed to go to that nudist resort with me after that. I tried to make it clear that we were still friends and just hoped that people could, you know, read between the lines."

Adam was busy writing notes on his pad before stopping and looking in his briefcase.

"Would you mind if I took video of the rest of this meeting?" he asked.

"What for?" Audrey said.

Adam held up his pen. "So I don't have to take as many notes, for one. And for another, I want to see how Dani looks when talking on camera."

"Why would that be important?"

"I'll get to that."

Dani and Audrey looked at each other, and Dani shrugged. "Sure, I don't mind."

Adam took a small camcorder from his briefcase and set it on the table pointed at Dani. Once he made sure it was running with Dani in the frame from the shoulders up, he resumed questioning.

"Has your friend Samantha read the book?"

"Not yet. I'm waiting to get a final copy to give her. I did tell her that it kind of made her look mean."

"Did she seem upset when you told her about how she might come across in the book?"

Dani shook her head. "I don't think so."

"Audrey said your editor wanted readers to have someone to root against. That would be this Dr. Slater for most of the book. What can you tell me about her? Was this sociology project of hers serious?"

"It was," Dani nodded.

"Her first article on the project will be published in *Cultural Sociology Journal* next month," Sylvia said.

"Is she still collecting data?" Adam asked. "Since you are still going nude?"

Dani shrugged. "Probably. They have all those ultra-high def cameras everywhere on campus."

"Why did you continue going naked? You said in the book that you did it to save Dr. Slater's project, along with her job. Was that the reason?"

"No, not really. It's complicated. I just know that for two months, I was special. Everyone looked at me everywhere I went. People treated me like a rock star or something. And when I put clothes on after the semester ended, I was like everyone else. Just another face in the crowd. A nobody."

Adam was nodding, not because he was agreeing but because he was trying to get her to open up and keep talking.

"So when I was back here on campus after the break," she continued, "I realized that I still had that opportunity to stand out from the crowd, and that if I didn't continue taking it while I could, then I would probably regret it when I didn't even have the chance anymore. Do you know what I mean?"

When Dani paused, Adam looked down at his list of pre-written questions and closed the tablet.

"I think I do," Adam said. "Now, I hope you don't take this the wrong way, but is there an element of sexual excitement by going nude all the time?"

Dani shook her head. "No, not really. I think it would be if I only went naked just every once in a while. But going like this all the time, it just becomes a part of who I am."

"But in the book," Adam said, picking it up and thumbing through some pages, "you talk about feeling aroused and at one point having to duck into the Science Building just to find a bathroom and give yourself some relief."

Dani's face blushed a deep red. "Well, that was my editor again. He wanted to play up the sex. He told me that people would want a read like *50 Shades of Grey* or something. Said it would sell more copies. The only problem was, I wasn't sexually active."

"So those parts aren't true?"

"Oh no, they're true. That was the only 'erotic content' I could honestly put into the book," Dani said, making air quotes with her fingers as she said the words erotic content. "Like I said, it was very important to me to not write anything that didn't happen or wasn't honest. And there was an adjustment period to the project. When you've been told all your life that your body is impure and has to be covered, and then you're told you have to go naked everywhere, that ingrained belief in its impurity becomes almost self-fulfilling. If you know what I mean. So yes, I felt sexually aroused by my nudity at the beginning. That gradually wore off as I got more used to it. And that time in the Science Building; yeah, that did happen. I wrote it and hated what I had written, but my editor insisted that I keep it in."

Adam nodded as he watched Dani talk on the viewfinder screen on his camcorder, containing his excitement as he realized his idea might actually work. The three women in the room would just have to buy into it.

"Ok," he said. "I came to talk about film and TV rights, so let me tell you my proposal. I don't think a movie adaptation of the book will work."

The surprised looks on all three faces almost made Adam laugh, but he held back.

"Why not?" Dani asked.

"A lot of reasons. Number one, there's a lack of external conflict. The appeal of the book is you telling your story, what you are feeling. That's all internal conflict and very difficult to portray onscreen. It would take a hell of an actress to pull it off. Which brings me to another issue, casting. I don't know of any A-list actress who would take the role because of the constant nudity. And without a big name in that role, it would be relegated to the low budget B movie bin. And without that strong external conflict, it would just be seen as a naked girl running around."

"So why are you interested in the book?" Audrey asked.

"Because of Dani here. The main reason a movie wouldn't work is because it wouldn't have her. It would, presumably, only be an actress playing her. People have seen her on the web or on TV. I think that's what people want to see. What I want to propose is a reality TV series. Short episodes, maybe only a half hour each, focused on Dani going about her normal day-to-day life interspersed with shots of Dani sitting down in front of a camera talking about her philosophy like she was just doing."

"A reality series?" Audrey asked.

"Exactly. Some successful television shows have been reality series. And Dani's story and situation are very compelling. People are interested in it. I think they'll watch it."

"They'll watch it just to see a pretty naked girl," Audrey said.

"And they'll keep watching because of Dani's personality and outlook on life. She's positive and has something that people will respond to. That's why I wanted to come out here for a meeting rather than do business over the phone like every other project I've worked on. I needed to meet her and see how she talks when the camera is running. And these past few minutes have convinced me."

Dani looked at Audrey, and Adam could tell they really wanted to talk about things. He could also tell that Dani was really excited about the proposal.

"So you don't want to option the film rights of her book?" Audrey asked.

"Like I said, I don't think a film adaptation would work. But if we move forward on a reality series, that's going to keep others from optioning it."

Audrey looked at Dani. "What do you think? It's you who would be the focus of this reality series? Do you think you are ready for the spotlight?"

"I've already been in that spotlight since the experiment started," she said with a shrug of her bare shoulders, "and especially since that *Stossel* show."

Audrey was still looking at Dani with questioning eyes.

"What would you need from us right now?" she asked Adam.

"Well, I don't have the funding to shoot a pilot right now. I'll be meeting with someone at Netflix this week to try to secure that. I have a friend on their review board. If I can't sell it there, I'm probably not going to be able to sell it anywhere else either."

Adam took two copies of a printed contract from his briefcase and slid them toward Audrey and Dani. "That's a two-week option agreement. I pay you five hundred dollars for exclusive rights to your story, including the book, for two weeks. If I can't get a deal with Netflix, you keep the five hundred, and you're free to option the book to anyone else. If I do get a deal, we start production on a pilot episode this month. I'm proposing that you, Dani, get paid ten thousand per episode to start. It's all in there."

Audrey was already reading the agreement. Dani just stared at it as if in a daze.

"Five hundred dollars for two weeks," Audrey mused.

"Yes," Adam said. "I'm betting my own money that Netflix will go for it. If not, you're not out anything. The book won't even be out then, so you'd be free to negotiate with anyone else. But if Netflix does go for it, we could get a pilot episode together before the book comes out. The marketing of both the show and the book could be tied together."

Everyone looked at Dani.

"What do you think?" Audrey asked. "You would be putting yourself out there in a way that no one has ever done before."

Adam couldn't help but see Dani's eyes shine as she smiled, and he knew she would say yes. This Dr. Slater really hit the jackpot by finding her, a latent exhibitionist, to use in her study on reactions to nudity.

"Like I said, I've already had the spotlight on me for the last few months. I don't see a downside to this."

Audrey looked to Silvia. "How will the university feel about a film crew following Dani around?"

"Dani has been huge for this university. Our enrollments are hitting new records. If Dani wants to do this, then I don't see how the university could refuse any reasonable accommodation."

"The crew would be small," Adam said, to reassure Silvia of the reasonableness of any future requests, "just me, a sound guy, and lighting guy. We'll have a makeup artist set up somewhere before each shoot. But other than that, this will be a small, inexpensive production. Especially since we'd be confined to campus. That's why I think Netflix will go for it."

"Actually," Silvia said, "you wouldn't be entirely restricted to the campus."

"How is that?" Adam asked.

"We have arrangements with Deal's grocery store, Mary Ellen's bar, and a Denny's in Palm Springs. Dani is as free to be nude there as she is anywhere on campus."

"Really," Adam said. "Those businesses just let her walk on in?"

Silvia shrugged. "Fame has its advantages. And Dani is usually a big hit wherever she goes. The Denny's is the same one we went to after the Coachella Music Festival. They called me a couple of days later and made it clear that Dani, Naked Dani, was welcome back any time."

Despite the video camera still running, Adam wrote down the three off-campus locations. They would have to take advantage of all of them during a full season of shows, if the project got that far.

"How is she going to get to these places?" he asked.

"The university has a pool of vehicles," Silvia replied. "We can appropriate an older one for the show if we need to."

"Awesome!"

"Are you sure you want to do this?" Audrey asked Dani.

"Yes," she answered, looking at Adam's camcorder as she spoke. "Absolutely."

"OK," Audrey said, motioning toward Adam to see the contract.

He slid it over to her, unable to hide his smile.

2

Dani

Danielle Keaton went straight from her meeting with the TV producer to an art class where she was scheduled to model. That meeting had lasted longer than she had expected, and she'd had to apologize and leave right after signing the contract. She arrived at the art studio three minutes before the scheduled start of class. She did her short gesture poses, one to two minutes each during which she spent her time trying to come up with the next pose. After ten of those, she finally settled into a standing pose with one arm holding a pole that would last for at least twenty minutes. Dani always enjoyed this time of solitude. And it was solitude even though she was the center of attention in a room of fifteen or more people. Nobody talked to her, and she didn't talk to anyone else. She could be alone with her thoughts.

Those thoughts naturally turned to the prospect of starring in a reality series that would be seen all over North America and maybe even the world. She viewed her participation in Dr. Slater's nudity study as her liberation. She had been freed from the idea that everyone had to wear clothes all the time. That so few other people on campus followed her example was something that still perplexed her.

Society had conditioned certain expectations into people, and one of those expectations was that you wore clothes when interacting with others. Dani knew that. She had been subject to that conditioning herself. The Nudity Project, as she thought of it, was not something she ever would have considered had she not been coerced into it. Her world had been about to crash down on her because of a stupid, selfish mistake, and Dr. Slater had offered her a way out. That the sociology professor had manipulated the severity of her circumstances was not something she found out about until after the project had officially ended. But by that point, Dani was too enamored of her ability to be nude in public to even be angry at her. Instead, Dani forgave Dr. Slater and committed to an even longer period of public nudity even though there was no one to hold her to it.

Perhaps this new reality show would encourage others to strip down and go nude in more places, especially here at Coachella Valley University. Dani had become a celebrity all over the valley and even throughout Southern California. This reality series, if it got off the ground, would expand that to the rest of the continent. The butterflies in Dani's stomach fluttered, and if she hadn't been in a pose in an art class, she would have been bouncing all over the room. She wanted to tell someone about the show, but she realized with some chagrin that she didn't have any close friends on campus.

A few months earlier, she would have gone running to Greg with the news. Dani fought off a pang of resentment as she thought of him. She should have known it wasn't going to work when she first went out with him. He was in his final semester of work on his PhD after all.

Greg had just returned from a trip where he had interviewed for positions at three different universities. Dani was one of the few people taking classes over the summer session. The campus was almost a ghost town. Not many classes were offered over the summer because most students didn't want to stay and endure the extreme heat of the desert. He had texted her while she was in a literature class, asking her to meet him at the deli in the Student Union Building. At the time, she hadn't seen him for a week, and she had to force herself to remain in her seat for the rest of the class. People who sneak out of class early are almost always noticed by everyone in the room; naked people who sneak out early are noticed even more.

Greg was sitting alone at a corner table when Dani finally made it to the deli. At the time, she was too excited to see him to notice that his eyes didn't light up like they usually did when he saw her. A hush fell over the deli as the naked girl walked in. By this time, she was used to these moments of stunned silence, and she wondered when the people on campus would be used to seeing her.

Greg stood up as she got to the table, and she threw her arms around his shoulders.

"Hey there," he said, putting his hands on her shoulders but not, Dani would think later, returning her embrace.

She kissed him, stopping only when she felt the eyes of the others in the deli looking at them.

"I missed you," Greg said.

"I missed you too. How was your trip?"

They sat down, Dani pausing to put the little towel she carried in her hand purse down on the chair before she put her bare bottom on it.

"It was great," Greg said. "We should order though. What do you want?"

"I don't know," Dani replied. She remembered that, before his somewhat cold greeting, she had felt like flirting with him. "Why don't you surprise me."

"OK," he said and got up to go to the counter and place their order.

Dani watched him go, wondering why he didn't seem like his usual self. He said nothing when he sat back down with their drinks, a Diet Coke for him and a Sprite Zero for her, and Dani had to prompt him.

"Where all did you go?"

He paused for a moment before answering. "Los Angeles."

"I knew that. Where else?"

"Chicago and Austin."

"Texas? Awesome!"

"Yeah. I really liked Chicago though. I finally got to go to a game at Wrigley Field. Always wanted to do that."

The lady at the counter called out a number, and Greg got up to retrieve their tray. "That's us," he said as he walked away.

It was then that Dani got her first sense of foreboding, that something was not only not right but just downright wrong. She had tried to ignore it, but it remained even after Greg sat down and slid a tuna salad sandwich toward her.

"Well, there's not an easy way to say this," he said after they had each taken a couple of bites, "so I'm just going to come out with it. DePaul University offered me an assistant professor position."

"DePaul? Where is that?"

"Chicago."

"Chicago," Dani repeated. "What about Pepperdine or USC? Didn't you interview with them?"

"I did. I haven't heard from them though."

"Well, are they still thinking about it?"

"Dani, I'm going to take the DePaul job."

"Oh." Dani took a drink of her Sprite Zero. She had known Greg had been interviewing, of course. That was why he had been out of town. He had successfully defended his dissertation during her trip home between the spring semester and summer session. His Doctor of Philosophy degree would be officially conferred during the university's August commencement a couple of weeks from then. He had said that he had applied to colleges in the region, but his job search had apparently extended beyond that.

"I'll be teaching courses this fall," Greg said, just to highlight the immediacy of the situation.

Dani, stunned, merely nodded. She felt an aching pressure in her chest. Chicago sounded like a million miles away. Still, this was the twenty-first century. Long distances were not same as they used to be. Dani and Greg could communicate on social media and FaceTime.

"When do you leave?" she asked.

"Next week."

"Oh wow. Well, I'm glad I got that laptop then." She had retired her old desktop and bought a new MacBook with the advance from her book.

Greg looked into his drink cup and said, "I think we should take a break."

"A break?"

"Yeah. I'm not going to be any good at the long-distance romance thing. I need somebody with me, physically. You know?"

Dani felt like she was being pulled down by an invisible weight.

"What have we been doing these past three months?" she asked.

"I like you. I like you a lot." His gaze remained on the top of his drink.

"Look at me," Dani said.

He seemed to have to force himself to look at her. "I'm going to have to make a life in Chicago. And you're going to be here. It's just better if we go our separate ways."

Dani started to say something else, but the words seemed to constrict her throat. She looked around at the people in the deli. Only two of them appeared to be paying any attention to her, but as long as she was naked in public, she still felt like all eyes were on her whenever she wasn't looking at them. And in her sadness and hurt, she felt angry at Greg for doing this, breaking up with her, in public when he also knew that she would be a spectacle just from her appearance. Afraid that trying to speak would prompt a crying fit in front of God and everybody, she stood up without a word, grabbed her hand purse from the table and her little black cloth from her chair, and walked out of the deli.

"Dani," she heard him say, "wait!"

He had stood up and tried to reach for her arm as she walked past, but she snatched it away from him. There was a unisex restroom in the building just around the corner from the deli, a "one-seater" her father had always called restrooms like that, and she thought she could lock herself inside and have a moment of privacy. But when she rounded the corner, she saw someone waiting outside the door, so she put her head down and marched outside, almost running into a couple of students who had just walked in and slowed down to relish the air conditioning of the student union.

And that had been that. Dani had gone on national television on *Stossel* and proclaimed her virginity and then had given that virginity to Greg just a few weeks later. She never would have done that if she had suspected that they were not in a long-term relationship. What had it been to him, just a summer fling? One more notch on his bedpost? She had wanted to throw up. In spite of all the things she had wanted to say to him, she never said another word. If he wanted to talk to her, he could call her. He had her number. But he didn't call or text. Dani walked by his place a week after that and saw a U-Haul truck parked outside his side of the duplex in which he lived.

Now, standing nude on a platform as sixteen art students drew her, she thought back to that first time she had seen Greg. He had been talking to the sociology department secretary as she went into an empty office to take off her clothes, that insane day that the nudity experiment had started. Greg had volunteered for the first shift, following her around and recording everyone's reactions to her naked body. Dani had been so frightened and embarrassed, doing things that she couldn't even have imagined just an hour before, and Greg had been so kind, patient and caring, that it seems little wonder that she would have developed a crush on him.

Her current situation in the art class mirrored her entire life at Coachella Valley University for the past seven months, naked in the middle of everyone but separated. It this case, it was the model stand and the model-student dynamic that separated her. In general life, she felt she had to keep herself distanced from everyone. Whenever someone tried to engage her, she could never tell what their real motives were. Did they just want to be close to her because she was somewhat famous? Did they think she might be an easy sexual partner? Or were they just envious that she was so free? With Greg, she thought she had found someone who loved the real her, but even that was a lie. The people she used to hang with before she got involved with Dr. Slater's nudity project had shunned her when they saw her naked the first time. Most of them had apologized for that, but she still felt that she had to keep them at arm's length.

The result was that she had no one to share the news about the reality show with. And she was almost bursting to tell someone. She glanced at the clock, just visible in her peripheral vision. There were still ten minutes left in the pose and then another two hours left in the class. But after that, she would have to call Samantha back home in Texas and tell her about the meeting with the TV producer.

3

Michael

Michael Cooley stood looking at himself in the full-length mirror on the outside of his dorm room's closet door. He wore nothing except a Los Angeles Dodgers baseball cap, something he hoped would keep the desert sun out of his eyes. And since everyone who knew him knew he was a devout San Diego Padres fan and therefore hated the Dodgers, he also hoped that the hat along with the sunglasses he was about to put on would help disguise his identity. The university had cameras all over campus, and because of all the stories about Naked Dani, Michael knew that they were 4K UHD cameras. He knew he would be seen and that he might even be recognized by campus authorities. That would be all right since Dani had proven for the past five months that walking around on campus in one's birthday suit was legal, although it was still hard to imagine doing it in front of a campus police officer. Michael just didn't want word of this little adventure reaching his mother. She could be a bit overbearing and hypercritical.

When Michael had arrived on campus after the summer break for his third year here, his mother had followed him in her car for the entire two hour drive and had insisted on helping him move into his dorm, even though he brought only one large suitcase full of clothes, his television and PlayStation4 console, his laptop computer, and one box of miscellaneous items: movie and game discs, phone and laptop chargers, a surge protector, and paper and pens. Once they had gotten everything put away, his mother had hung around in the room for forty-five minutes until she finally asked Michael to give her a tour of the campus.

"Now?" he had said. "It's like a hundred and ten outside."

"I want to see where you have been spending your days here," she replied. "And a little dry desert heat never hurt anyone."

But once they had gotten outside, she had immediately started fanning herself with a copy of a church worship service guide she found in her purse, which had probably been there since the previous Easter. Michael took her to the Student Union Building and to each building where he'd had classes the previous semester. But Mom had seemed more interested in looking at the passersby than at anything he was showing her, and Michael thought he knew what, or whom, she was looking for. The day after the live *Stossel* episode that had been shot on campus aired, she had called him asking if he knew "the naked harlot". He told her no, and that had been accurate. He didn't really know Dani, but they had met on the first day of her nudity study. Dani had looked frightened and embarrassed, and Michael had thought for a few moments that she might need to throw up. He had offered her some words of encouragement and that had seemed to cheer her up.

Thankfully, his mother had not caught even a glimpse of Naked Dani's bare flesh even though Michael knew she had to be on the campus somewhere. It was common knowledge that she had taken classes throughout the summer session despite the brutal heat in the valley. It had been after six PM when Mom had finally, mercifully, left, and Michael knew that it had only been her reluctance to drive after dark that had pulled her away.

Michael had, of course, seen Dani several times since that first day. Everyone on campus had. But he had never spoken to her again. For a while, she always had at least one of those graduate assistants always around her, recording everything. It would just be his luck if his mother ever saw a video of him talking to her. Since the scandalous hearing at the beginning of summer, where it was proven that the dean of the sociology department along with the former president of the university had manipulated academic punishments in order to coerce volunteers for her nudity study, Dani had seemed like a celebrity. Whenever he had seen her during the current fall semester, she always had someone with her, talking to her about something.

In all the time since that first day Michael had seen Dani without her clothes in public, he had wondered what it felt like to be so naked and exposed to everyone and everything. How had Dani gotten so used to it that she was now doing it of her own accord, even after the nudity study had supposedly ended? There had to be something about it. And so Michael stood at the mirror, looking at his own body and contemplating what he was about to do. If he were going to go out like this, it would have to be soon, and today was as good a day as any. He had just gotten word that he had been hired as the resident assistant for this floor of his dorm, beginning next January when the spring semester started. He couldn't very well hold such a position of responsibility while also walking around campus in his birthday suit.

Michael took a closer look at himself in the mirror. The hat hid the dishevelment of his dark brown hair. The acne scars on his cheeks had faded a bit since he graduated from high school, but they were still there. His neck was so long and thin that his Adam's apple jutted out and moved up and down like a dribbled basketball with each swallow.

From the neck down though, he was more impressed with himself. Being a full-time student gave him access to the campus fitness center, and he took advantage of that after his first encounter with Naked Dani. Having been a skinny nerd in high school, he had felt embarrassed at the low weight he lifted when he first started exercising, and the soreness after those early workouts was almost enough to make him quit. It took him a couple of weeks to realize that no one was paying attention to how much weight he used, and he could concentrate on the exercises themselves. The post-workout soreness, which was always worse the second day after, eventually eased up enough to allow him to keep going. Now, his deltoids and pectoral muscles were larger and more defined than they had ever been, and his tall, thin frame made them that much more noticeable. His belly was flat, but he had never been able to get rid of enough body fat to see the six-pack shape he hoped for. Still, his body was lean enough that he could see a pronounced V shape to his abdomen, the bottom of which was hidden by his pubic hair.

Michael's legs had good size and definition. As a fan of the Marvel Comics character The Incredible Hulk, he followed Lou Ferrigno on Facebook and Instagram, and Lou was always emphasizing leg day in his posts. But it was the sight of his own genitals that jarred Michael the most. Long and thin with a visible bulbous head thanks to his circumcision, his penis hung between his legs like a venomous snake emerging from its hiding place in the weed-like pubic hair. His scrotum was pulled up tight and barely visible in the overworked air conditioning of the dorm room. How could he be contemplating going outside with that visible? It was obscene. No, Michael had to remind himself, people are only taught that it was obscene. How could something that roughly half the population possessed be considered, in and of itself, so taboo that it could not be seen?

After six months of nudity, no one seemed to think that any part of Naked Dani's body was obscene. Michael remembered the first time he had watched Dani's appearance on *Stossel*. He hadn't been able to get a ticket to the studio, so he had watched it as it aired on the television in his dorm room. They had showed video from the university cameras, and John Stossel had said it was from the first day of the nudity project. Michael had held his breath, both hoping that they wouldn't show footage of him talking to Dani that his mother might see and wishing that he didn't have to worry about such things. In the clip that had been broadcast, Dani was walking by herself across the Commons, the large grassy area in front of the library between two rows of buildings. The reactions of the passersby ranged from disbelieving, almost comical, double takes and stares of astonishment to looking away and seeming to pretend that they didn't see what they had just seen.

And now, looking at himself in the mirror, Michael wondered what the reactions would be to the sight of him and this appendage that Dani did not have. There was only one way to find out.

He stepped away from the mirror and sprayed a liberal dose of sunscreen all over his body. After putting his sunglasses on and slipping his feet into a pair of sandals, he took another look at himself in the mirror. The sunscreen made his body seem to glow, something that could only attract even more attention to himself. It couldn't be helped though; he didn't want to get a sunburn.

Michael didn't have a pocket or a bag, so he would just have to carry his keys loose along with his cell phone. He didn't want to leave his dorm room unlocked, and he sure didn't want to lock himself out while naked. Opening the door, he peeked outside into the corridor before telling himself that he shouldn't be so tentative. If he was really going to do this, he should just do it boldly. No one was in the hallway anyway, so he turned the lock on the inside doorknob, made sure his room key was included on his keychain like it always was, and stepped out into the hall. When he heard the click of the door, he knew he was committed to this adventure. He did rush over to the back stairwell and bound down to the ground floor. He may not mind having people see him out on campus, but he was happy to avoid the people he lived with and saw multiple times a day. That must have been one of the most difficult things for Dani early on, letting the people she saw all the time see her naked.

Michael told himself to forget about Dani. This was his experience, and it was going to be different from Dani's, especially since he was a guy. He stopped at the bottom of the stairwell and looked down at himself. His penis had bounced around on his way down and seemed even larger than it had been in the room. This was all such a new experience. Michael's previous times nude had been while bathing or changing in very small rooms. He had never been naked outside, had never before walked more than ten feet or so while nude. Taking a deep breath, he pushed open the door of the stairwell, stepped out, and then walked out the exterior door and into bright sunshine.

A girl in shorts and a sports bra was jogging on the concrete walkway up to the back door of the dorm, a water bottle in hand, her phone clipped to her waistband, and Bluetooth earbuds in her ears. She took just a cursory glance at Michael as he stepped away from the door and past her before her head jerked back around.

"What the fuck, dude!" the girl exclaimed, shaking her head, before bursting into the dorm building.

Michael stopped and contemplated going back inside. That was not the reception he had anticipated. But that girl had just gone in, and he didn't want her to think that he was following her. A parking lot was next to the dorm, and Michael felt a surge of panic when he saw a white Buick Regal trolling by. His mother had come for a surprise visit. On a Tuesday in the middle of the afternoon. Surely, she had to have seen him by now. What would he say to her about being outside his dorm without clothes. But no, the Buick turned out of the parking lot and onto the street. There were plenty of free spaces, so it had apparently just left. Michael exhaled, and only then had he realized that he had been holding his breath. He looked back at back door to the dorm. The girl had to be well on her way to wherever she was going by now. He could duck back in and sneak back to his room.

No, Michael told himself. Dani hadn't had the option of running back to her room and getting dressed that first day, the day he had talked to her. So he wasn't going to do that either. With new resolve, he walked forward, away from the door and toward the corner of the building. Once he passed that corner, he would be visible to the Commons and to the normal university crowd. He checked his phone and saw that it was 1:47, a busy time of day with one set of classes getting out and the 2:00 classes starting soon.

As he turned that corner and saw all the foot traffic, it suddenly hit him that he was naked outside, in the sunshine, for the first time in his life. Only one person had seen him, but Michael could see that that was already changing as people's heads began to turn. He had his keys and phone in his right hand. His left hand brushed his hip, feeling nothing but bare skin. The sensation of his penis swaying with each step was both stimulating and terrifying, but he kept walking. Six people were walking toward him in the direction of his dorm. Michael's gut tensed with anticipation and nervousness. The jaws of three of the people dropped in expressions of shock, one of the girls mouthing the words "Oh my god!" One of the other guys pulled his phone out of his pocket and appeared to start shooting video. Michael's first impulse was to hide. If anyone was going to take video of him, Michael would have rather it been a girl. Not that he was homophobic, he told himself, but he soon realized that if he had to tell himself he wasn't, then maybe he was.

"How's it hanging?" one of the girls said as they all came within close proximity of each other.

The six approaching people all laughed.

"Can I get a picture with you?" the girl who had mouthed "Oh my god," asked.

"Sure," Michael said without even thinking about it.

The girl ran forward, turned, and faced the other five, putting her arm around Michael's waist.

"Hold on," the guy with the camera phone said as he worked to adjust some settings, probably switching from video back to still photography Michael thought.

The other four people crowded around Michael as he did this, and then the guy with the phone seemed to take several photos.

"OK, Matt," he said, and he and another guy switched places so the phone guy could get in the picture.

"Cool," Matt said.

"Thank you so much," the first girl said to Michael as her hand slid down his lower back.

"N-no problem," Michael said with a stutter.

The six of them walked away, the one guy taking his phone back from Matt and looking through the photos.

"Text me all of them," Michael heard one of the girls say to the guy.

Michael kept walking the opposite direction and didn't hear anything else they said to each other. He soon passed the shadow of the buildings and walked under bright sunshine. It was already late October, but the afternoon temperature was still around ninety degrees in the valley. The heat felt good on his bare skin. Michael hoped he got enough sunscreen on his backside and other parts that had never been exposed to the sun before. He wondered how the photos turned out, and he almost wished he had given them his number so that they could have texted him copies. Two girls walked past him, walking onto the grass to avoid getting too close, one of them giggling and whispering something to the other. Remembering the feel of that girl's hand on his lower back and sliding toward his buttocks, he glanced down and saw that he was aroused although not fully erect. That was one thing that Naked Dani didn't have to worry about.

Michael continued walking, taking the same route he had taken his mother on during the tour she had requested at the beginning of the semester. At one point, an older man in a short sleeve button down shirt with a tie shook his head and uttered "Oh good Lord," before ducking into the Life Sciences Building. Michael heard the word "penis" several times as people commented to companions about his appearance. "I'm more than just my penis," Michael wanted to say, but he remained quiet as he continued his walk.

About two-thirds of his way around the campus, he finally saw her, Naked Dani, walking out of the Student Union with a red slushy in her hand. Her skin looked darker than he had ever seen it, and she had let her hair grow longer. She looked stunning, the muscles of her thighs flexing with each step, the curve and sway of her hips mesmerizing. And she seemed to be walking alone, which was unusual in all the times that Michael had seen her. And here he was just as naked as she was. It occurred to him just then that she might take offense at his nudity, that she might think he was infringing on her turf.

Dani glanced in his direction, did a double-take, and turned to walk in his direction. Michael took a deep breath, trying to think of something to say if she wanted to talk.

"I hope you're wearing sunscreen," she said when she got near.

"I am," he replied, unable to think of anything witty or charming.

Dani stopped and looked him up and down. Michael felt a jolt in his loins at her gaze.

"You inspire me," Michael said and felt ridiculous as soon as he said it.

"I do?"

"Yeah." He looked down at himself, then back up at her. "This feels amazing. It's so freeing. I guess I don't have to tell you that."

"No, you don't." After a pause, she said, "So you just wanted to see how it felt?"

Michael shrugged. "Yeah, I guess so."

Fearing what might happen to a certain body part of his if he remained under Dani's gaze, Michael turned and took a step in the direction in which Dani had been walking, hoping she might walk with him and feeling relieved when she did.

"Do you remember when I talked to you on that first day?" Michael asked.

"First day of what?"

"The first day you went like this. Naked. You looked pretty shook up."

Dani turned and took a long look at his face as she sucked on the straw in her slushy. "Oh my God, that *was* you. Yes. You saved me; you really did. I was about to quit the whole thing and just pack up and go home. People had said some rude things, and I just didn't think I could keep doing it. But you. You said I was brave and beautiful and awesome. So yes, I remember. Thank you."

"I don't even remember what I said. I was kind of in shock. I mean, I'm not used to seeing girls with nothing on. And I'm not used to talking to them either."

Dani laughed. "I remember what you said because I tried to write everything down. In fact, you're in my book."

"Your book?"

"Yeah, I have a book coming out in a few months, about the whole experiment and everything."

"I'll have to read it. What's it called?"

"*The "Volunteer"* with the word Volunteer in quotation marks, because—well, I didn't really volunteer."

"I'll have to read it," Michael repeated. "You said I'm in it?"

"Yep. End of Chapter Four, I think. You and your silent friend."

"Oh yeah. Dave was with me then."

They continued walking, and Michael didn't even care where they were going. People continued to give them stares. They were used to seeing Dani naked on campus, but seeing him naked was new. He wondered if they thought he might be Dani's new boyfriend, and, for some reason he couldn't explain, he wanted them to think that very thing.

"Are they still doing the study?" Michael asked.

Dani shrugged. "I don't think so, but they have so many cameras, they could be. I mean, Dr. Slater told me that she had wanted it originally to last an entire semester. They just couldn't get someone to do it until they found me after spring break."

"You don't have to be naked now?"

"No."

"So why are you still doing it?"

She stopped near a trash can as she finished her slushy, and Michael stopped with her. "Because it's freeing. And because when I graduate and leave this university, I won't have this freedom again. So I might as well take advantage of it while I can."

"That's awesome. You've come a long way since that first day."

"Yeah," Dani said as she threw her empty cup away. "It really did change me. I feel like I've been liberated. When I started doing the project, I was so afraid that my parents would find out. And then when they did, it felt like a burden lifted."

Michael thought of his mother and what she might do if she found out he had taken this little naked walk.

"Now that you've got a taste, are you going to be naked on campus more often?" Dani asked as they resumed walking.

"I doubt it. I'm going to be the RA for my floor next semester, and I don't think the university housing administration would look kindly on a naked resident assistant."

"Who knows what the administration might look kindly on at this mixed-up university."

"Well, yeah. I guess that's true. They did pretty much make you go naked everywhere. I can't believe that Dr. Slater didn't at least get fired."

Dani shook her head. "The only thing that would have done was make my two months of constant nudity a total waste. And I didn't want to have done it for nothing."

"So you really don't hate her guts?" Michael asked.

She shook her head. "I don't have the time or energy to hate anyone. Yeah, she used her authority in an abusive manner, but she showed me so much about myself. This thing that I could never have even thought of doing on my own became something I love. And now look at me. I have a book deal, and there may even be a TV show."

"A what?"

"Well, it's not definite. A producer came to talk about the movie rights to my book, but he came up with the idea of doing a reality show instead of a movie."

"What, here at CVU?"

"Yeah, that's the plan. But it's far from a done deal yet."

Michael couldn't help but look around for a camera crew as he held the hand with his cell phone and keys over his genital area, but as soon as he did, he realized that the university had cameras everywhere. Whoever was on the other end of those cameras already had a copious amount of footage of Michael naked on campus.

"It's too bad you're not going to stay au naturale," Dani said. "You could become a TV star."

"Haha. I don't think my mom would like that too much."

"She'll get over it. My parents did. Well, mostly."

Michael was surprised to see that they were walking right beside his dorm building.

"Dad still has issues," Dani continued.

"This is my dorm," Michael said, feeling awkward as he did so.

"Oh. I'm one building over, at Holcombe."

"Yeah, well, thanks for walking with me."

Michael found that he didn't want to go in, and he especially didn't want to get dressed. He wondered if Dani would consider walking another lap around the campus with him."

"Cool. Well, I hope to see you around again." She held out her hand, and Michael shook it without thinking.

"I hope so too."

As Michael struggled to get the words out of his mouth, asking her to walk with him more, she turned and walked away. He watched her go, marveling at the purity of her form, the straight curves and tan skin, and wondered why people *always* had to wear clothes at almost every other place. A few nearby giggles made him realize that he was a naked guy standing by himself outside, and he scurried back into the building.

4

Adam

Adam pitched the show concept to the Netflix board as *Duck Dynasty* meets *Girls Gone Wild*. He had thought that the two seemingly opposite ideas mixed together would appeal to them, but they didn't seem to like any of it, not even when he tied the production of the proposed series to the release of Danielle Keaton's book on the nudity experiment.

"We don't want adults-only programming on Netflix," one of them said.

"It's not adults-only," Adam countered, "it's just nudity. No sex. You have nudity with current Netflix shows now, and that nudity is usually tied to sex. That's more adults-only that what I am proposing. Dani has been the subject of news stories and was on *Stossel*. People are curious about her."

"Yes, but the nudity in our current offerings is not the focus. It's just brief and fleeting, something to give realism to the story."

"Something to make people watch," Adam said.

"That's not why the nudity is there."

"Oh, come on. You mean to tell me that people aren't going to be more likely to watch something because they heard that ... well, Alison Brie, for instance, has a nude scene in it?"

Adam realized that he was doing something he didn't want to do, getting combative in defense of his idea, and he resolved to tone it down.

"That may be the case for some people, but that's not the reason for it."

The members of the board didn't respond to the video of Dani speaking toward the camera in the way he had hoped.

"You should have pulled the camera back," the most vocal member said, referring to the fact that only Dani's head and shoulders were visible.

Adam thought about pointing out how he had just contradicted his earlier statement about people not watching shows because of nudity, but he remained quiet. He knew at that point that they were going to pass on the project. They voted it down 5-4.

"Thank you for your time," he told them as he packed up and left the room.

Now he had to decide whether to shop the idea to other networks or move on to another project. The problem was, he didn't have another project, and he had bet five hundred dollars on this one. When he had first read the book and come up with the idea of a reality series, the idea had just been a shot in the dark, a move of desperation. He was in desperate financial straits. The lease payment on his Corvette was due, and it wasn't going to pay itself. Many times, Adam wished he hadn't bought the 'Vette at all. He had rationalized it at the time by telling himself that if he was going to play the part of a big-time TV producer, he had to look like a big-time TV producer. Maybe he should just cut his losses, get rid of the Corvette, dissolve his production company, and go back to operating cameras for other people. If he didn't score with a project soon, that's exactly what he would have to do.

As Adam was stepping into the elevator that would take him down to the ground floor, he heard his name called. He stopped on the elevator threshold, preventing the doors from closing, and saw George Blanchard, his contact here at Netflix and the reason he got the pitch meeting in the first place, ambling toward him. There were two people in the elevator already, so Adam mumbled "Sorry," and stepped out of the way of the doors and back into the hallway.

"Man, I'm sorry about that," George said, out of breath from running to catch him. He was overweight, and his shirt seemed to struggle to stay tucked into his pants. "I really thought they would go for it. I mean, an attractive girl who stays naked everywhere she goes, who wouldn't want to watch that?"

"Was there something wrong with my pitch?"

"No, your pitch was fine," George said. "*Duck Dynasty* meets *Girls Gone Wild*, fucking brilliant."

"Why didn't you say that in the meeting?" Adam asked. He knew George had been in the television industry for thirty years; the other board members would have listened to him.

"That board is Vic's thing."

"Is he the one that did the most talking?" Adam asked. They had all introduced themselves at the beginning of the meeting, but Adam couldn't remember all of their names.

"Yeah, that was Vic."

"He didn't seem to like the idea, but he also didn't know exactly why he didn't like it."

George looked up and down the hall, grabbed Adam's arm, and pulled him toward a nearby copy room.

"I think I can sway him," he said as he pulled the door of the copy room closed. "Look, I've seen that naked chick on Youtube and *Stossel*."

"She's more than just a 'naked chick'," Adam said. "That's why the show will work."

"Yeah, of course she is. She seemed really smart in that tape you played." George leaned close and spoke in as quiet a voice as he could manage. "If you could get me a finished pilot, I think we can change Vic's mind."

Adam tried not to pull away despite the stale stench of cigarettes on George's breath. He thought of the expense of a full pilot, the production costs, graphics, music, talent, union fees, taxes.

"I can't afford to shoot a pilot," he said. "I'm pretty strapped right now."

George nodded and seemed to consider something. "Fine. I'll put in forty thousand, my own money."

The wheels started turning in Adam's head. Forty thousand wasn't even half of what he would need to produce a quality episode from scratch. But if he had to, he could beg, borrow, and steal whatever he needed, and defer payments on a bunch of other things. The bad part of that was that if the show wasn't picked up, he would never be able to make good on those deferred payments. If he went through with this, he would be risking his entire production company on it. Did he really trust that George would come through once a pilot was finished? But if he didn't take this shot, would he be able to live with himself? He had talked with Dani, seen her in the flesh (in more ways than one), and he believed in her. She would make this show. He knew she would.

"Will that get you over the hump?" George asked.

Adam nodded. "Yeah, I think that's doable."

"Good. If the show's picked up, pay me back sixty. If not, well, I've just lost forty grand."

Adam thought that it must be nice to just have forty thousand dollars lying around, but he only said, "All right."

"I'm betting on you being able to produce a great show. If you do, I can get board approval without any problem. And if not, well.... I know people at other networks."

Adam had worked with George as a camera operator on three of his previous productions, and they had talked at length about the ambitions Adam had. Having his name as a producer on a nationally televised series was at the top of that list, so this could be the big break he was looking for.

"Just one other thing," George said.

"What's that?"

"I want access to the set. And I want to meet this Naked Dani or whatever her name is."

"I think that can be arranged," Adam said.

"Good." George held out his hand, and Adam shook it. "I'll email you the paperwork today. Just sign it and scan it back to me."

"Okay."

"And when you do that, send me your account info. I'll wire the money to you right away."

George opened the door of the copy room and led Adam back out into the hall just as two members of the programming committee walked past.

"Nice seeing you Adam," George said in a louder voice as they stopped in front of the elevator doors. "Thanks for coming in. Good luck to you."

"Thanks." Adam shook his hand one more time and then pressed the elevator down button as George walked away.

Adam's mind was already running a mile a second as he stepped back on the elevator. He had envisioned a roommate for Dani, probably an aspiring actress who resented Dani's nudity and had had the idea of using the first episode as their first meeting. That would have to wait now. He had to shoot enough footage to get a thirty-minute episode, and he had to shoot it fast. If the show was picked up, they could stick the pilot somewhere in the middle of the season. But if the roommate wasn't in that episode, they would have to avoid the dorm as a shooting location. Sylvia had said that Dani was free to go naked to three or four places off campus in the area. That was what they would have to do for this episode, get Dani out in public with a bunch of people not associated with Coachella Valley University.

Adam was already on the phone with Sylvia before he got to his car, but he got her voicemail.

"Sylvia, Adam Munch. I got the funding for just one episode, a pilot. So we need to shoot something good to get approval for the rest of the season. I was thinking one or two of those places off campus. And you said Dani could have a university car to drive. We'll need access to that and probably another vehicle for crew and equipment. Call me later this afternoon."

He disconnected and sat in his Corvette thinking about the calendar. It was late October already. He had to get everything shot before Thanksgiving, he thought. But then he remembered that he needed to edit, do the graphics, and get someone to write music. He didn't have until Thanksgiving. He had to get the raw footage shot by Halloween which was this Monday. Today was Friday. He had the weekend to prep to shoot as much footage as he could get on Monday. If Sylvia hadn't called him back by the time he got to his office, he would call her again. And if he couldn't reach her then, he would have to call Audrey or even Dani herself. Adam was sweating by the time he started the engine to get the air conditioning going and start driving back to the production office. On the way, he had another idea for further funding through product placement. Adam was going to be spending the rest of the morning on the phone.

5

Dani

Dani was on the way to her Monday morning political science class when her agent Audrey Lambert called her and told her that the reality show was a go. The whole proposal had sounded too good to be true, especially the ten thousand dollars per episode that she would get, and she hadn't expected it to happen.

"Just for a pilot episode," she said.

"What does that mean?" Dani asked.

"It means that Mr. Munch couldn't sell the network on an entire season of shows, but they did agree to let him shoot one episode and see how it plays."

"OK. When do we shoot that?"

"Actually, since this is time sensitive, he's on his way to campus now with a small crew. He should be there in a couple of hours. What's your schedule like for this afternoon?"

"Wow. I wasn't expecting that. Um, I have 20th century American lit from 2:00 to 3:20. After that I'm free."

"OK. Sylvia's going to meet them when they get to campus. Keep your phone powered on and check it as often as you can. She'll text you if they need you to duck out of class early. You don't have a test or anything, do you?"

"No, I don't think so."

"OK. I won't be able to make it today, but you'll be fine."

This was happening too fast, Dani thought. "Do you really think we will start shooting today?"

"I don't know. Just work with them when they get there. Talk to you later."

She disconnected, and Dani stopped walking for a moment. How was she supposed to keep her mind on either of her classes with this show taping coming up, possibly even later that day? A guy in a Harry Potter Hogwarts robe walked past, looking at Dani up and down, and she remembered that it was Halloween. Given her commitment to constant nudity, she reminded herself to get an apple later so that she could tell people her costume was Eve from the Bible. She wondered if Adam wouldn't somehow incorporate Halloween into the show taping today. Holy crap, she was shooting today! Dani took a deep breath and continued to her class.

She was only able to eat about half of the lunch in her dining hall, and then she only got through the first forty-five minutes of her American literature class before her phone vibrated on her desk. The text was from Sylvia. "MEET ME AT HOLCOMBE LOBBY ASAP."

There was no easy way for anyone to sneak out of a small advanced-level class; it was even more difficult for a naked girl who tended to draw everyone's attention anyway. Dani mouthed the word "sorry" to the professor as she slipped out the door with her Kindle and purse in her hand. Simply nodding at people who greeted her, she hurried back to her dorm, at an almost jogging pace. She entered Holcombe Hall at the back entrance like she usually did. When she made it to the lobby, she saw Sylvia waiting alone for her by the front door. Dani had expected a whole film crew, and she had to hide her disappointment from Sylvia.

"There she is," Sylvia said, and it took Dani a couple of seconds to realize that Sylvia was talking on her Bluetooth headset.

Sylvia motioned to Dani and walked out the front door. A white Toyota Camry that was at least five years old was parked in the No Parking zone on the street in front of the dorm. Sylvia motioned to Dani to get in on the passenger side as she walked out into the street to get behind the wheel.

"Ok, we are about three minutes away." Sylvia shut her door and started the car. "No, she has her handbag and Kindle. Oh." Sylvia leaned over to look at Dani's feet. "Yes, she has her sandals on."

Sylvia pulled out into the street and did a U-turn.

"Ok, see you in a minute." Sylvia pulled her Bluetooth piece from her ear.

"Where are we going?" Dani asked.

"Deal's. Adam has some scenario where you go to the store for some new sunscreen that you read about."

"Okay."

Although Deal's grocery store had reached out to Dani through the school, saying that she could shop there at any time, she had never actually gone there while nude. In fact, her off campus excursions had only been to the Coachella Music Festival and to the Denny's afterward.

"Are we sure it's going to be okay for me to be there like this?"

"Yes. Adam has been there for a few hours now, getting everything set up."

"A few hours?"

"Yeah, you'll see. They have a trailer in the parking lot. You'll get hair and makeup done there."

Deal's was a holdover, an anomaly, a small independent grocery store in an era of chain supermarkets. Dani had been there a few times in her first two years at CVU, before Dr. Slater's nudity experiment turned her life upside down. The building was older; the floor tiles were cracked in many places, and the freezers in the frozen food section were dented and rusty in places.

The parking lot at Deal's was more packed than Dani had ever seen it. Rather than try to find an open parking spot, Sylvia drove right up to the white motorhome that sat in the back corner of the lot, close to the street. She stopped the car and looked at Dani.

"Okay, go on in."

Dani looked around at the parking lot, all the people walking into and out of the store, to and from their parked vehicles, and at the police car near the entrance to the store.

"And it's okay for me to be naked here?"

"Yes, it's fine." Sylvia shooed her out with her fingers. "Now go. They're waiting on you."

Dani took a deep breath and stepped out of the car. She was used to being naked in the familiar territory of the CVU campus, but this was something new. It was somehow more public than a university campus. She only had to take four quick steps to get to the motorhome, bounding up the stairs and through the front door.

There wasn't as much light inside the motorhome when she shut the door, and it took her eyes a few seconds to adjust. There was a sofa directly across from the door and several folding chairs set up to her right. To her left was a long desk with mirrors on the walls above. The mirrors were surrounded by lights with big round bulbs. She did a quick scan but didn't see Adam Munch anywhere.

"You must be Dani," said a woman with close cropped spiky blonde hair.

Dani merely nodded.

"I'm Mandy. I'll be doing your hair and makeup." She swiveled a chair toward Dani, wordlessly inviting her to sit.

"And where is Adam?" Dani asked as she put her towel on the seat and sat down.

"Who?"

"Adam. Mr. Munch."

"Oh, he's inside making sure the set is ready."

"The set? I thought this was a reality show."

"Sorry," Mandy said as she began wiping the oil from Dani's face. "I'm using the jargon. It is a reality show, but he's still got to get everything ready. Now, let me get this base on you."

Dani sat quietly while Mandy applied make up to her face and styled her hair. When she finished, she had Dani stand in the corner as she sprayed something all over her body, having Dani turn all the way around.

"This will give your body a nice even shine for the camera," Mandy told Dani.

Dani couldn't help but think about the only other time she went through this process when she was a guest on the *Stossel* show. If the network ordered more episodes of her reality show, she would have to get used to this.

"There's the star of the show," she heard Adam say after he stepped into the trailer. "She's looking great Mandy."

"Thanks boss. I think she's about ready."

"Good." He stopped to stand next to Dani and speak in a lower voice. "Sorry this is such short notice. We have a very small window to get a finished episode done."

"But here, at a grocery store?" Dani said.

"Yeah, a couple of reasons for that. This episode has to be good enough to persuade the network to order a complete season. So I wanted to get you in a new location. People are used to seeing you at the college campus. This is something new, something different. There's also financial reasons. I got a product placement deal with Sunguard. You're here at the store specifically to buy some of their sunscreen."

"I've never heard of them."

"Doesn't matter. You don't have to use the stuff. We'll shoot footage of you going into the store and buying several bottles of it. Later, back at your dorm, we'll shoot you using your last sunscreen, which will then prompt your trip to the store here."

"And you'll just put that scene before this?"

"Exactly."

"That doesn't exactly sound like 'reality' television," Dani said.

"In this business, reality is just an illusion." Adam paused, then turned toward the door of the trailer. "You ready?"

"And it's okay for me to be like this out there?"

"Yeah. Everything's clear with the store owner."

Dani sighed and stepped forward.

Adam opened the door, and the two of them walked down the steps into the bright desert sunshine. A large boxy looking white car was parked next to the motorhome in the spot where Sylvia had dropped her off. A guy Dani had never seen before handed a keyring to Adam.

"Sorry," Adam said, relaying the keys to Dani. "Old Crown Vics were all they had available in the university motor pool. Now, what I want you to do is drive around the block over there." He pointed to where he wanted her to go. "We'll shoot your approach, getting out of the car, and walking into the store."

"And what do I do when I get inside?"

"Just stop. We'll have to reset the cameras. I only have one other camera operator besides myself. We do have cameras inside the car, so we can use some of those shots. If you feel like talking when you're driving, go ahead."

"Talking to myself, you mean?"

"No, talking to the viewers. Or the camera, or however you want to think of it. In fact, while you're driving around the block, talk about how you've never been to this store before since you stopped wearing clothes. And say it like that, 'stopped wearing clothes.' Don't say nudity project or going naked. I think I'm going to call the show *The Girl Who Stopped Wearing Clothes*. It's got a ring to it, with all of the books and movies with Girl in the title. You know, like *Girl with the Dragon Tattoo*."

"Yeah, I've heard of it."

"And don't worry about saying anything dumb or stumbling over your words. We'll edit it all together. For a show like this, we will probably shoot fifty or sixty times the footage actually used in the finished show." He pointed toward the store entrance. "You see that parking spot with the orange cone?"

"Yeah."

"That's where I want you to park. The cone will be moved right before you get there."

Dani nodded and got into the car, dropping her towel onto the seat before sitting down.

"And don't worry if it doesn't seem to work," Adam continued as Dani fastened her seat belt and adjusted the seat position and the rear-view mirror. "We can always shoot more driving stuff later."

"Ok." Dani started the car, and Adam shut the door.

She saw Adam say something into his walkie-talkie as she put the Crown Victoria into gear and drove toward the parking lot exit.

"It has been a while since I've driven a car," she said, remembering that she was supposed to be talking as she drove. "I guess I'm not supposed to say this for the show though. Is this supposed to be my car? I'd never drive something this big. Looks like a police car and feels like a tank."

She took a right turn, intending to swing around and head back to the grocery store.

"This is the first time I've ever driven in California. I've always gotten rides to and from the airport or anywhere else here. I hope I don't get lost."

Dani stopped at a red light, and a pickup truck pulled up next to her in the right lane. She kept her gaze straight ahead, but in her peripheral vision, she could see the guy driving the truck talking animatedly with the guy in the passenger seat. Dani took a look down at herself, the shoulder belt across her chest right between her breasts. The pickup was higher than the Crown Vic, so she knew that the two guys had a clear view of her from at least the waist up. The passenger was leaning across the driver, both of them looking at her. Dani refused to look their way even though they appeared to be trying to get her to roll her window down.

She was used to people looking at her, of course, but it was normally within the safe confines of the university campus. This, being out in an open public place, even though she was inside the car, was new. Dani felt more vulnerable than she had felt since the early days of Dr. Slater's nudity experiment.

"I guess I should be talking," she said, remembering the cameras and microphones hidden in the car. She was tempted to look around and try to find them, but she wanted to keep looking straight ahead until the two guys in the truck had moved on.

"It's strange being away from the campus," Dani said. "I've found a comfort zone there, and being outside of that makes me anxious or nervous. Or something. It's weird."

The light turned green, and Dani let the pickup truck pull away from her before proceeding through the intersection at a slow pace. She made another turn and started back toward Deal's grocery store, pulling into the parking lot and parking in her assigned space. The orange cone was indeed gone. She saw Adam with a camera mounted on some kind of stabilization apparatus strapped to his body near the store entrance, the camera trained on the car the entire way. Dani parked the car and sat for a moment, looking at the people walking in and out, some of them noticing Adam with his camera, others not.

Most of the people she encountered on campus were fellow students, almost all of them in their early twenties. Dani couldn't help but notice that the crowd at Deal's were of all ages, older people, young mothers with small children, teenagers, and everyone in between. And she was about to step out and walk naked amongst all of them. The fear and shame that she had felt when she first walked naked out of the sociology department office and all the way across campus back to her dorm the previous spring came flooding back. Dani looked at the car's dash. She had just put it in park, so the motor was still running. She was tempted to slip the car back into reverse, back out of her saved parking space, and head back toward the safety of the CVU campus.

The motion of Adam's arm snapped Dani out of her momentary reverie. He was gesturing for her to get out of the car. She took a deep breath and said, "Here goes nothing," before remembering that the car was wired for sound and wished she had remained silent. She cut the motor and opened the door. Adam was just outside the shadow of the entrance, shooting her approach. She tried not to look directly at the camera as she closed the car door and walked toward the store. A young mother with a boy who looked to be about five years old stopped and stared. Dani could see the woman in her peripheral vision, but she didn't dare make eye contact with her. Exposure to nudity harmed no one, including children, Dani thought, but she feared what the parents of children who saw her might do or say just because of society's conditioning that kids should somehow be shielded. Dani, of course, thought that the main issue parents would have was the questions posed by children after seeing nudity that those parents just didn't want to answer.

The woman surprised Dani by not trying to cover her son's eyes or turn him away but allowed him to stare at her. The child also surprised her by not appearing to ask his mother why that woman didn't have any clothes on. This was, after all, California, Dani thought. The situation would be much different in her home state of Texas. In fact, her public nudity wouldn't be tolerated at all.

Other people had stopped what they were doing to watch her. Dani tried to hold her head up high and keep walking toward the entrance. Adam's face was hidden behind his camera, and she saw that he had started panning around to the people watching her, their expressions varying from shock to amusement. Dani quickened her pace as long as Adam's camera was looking elsewhere, although she doubted that the inside of the store would offer her much sanctuary from the staring eyes. This was all so surreal, just as those first few times naked on campus had been back in March. The nervous flutters and tingling she felt in certain body parts was familiar, and she realized just how comfortable she had become on campus. Dani found that she missed this nervous excitement of being naked in a new public place, and that finding surprised her. Life had become so surreal these past several months.

Dani reached the front door of the store. Adam had circled around and was now shooting her from behind. She was tempted to turn around and try to catch his attention, but she resisted it. There was someone with a shoulder mounted camera just inside the store. Adam had told her to walk inside and stop so that they could set up another shot. All the customers waiting in line, the baggers, and many of the cashiers had stopped what they were doing to watch Dani. Standing still here was the least natural thing she thought she could do. She wanted to keep walking and get out of the view of so many people.

"Okay," she heard Adam say from behind her. "Hold there for just a minute."

Dani stopped, and Adam rushed by her, motioning to the other camera operator into another position. A lady who looked to be in her forties pushed a shopping cart past her, her groceries bagged and a long receipt in her hand.

"I wish I had that kind of confidence," she said to Dani.

"Yeah, me too," Dani answered once the lady had passed, feeling less than confident.

Adam scurried back to her. "Okay, pick up one of the handheld baskets and walk over to the pharmacy area and find a store employee named Dave. He'll have a name tag on. He's signed a release and everything. Ask him where you can find Sunguard sunscreen. He'll show you where it is. Take four bottles of it and head toward the registers. Just keep going, and we will follow you since the lighting will all be the same inside. Okay?"

Dani had to pull her attention away from all the onlookers to listen to what Adam said. She nodded, telling herself to remember the name Dave.

"When you get to the registers, go to number 3. It's empty now, but someone will be sending a checker there when you approach."

"Dave. Sunguard. Register three. Got it."

"Great," Adam said and scurried off toward the pharmacy section.

Dani stood waiting, still aware of the scrutiny of more than a dozen grocery shoppers and store employees, until Adam got turned around with his camera pointed at her. That the simple act of walking into a grocery store had become such a major production for a television show seemed insane to her. But then again, how many people go to the grocery store in the nude?

Adam motioned to her, and she picked up a basket from the rack near the front door and started walking toward the pharmacy area. A young kid wearing a store smock, with acne on his face and braces on his teeth, was near the skin care products. Dani was surprised when she saw that his name tag identified him as Dave. He ought to be in a high school somewhere at this time of day, she thought. When he saw her for what must have been the first time, his jaw dropped, and he seemed to freeze in place. But she played her part well, stopping for a few seconds and looking around at all the shelves.

"Excuse me," she finally said to him, "I'm looking for Sunguard sunscreen."

Dave seemed to snap to life. "Oh, yes. It's right over here." He walked backward to the endcap of the aisle, unable to take his eyes off Dani. "We have a special display of it here. Did you want the regular cream or the spray on?"

"The spray," she said, feeling like she was in a commercial.

"The spray-on is on the top shelf right there."

"Thank you." She couldn't remember how many Adam had told her to get, so she grabbed five of the SPF 90 bottles and dropped them into her basket.

"Is there anything else I can help you with?"

Dani shook her head. "No, I think this is it."

She started walking back to the front of the store, wanting to get done with this shoot and back to the familiar confines of the CVU campus. Dave walked just behind her for a little way, saying "Thank you for shopping at Deal's," before walking right into the shopping cart of a middle-aged lady who had come to a sudden stop when she saw the naked girl.

"Oh, I am so sorry ma'am," Dani heard Dave say to the woman, and she had to stifle the urge to laugh. Adam had kept his camera on the store clerk and the woman, so at least there would be a little slapstick comedy in what Dani had thought was going to be a mundane store trip.

Dani remembered Adam's instructions and didn't stop until she got to the front of the store. The light for register 3 came on right as she stepped into the lane. The cashier was a heavyset woman with short blonde hair and a small Band-Aid on the side of her nose. Dani thought that it might be there to hide a piercing that the store management didn't like. Her name tag identified her as Tara. Lane 2, behind Dani, was still closed, and Adam was standing where a customer at that register would be, taking footage of the exchange. The other cameraman was at the end of the station, next to a young bagger who stared at Dani with eyes that seemed unnaturally large.

"Good afternoon," Tara said with a smile.

"Hi," Dani replied as she set her basket on the conveyer belt.

Tara picked up one of the bottles as her lips moved, counting the bottles in the basket. She punched in a number and ran the bottle over the scanner. "Sunguard sunscreen. I guess you would need a lot of this."

Dani smiled back at her, thinking that she must have been told to say the name of the product for the show. "Yes, I go through it pretty quick."

"You know, I saw you on that show, *Stossel*, and I love what you're doing. They make you do this, and then when they want you to stop, you say no and keep doing it. It's like, 'I'll show you.' That's awesome." Tara's voice was raspy and shaky, and Dani could tell how nervous she was.

"Thank you," Dani said.

"We've had a few celebrities come in here, being close to Palm Springs and all, but I think you are my favorite. You're amazing."

"Thanks. I wish everyone felt that way."

"If you keep doing this, maybe people will change."

Dani nodded as she took her bank card out of her hand purse. Adam hadn't given her a way to pay for this, but she supposed he would pay her back. "That's what I'm hoping." She inserted her card, chip first, into the reader.

"Good luck to you," Tara said. "And stay safe."

"I will." The card reader displayed a message to remove her card as her receipt printed on Tara's register.

"Thank you for shopping at Deals. Please feel free to come back anytime." Tara handed the receipt to Dani.

"Thanks. I'll do that."

Dani folded the receipt around her card, stuck it back into her purse, and took her sack of sunscreen from the wide-eyed bagger who could only mouth the words "Thank you." She walked past the other registers, cashiers and customers all staring at her in silence. It was all she could do not to break into a run to get out of the store. When she got to the doors, she turned right and walked outside.

"Cut!" Dani heard Adam yell as soon as she stepped across the threshold.

Dani stopped at the loud, sharp voice even though all she really wanted to do was run to the car and drive back to campus. Of course, it also occurred to her that she had no idea where to park the thing once she got there.

"Dani, that was great," Adam said, rushing over to her.

"Thanks."

She turned and looked back into the store. Several people with iPads were talking to the customers who had finished checking out. One of them signed something on the iPad screen before the interviewer took the tablet back and appeared to take a quick photo of the customer.

"Hopefully, we won't have to blur anyone's faces," Adam said when he saw what she was looking at. "Now, let's get a shot of you walking to the car and driving away."

Dani sighed in relief that she wouldn't have to redo her walk through the store or her purchase of the sunscreen. Maybe that was the only difference between a reality show and a regular one, she thought: they do everything in one take.

6

Michael

Michael Cooley was proofreading his paper on the Spanish American War for the third time on his laptop when someone rapped on his door. It was a Sunday afternoon, and his roommate Dave wasn't due back from visiting his parents in San Bernardino until after ten o'clock that night. Michael clicked the Save button for the fourth time in the last five minutes and got up to answer the door, thinking it was Ted or Bill wondering why he wasn't down in their room watching football even though he had only ever watched one Rams game with them and hadn't paid much attention to the TV even then. The truth was, he could never get into football since his dad had died of a stroke at 46 years of age. His mother had, of course, blamed it on the three concussions he had suffered during his high school and college playing days. Michael had been in eighth grade when the stroke happened and had played football for his middle school team. His mother had forbidden him from playing in high school, but she didn't have to. Michael had never been good at football as a kid and only played because he thought his father expected him to.

When Michael pulled open the door of his dorm room, he was surprised to see a vaguely familiar middle-aged woman in a business suit standing in the hall.

"Hello," she said. "You're Michael Cooley." It was a statement, not a question.

"Yeah."

The woman held out her hand. "I'm Dr. Lorraine Slater, sociology department."

Michael shook her hand, more as an automatic response than a conscious decision. As he did so, the name she had given him registered in his brain, and he realized why her face looked so familiar. She was the architect of Danielle Keaton's naked in public project.

"Nice to meet you, I guess."

She smiled and chuckled. "I can see that my reputation has preceded me."
Michael couldn't help but laugh with her. "Sorry."
"That's all right. May I come in? I have something I'd like to discuss with you."
Michael turned and looked back into his room. The dirty clothes hamper was full, but no clothes were falling out of it, nor were any scattered anywhere else in the room. His bed was unmade, but he never made his bed anyway. All in all, the room didn't look half bad for a college dorm.
"Sure," he said, stepping back and letting Dr. Slater in.
She walked into the room like she owned it and sat in Michael's desk chair. Michael shut the door of his room and had to fight an urge to lean over her and click the save button on his laptop keyboard again. He sat on the edge of his bed facing Dr. Slater.
"You know, of course, about the study on public nudity I spearheaded last semester."
Michael nodded. "Sure. Everyone knows about that. I mean, it was all over the news."
"Yes. That was most unfortunate."
"Why is that?"
"Because the point of the project was to study the public's reaction to nudity when encountering it over a prolonged period of time. But when the public knows they are being studied, they tend to alter their honest reactions."
"Oh. Yeah. I can kind of see that," Michael said.
"What most people don't realize is that Miss Keaton's part in the project was only supposed to be a first step."
"A first step?"
"Yes. The second step is to explore whether the public would accept a nude male as readily as they did a nude female, assuming, of course, they did accept a nude female, as they appear to have done. The news story about the recruitment methods used to gain Miss Keaton's participation in the project might alter the results of this second step. Miss Keaton's continued nudity might also have an effect on those results, but given the tenuous status of my standing with this university, I would like to continue."
"Un huh," Michael said, trying to figure out why she was telling him, out of all the students on campus, about this.
"I don't have the staff or the resources that I used to have, but since Miss Keaton has continued with her public nudity, the department has continued to monitor the reactions to her."
Dr. Slater stopped and gave Michael a curious look.
"I guess that makes sense," he finally said when she seemed to refuse to go on.
Dr. Slater smiled. "I saw something interesting in the video files this past month. You and Miss Keaton were speaking near the Commons.

You were — well, you were as naked as she was."

Michael took a deep breath, feeling embarrassed, thinking about Dr. Slater watching his naked body on a video monitor somewhere. For an older woman, she was still quite attractive, with a nice figure, long brown hair with just a touch of gray, and minimal wrinkles around her eyes and the corners of her mouth. His face was probably turning red. "Yeah. I saw Dani on the first day. The first day she went naked, that is. And I had wanted to do that ever since then. I mean, if she can do it, it must be legal for everyone, right?"

"That's correct."

"It took me a few months, but I finally worked up the courage to go out and take a walk in the daylight. It was just luck that I ran into Dani."

"And how did it feel to be outside in the nude, in broad daylight?"

"It was…". Michael paused, trying to find the right word. "Weird. Scary. Every time someone would see me, I never knew how they were going to react. But it was freeing too. The sun and the wind all over me. People don't realize how good that can feel."

"It was a positive experience for you then?"

"Yeah, I would say so."

"Good," Dr. Slater said, "because I want you to be the central figure in this next step."

"Me?" Michael was already shaking his head, thinking of all the press that Dani had gotten. There was no way he could allow his mother to see him doing what she had repeatedly condemned Dani for doing.

"Yes, you. You would do just what Dani had done, spend the entire semester on campus nude. Go to classes, live in the dorm, eat in the dining halls. All free of clothing."

"No, no, no, I couldn't do that."

"Why not? You've already walked across campus in the nude, and you said it was a positive experience."

"That's different."

"How so?"

"I can't just go naked here in the dorm. These are guys I live with and see every day. And they're not going to like it. Especially if I'm naked around their girlfriends. I'm liable to get my ass kicked. And not only that, but I was hired to be an RA next semester. I don't think it would go over with residence hall administration if one of their new RA's suddenly refused to wear clothes right after being hired."

Dr. Slater gave him a wry smile. "Don't worry about residence hall administration. I'll handle them. And as for how the other guys will react, well, that's exactly the thing that I want to study. Common perception says that people will react more harshly to a nude male than to a nude female. I would like to challenge that, but to do so, I wanted to start with a female. That's why we started with Miss Keaton, and she has garnered a far greater level of acceptance that I ever anticipated. Much greater than Andrew Martinez ever got."

"Who?" Michael asked.

"Andrew Martinez. He was a student at Berkeley in the early 1990s, became known as the Berkeley Naked Guy. You can Google him. I was at Berkeley at the time, and he developed a following. Most everyone else just accepted him as he was, but the authorities at the university enacted legislation to stop him from attending classes in the nude. The city of Berkeley soon followed suit. Andrew was the inspiration for this study."

"The early 90s?" Michael asked. "How long have you been working on this?"

"Oh, I've contemplated this study for years, but it was only recently that the time seemed right. That, and we have much better surveillance technology now and can better measure the public's reaction, especially over a long period."

"How long of a period?"

"Well, I'd like you to be nude for the entire semester."

"You mean next semester?"

"Yes. Although we could start now if you wanted and keep going all the way through next spring."

Michael shook his head, thinking again of his mother. "There's no way I could do this."

"If I remember correctly, those were Danielle's exact words when I first brought the subject up with her." She pulled a multipage document from the binder she carried and offered it to Michael. "Take a look at what I'm offering."

Michael took the papers from her and glanced down. From the heading on the first page, the document appeared to be a contract between the university and himself.

"I'm not in the same position with the university that I was when Phase One of this study began," Dr. Slater said as Michael skimmed, "but I think you will find some worthwhile incentives for participating in this."

"You mean what might happen to me if I don't?"

Dr. Slater's smile dropped. "No, nothing like that. I think I learned my lesson with what happened with Miss Keaton." Her smile returned, but the way her eyes remained fixed on Michael just highlighted how forced it was. "You will find that there are several incentives to participating, like the six hours of sociology credit, with a grade of A. That will help both your tuition costs and your grade point average. Miss Keaton got the same deal, and she wound up switching to a sociology minor. And why not, with those six hours of advanced credit. She only has to take two more courses to complete the requirements for a minor. You may want to do the same thing."

Michael's mind was overcome with thoughts of constant nudity and constant attention so that he barely heard what Dr. Slater said about the sociology credits. He thought about that group of six people who had stopped him that day he took his naked walk. They had thought he was brave, and the way the girls had giggled made him think they found him attractive. When it was happening, he had been too nervous and afraid to really enjoy the experience, but afterwards, he had grown to cherish that memory. And now Dr. Slater was proposing that such experiences become part of his everyday life. Michael wanted to take her up on it. The more Dr. Slater talked, the more desperate he became to do it.

The only thing stopping him was the thought of his mother. He didn't want her to know about that first naked excursion much less that he might be the next participant after Naked Dani. And he sure didn't want her seeing him naked on campus, either in photographs or in person. He wondered how long he would be able to do it while keeping it from his mother. Dani had gone a couple of weeks, hadn't she? He couldn't remember. But she was the first, the only naked student on campus at the time. Of course she was going to make news. Michael would only be following in her footsteps. The story would be old news by then. Maybe he could get away with going naked for an entire semester without Mother ever finding out. She wasn't exactly a news hound anyway.

"I'll have to think about it," he told Dr. Slater.

"Of course. This phase doesn't officially start until January, but I will need to know something from you before the Thanksgiving break."

"Sure. I can let you know before then."

She handed him a business card. "My office hours are here. If you decide to do this, and I hope you do, you'll have to sign a few things and pick up a necklace microphone."

"A microphone?"

"Yes. Like I said earlier, I don't have the staff to follow and record audio from all of your waking hours. We'll have to pick our spots. But we will get as much audio as we can. The details are in the document. I suggest you read it thoroughly."

"I will," Michael assured her.

They sat looking at each other for a moment, and Michael couldn't help but wonder if she were imagining him naked now. Or maybe that was just his wishful thinking.

"Well," she said at last and stood up, "I'll let you read that. Please get back to me as soon as you decide."

Michael stood up as well and walked the three steps to the door and opened it for her.

"Thank you for bringing this to me," he said.

Dr. Slater's face seemed to relax. Michael thought that his thanking her made her think that he was going to say yes.

"You're welcome. I'll look forward to hearing from you."

Michael watched her walk away down the hall until she disappeared around a corner. When he stepped back into his room, he closed the door and checked the time on his phone. Dave wasn't supposed to be back for several hours, and Michael wasn't expecting any other visitors. Removing his clothes took all of three seconds. He stood at his closet mirror looking at himself for just a moment before telling himself to just act normally, like he would do while clothed. The laptop had gone into power save mode, so he had to wait a few seconds after sitting down for the screen to come back on. The paper on the Spanish-American War was still there, so he resumed his proofreading. Being his third time through the essay, he read to the end without finding any other errors, clicked save, and submitted it to his professor via the university's Blackboard app.

Once that was done, Michael took a moment to think about what he would do next if he were wearing his normal attire. Whatever it was, he would have to get used to doing it without clothes if he took Dr. Slater up on her offer. That also meant that Dave and everyone else in the dorm, not to mention everyone else on the university campus, would just have to get used to him. Michael googled Dr. Slater's name and got several pages about last semester's "Naked Study Scandal" as it was called in the news. Even though his search engine results were set to moderate, which should have censored any full-frontal nudity, there were still several photos of Dani that showed up in the list. Apparently, her nudity had somehow become special, an allowable exception. Of course, she had been shown nude on a major television news network, so maybe Google figured that there was no need to censor what everyone had already seen.

Rather than click on any of those results, Michael typed "Berkeley Naked Guy" in the search engine, and read the Wikipedia article about Andrew Martinez, how he had gone to classes wearing only sandals and a backpack until the university had banned public nudity in December of 1992. Michael wondered about the membership of whatever governing body had prohibited nudity at the university, seeing them all as elitist old men in his mind's eye, and whether they would have done so if it had been an attractive young female going naked in public. He continued reading about Andrew Martinez, who, after he started wearing clothes, traveled quite a bit but later exhibited signs of mental illness. Martinez had various legal troubles before committing suicide in a jail cell in May of 2006.

After finishing the Wikipedia article on Martinez, Michael clicked on a link about Stephen Gough, the so-called Naked Rambler who had walked nude across the United Kingdom a couple of times but kept getting arrested. According to Wikipedia, which Michael knew wasn't the best source of information but was at least accessible for quick research, Gough was released from jail several times but would be re-arrested after just a few steps because he would walk away in the nude. He also appeared nude in court so often that they stopped allowing him in court. Gough was, apparently, still alive and still practicing what was described as "unlimited naturism". At the bottom of that page were several links to other Wikipedia articles, one of which was on Naked Dani. He clicked on it and read with interest. There were also a couple of uncensored photos of her attached to the article, one of her on the

Stossel show and another of her on stage with Miley Cyrus at the Coachella Music Festival. The article was fun to read, especially since he had a personal connection to it, having talked with Dani during her first day of nudity and then during his brief naked excursion outside the other day, but it didn't tell him anything he didn't already know.

From there, Michael clicked on an article about public nudity in general and read about the history of nudity in various places. There was a separate article about public nudity in San Francisco, and since San Francisco was in the same state, albeit several hundred miles from Coachella Valley University, he clicked on it and read about how the city had enacted a public nudity ban in 2013. There were several public nudity activists working to reverse this ban, and one of those even had her own Wikipedia article. She was from Russia and went by the name Gypsy Taub. Gypsy had also been detained several times after stripping down in city council meetings in San Francisco and Berkeley.

Michael barely had time to register the beep of a keycard being used at the door to his room before Dave burst in trailing a suitcase on wheels, interrupting his reading. Michael's first impulse was to close his laptop so Dave couldn't see the photo of Gypsy Taub nude in front of San Francisco City Hall with a hat that displayed her opposition to the city official who had written and proposed the nudity ban, an official with the unfortunate name of Weiner. But Michael also realized that he himself was still naked. As Dave stopped in the doorway with his girlfriend Debbie behind him, their mouths hanging open in astonishment, Michael realized with some surprise that the dorm room window was dark. How long had he been surfing and reading Wikipedia?

"What the hell?" Dave said.

Michael jumped up to get some clothes, and Debbie failed to suppress a giggle.

"Sorry," Michael said, trying to find the words for an explanation.

Dave turned toward Debbie and said, 'What are you looking at?"

Debbie shook her head, still laughing but not turning her gaze away from Michael. "Now I'm really glad you agreed to leave early."

Michael eschewed the white briefs and picked up the denim shorts he had left on his bed. For some reason, he didn't want Debbie to see him in just his underwear even though he didn't mind her looking at him in nothing at all and probably wouldn't be jumping into his shorts if Dave wasn't there making a conscious effort not to look at him. If he took Dr. Slater's offer, he wouldn't have the option of even putting on shorts in front of Dave. But then again, Dave wouldn't be his roommate next semester. One of the big advantages of being the floor's resident assistant was getting a private room.

"I was looking up stuff on Danielle Keaton," Michael said in a feeble attempt at explanation.

"The nudie girl?" Debbie said.

"Yeah." Michael was careful not to get any hair or sensitive parts caught as he zipped up his shorts.

"What, you thinking of joining her?" Dave asked.

"I talked to her again the other day, and I just wonder what it feels like to do what she does all the time." It wouldn't hurt anything to at least plant a seed in his friends' minds about his upcoming participation, he thought.

"She stopped and talked to you?" Debbie said as she sat on Dave's bed. "What did you say?"

Michael pulled his t-shirt on and shrugged. "I don't know. I reminded her of when Dave and I talked to her on her first day of going naked. She actually remembered us. Even put us in that book she has coming out."

"What? Really?" Dave said as he moved clothes from his suitcase to the dresser.

"You never told me you ever talked to Naked Dani," Debbie said. "She's usually so standoffish."

"I didn't talk to her, not really. Mike did all the talking."

Debbie turned to Michael as he sat down at his desk and minimized the browser on his laptop.

"I see her walking across campus all the time, but I've never seen her stop and talk to anyone unless they were already walking with her."

"Well, she is making herself very vulnerable," Michael said, "so I'm sure she's just being careful."

"Yeah, maybe. It still seems like she wants attention, but then she doesn't want attention."

Michael shrugged. "I wouldn't judge her unless I walked in her shoes for a while."

"What, walk around naked like she does? I don't think so."

"There's got to be something to it," Dave said after having finished putting his clothes up and turning back to the conversation.

"Yeah, there is," Michael said.

Debbie's eyebrows raised. "Oh really? And how would you know that?"

Michael had never told anyone in his circle of friends about his naked excursion which was also why he hadn't told any of them about speaking with Dani again. Now that he had been asked to fulfill the same role Dani had in the sociology study, his naked walk didn't seem like a secret worth keeping.

"Why do you think Dani stopped to talk with me?" he said.

"You were outside naked?" Debbie asked.

"Yeah."

"When was this?" Dave asked at the same time Debbie was saying, "Oh my God!"

"I don't know. A few days ago."

"What did you do," Debbie said while laughing, "just forget to get dressed and go walking across campus?"

"No, I didn't forget. I wanted to know what it felt like."

"What *did* it feel like?"

Michael shrugged. "Strange. It was like I was either the center of attention or people went out of their way to avoid even looking at me. There didn't seem to be much middle ground."

"But what did *you* feel?" Debbie asked as Dave sat on his bed next to her and took her hand.

"Nervous. Excited."

"Excited? Like hard?"

"What? No, not like that. It was like the feeling you have on a roller coaster when you're clicking up that first hill."

"You want to do it again, don't you," Debbie said. It wasn't a question.

"I've been thinking about it."

"Obviously."

"What?"

"Hello? You were naked when we came in."

"Oh. Yeah."

After an awkward moment of silence, Michael turned back toward his laptop.

"I think you should take another naked walk," Debbie announced. "Right now." She had her phone in her free hand. "And I'll record people's reactions."

"Whoa," Dave said, letting go of her other hand. "Why are you so interested in getting my roommate naked?"

"Calm down baby. It'll be for science. And it's not like we didn't already just see him naked."

"Sorry about that," Michael said to Dave.

Dave shrugged at him and stood up. "Let's let Mike finish his homework or whatever it was he was doing. Come on; I'll walk you home."

Dave held his hand out to Debbie, but she didn't take it and kept looking at Michael.

"I think Michael should walk with us, dressed like he was when we got here. It would be so much fun."

Debbie lived in Folsom Hall, the largest women's dorm on campus. Michael imagined himself walking naked across campus on an early Sunday evening with people returning from their weekends away, Debbie stopping to talk to anyone and everyone she knew, making sure that they all got a good look at him before escorting him inside the crowded game room on the first floor of Folsom Hall. And then he thought of Dave tagging along behind looking embarrassed and ashamed, if he even stayed with them that long.

"Maybe some other time," Michael said.

"Ugh, you guys are no fun."

She stood and took the three steps to the door. Dave and Michael shared a look, with Dave sighing and shaking his head.

"Well, let's go." Debbie opened the door and walked out into the corridor.

Michael had only talked with Debbie a couple of times before this, and she had seemed like the polar opposite of Dave, outgoing while Dave was introverted, loud while Dave almost always spoke softly, flirtatious while Dave could barely talk to women. Still, Michael couldn't not be attracted to her with her curly blonde hair, simmering green eyes, and shapely body. And since she flirted with him every time she had seen him, Michael thought that she must be attracted to him too. So as much as he wanted to humor Debbie, he didn't want anything about her to come between him and Dave.

"Be back in a few minutes," Dave said and walked out after Debbie.

Michael, realizing that he had skipped dinner, put his socks and shoes on to go eat at the Student Union building. The dining hall adjacent to the dorm was now closed.

Debbie and Dave had never been a good match, he thought as he walked to the union. When the inevitable break up did happen, he just hoped that Dave wouldn't blame him for it.

7

Adam

The day after the grocery store shoot, Adam shot more than three hours of Dani sitting and talking in front of a blue backdrop in one of the studios in the Radio and Television Building on campus. He sat behind the camera, checking the view finder every few minutes to make sure Dani was still centered properly, and fired questions at her. Adam didn't have to ask many questions though. Dani would take each question and give such a multi-layered response that he only had to ask seven or eight questions the entire time. Once they were done with that, he gave her a pre-written speech about seeing a review of Sunguard sunscreen online and that she wanted to try it. That took three takes as she stumbled over the words that were not her own.

Adam then spent the rest of the day and most of the following night in the rented motorhome that served as the production trailer. It had been moved from the grocery store parking lot to one right behind Dani's dorm. Adam cut clips from those three hours and intercut them with shots from the grocery store until he had an eighteen-minute segment. The entire episode needed to be at least twenty-three minutes, and he planned on shooting a sequence to go before the supermarket scene. He kept a spiral notebook next to the keyboard of his workstation to jot down ideas about the next shoot or about future episodes as he edited video from the supermarket.

"Mr. Munch?"

Someone had grabbed his shoulder and was shaking it. Adam was surprised to find the side of his face on his desk, and he bolted upright.

"You okay?"

Mandy the makeup artist stood over him, still shaking his shoulder. Sunlight filtered in under the window blinds. Adam put his hands on his desk, checked to make sure his notes were still there, and looked up at Mandy.

"What time is it?"

"It's a quarter to eight."

His monitors were powered off, so he thumped the mouse, harder than he intended since it skidded across his desk and onto the floor, to bring them back to life.

"Shit," he muttered as Mandy bent down to pick up the mouse.

"Were you here all night?" she asked as she set the wireless mouse down on Adam's mousepad.

"Yeah, I guess so."

He tried to remember the last changes he had made to the video, couldn't recall if he had saved those changes or if he had even wanted to save those changes, and, just to be safe, clicked on the Save Project As button and saved it as a new project with a different name.

"I thought you were staying at the Fairfield like the rest of us."

"That had been the plan," Adam said.

The two empty bottles of Diet Mountain Dew next to his keyboard helped explain his overwhelming need to pee. Once he had taken care of that in the motorhome's tiny bathroom, he bent over low enough to get his mouth under the sink faucet, his butt bumping against the wall as he did so, and rinsed his mouth out as well as he could, wishing all the while that his toothbrush and toothpaste were here and not in that room at the Fairfield Inn. With an 8:00 AM call time, he wasn't going to be able to get back to his room until the end of the shooting day. He normally washed his hair every day, and when he didn't his hair always looked oily and flat. Like it did now, he thought as he looked in the mirror. Adam tried combing it with his fingers but achieved mixed results. Friends would usually say they didn't notice any difference in his hair on those rare non-wash days, but he never believed them because he always saw it when he looked at himself.

Dani was stepping up into the motorhome when Adam exited the tiny bathroom. It was still jarring to him to see an attractive naked girl just going about her business. Adam wondered how many people at the university had truly gotten used to seeing her in the eight months she had been doing this. The thought that some men might think about trying to take advantage of her crossed his mind, remembering that, according to her book, her chemistry professor had done that very thing. And that reminded Adam that his financier, George Blanchard, was supposed to visit the set today. Adam maintained a professional friendship with George, but he knew of the guy's reputation as a womanizer and that he used his position in the entertainment industry to curry favor among young women. It wouldn't have surprised Adam if George put up the money for this pilot just to get a shot at Dani. A few days ago, Adam wouldn't have cared. But after working with Dani at the grocery store and especially listening to her talk while just sitting in front of the camera, he had taken a more protective attitude toward her.

"Good morning," Mandy said to Danielle.

"Morning." Dani glanced from Mandy over to Adam as he returned to his workstation. "You're up early."

"I don't know whether I'm up early or up very, very late."

"I found him sleeping on the job here in the trailer," Mandy said.

"Burning the midnight oil?" Dani said to him.

"Something like that."

Adam looked around the trailer, but he didn't have a change of clothes to put on. He lifted his arm to sniff the shirt he was wearing and felt a knot constrict in his neck as he bent his head down. The shirt didn't have any noticeable smell, but the crick in his neck was going to bother him for a while. Sighing, he looked at the notes in his spiral notebook on his desk as Dani sat down in Mandy's make-up chair.

"You feeling okay?" Adam said to Dani.

Mandy had already started on her hair, snipping just a tiny bit here and there. "Sure," she replied without looking at him.

Adam felt like he should give her some kind of pep talk or creative instruction. She was his main talent on this production after all, but with his dirty clothes, oily hair, and aching neck, he didn't feel like himself.

"So, today is still Monday," he said.

"I thought it was Wednesday."

"It is, but for the shoot, it's still Monday. We're shooting what's supposed to happen before you went to the supermarket."

Dani shrugged. "Okay. I mean, I still have the same classes Monday and Wednesday."

"Good. We'll start on the front step of your dorm building with your last bottle of sunscreen."

"But I have lots of sunscreen."

"Not on Monday morning, you don't. I have an empty bottle you can use. I figure you'll try to spray some out before you go to class, and that's when you'll realize you're out. We'll shoot some of you on your way to class, and then we'll shoot some of you spraying the new sunscreen on, which is supposed to be right after you got back from the store. You'll need to record some voice over about not realizing your last bottle of sunscreen was almost empty, and then I'll intercut all of this the stuff we shot yesterday, and that should give us our 23-minute episode run time."

"Really?" Dani said. "So we'll be done today?"

"Well, you will. I'll still be working on this episode a few more days."

"Why on the front step of the dorm building?" Dani asked as Mandy swabbed a dab of makeup on each of her cheeks and started rubbing them into her skin.

"I don't want to show your dorm room this time since we don't know where this pilot will fit in with the other episodes."

"Why not?"

"Just trust me."

Mandy started the delicate work on Dani's eyebrows.

"You think that will be good enough?" Dani asked.

"I hope so."

"I mean, it seems kind of simple, running out of sunscreen and running to the store to get some more. You think people will watch that?"

"It's not just anyone going to the store for sunscreen. It's *you* going to the store for sunscreen. I am betting that they will watch you," Adam said as he took a good look at a very naked and very beautiful Dani. "I think they will." He turned to his work desk without waiting for Dani's reply, feeling the shame of his thoughts. For this production to work, he could not allow himself to even begin looking at Dani as a sex object.

"I hope you're right," Dani said.

"Yeah, me too."

Adam gathered his clipboard with today's shot list, roster of production assistants, and tentative schedule and headed out of the trailer. The air outside was dry and refreshingly cool. November brought cooler mornings to the desert, although the daily highs were still in the 80s and 90s. Kyle, his secondary cameraman, was unloading his equipment from his car. When he had heard he would be shooting Naked Dani, he had called in sick to his previous booking to do this. Normally, Adam would have objected and looked for someone else, but he had to get this footage fast, and he had worked with Kyle before.

Adam was still hesitant to bring up his roommate idea to Dani which is why he had declined to answer her question about shooting outside the dorm building. She'd had the luxury of a private room since the summer, and he figured that she would be hesitant to give that up. Adam also knew that with George Blanchard coming to visit the set, having all the shooting take place outside in the open would minimize any chance he might have at cornering Dani alone.

But Adam had enough things to worry about with the show production to really care about what George said or did with Dani. They were both adults, after all. And George was the reason Dani was going to make ten thousand dollars for a few days of work shooting this pilot. Wasn't George owed a little something for that? This was the way that Hollywood worked, after all. And yet, he just couldn't leave Dani to the wolves. There was something about her, a spark of idealistic innocence maybe that Adam felt the need to protect. That was, he thought, what gave Dani her appeal and what would, he thought, make the show watchable if not a bona fide hit.

Adam talked with Kyle about the shoot on the front steps of Holcombe Hall and that he planned to shoot Dani's walk across campus. He was glad that he didn't have to worry about the platoon of production assistants he'd had to have at the grocery store to get signed releases from the shoppers and store employees who had wound up on camera. Any student or employee on campus had agreed to the university's use of his or her image in any promotional material, and this reality series pilot had the endorsement of the university. And while he wanted to make sure he got the shots he needed, he was looking forward to getting back to his own studio office.

8

Dani

Dani felt like she was starring in a commercial for Sunguard sunscreen rather than an honest reality show about her life, but she went along with the pantomimed exercise in front of her dorm, trying to spray herself with a can of generic spray-on sunscreen before realizing that the can was empty. When she thought about it, that should have been obvious as soon as she picked it up and supposedly brought it downstairs from her room. But she did as Adam had asked and tossed the empty bottle into the trash can just outside the door of the dorm. She then stood squinting at the sunshine beating down on her before bounding down the stairs and walking at a fast pace toward the Commons.

"Cut!" she heard Adam call just before she rounded the corner of the building.

She stopped and turned, wondering if she would have to do another take.

"Perfect," he said as he and the other cameraman jogged toward her, passing her to take up positions on the path ahead. "Hold right there."

Dani stood in the desert sun, keenly aware that, as was being portrayed in the show, she wore no sunscreen. Adam and the second cameraman got set up, and Dani looked past them to a shady spot over the entrance to the Science Building. She would stop there when he called cut again.

"And action!" Adam yelled after getting a thumbs up signal from the second cameraman.

Dani resumed her brisk walking pace, glancing up at the sun as she went just to remind the viewers why she was moving so quickly. She zipped past the two cameras, ignoring Adam's call of "Cut!" until she made it to the shady entrance to the building. A steady stream of students was entering the building, most of them slowing to get a good look at the naked girl. Dani did not often stand still in one spot while out on campus simply because she didn't want to get drawn into conversations with strangers. She should be used to the looks she got from people, and in most ways, she was, but she still had to admit that she liked being the spectacle that she was even though she felt a great deal of awkwardness with it. And "like" was too mild a word. She loved it. If she didn't love it, she would have kept her clothes on after the study officially ended. A couple of male students started in her direction, and she prepared herself for whatever predictable questions they were going to ask her. But they turned away and ducked into the building when Adam caught up to her, trying to catch his breath as he stopped.

"Sorry," she said when he gave her an irritated look. "I didn't want to stand in the sun unprotected."

"Oh yeah," Adam said. "Sorry."

"It's all right, but I was thinking I could go through the buildings to get to class. Maybe run between buildings when I have to go outside. That might be funny."

"Yeah, that might work. We need a shot of you dashing into the building then."

Adam waved the other cameraman off, saying that he'll just do one angle of this quick shot. He motioned Dani back into the sunshine and then yelled "Action!"

Dani ran back into the shady overhang, slowed down, and walked into the building via the automatic sliding glass door.

"Cut!"

"We'll have to shoot with what we got," Adam was saying to the other cameraman as they both looked up at the lights. "I wasn't expected any interior shots, so I didn't bring a lighting guy," he told Dani.

"Sorry," she said. "I could go ahead and run outside."

"No, this is all right. It's supposed to be a reality show, right. We have to learn to shoot with what we have." Adam leaned in and said in a softer voice, "Be available for a quick reshoot tonight though if this doesn't look good."

He and the other guy set their cameras down near the foyer of the science building and made some adjustments to them, Dani knew not what. Maybe they were changing lenses. She stood off to the side, wondering if the actors she watched in movies had to do this much standing around during production. Adam stopped what he was doing and pulled his cell phone from his jeans pocket, glanced at the screen, and answered the incoming call. He said a few things, but Dani couldn't hear. So she took a few steps closer to Adam, but he ended the call and stuffed the phone back in his pocket.

"Shit," he said.

"What?" Dani and the other cameraman said at the same time.

"He's here." Adam looked at the other cameraman who seemed to have his camera ready and said, "We're going to have to take a break for a few minutes Kyle. Just hang loose."

Adam set his camera down beside Kyle and walked outside. Dani exchanged a glance with Kyle. He shrugged, and Dani followed Adam outside.

"Who's here?" she asked when she caught up with Adam.

"George," he replied. "The money behind this pilot episode. I didn't think he'd come. I mean, he said he was going to, but I figured it was too many hours out of his day to drive all the way out here." He sighed as they walked and glanced at Dani. "He has a bit of a reputation with the ladies, so watch him. Don't let him corner you alone."

"I can handle myself," she said, but as her hands brushed against her bare hips as she walked, she felt more naked than usual.

"There he is," Adam said.

The first thing Dani noticed were the wet patches around the arm pits of his striped shirt. He was a heavy-set man with a thick head of hair that was going gray around the temples and clean shaven which revealed the redness in his face. When he saw her next to Adam, both of them walking toward him, he stopped, his jaw dropping a bit. He looked around at the students walking in different directions, few of whom took any notice of the naked girl.

"George, you made it," Adam said, sounding much more cheerful about the visit than Dani knew he was.

"Yeah, well," he said and gestured toward Dani, "it seems to have been worth it."

He had the elevator eyes that Dani had gotten so used to from men who had never seen her before.

"George, this is Danielle Keaton. Dani, George Blanchard, executive producer from Netflix."

"Nice to meet you," she said, offering her hand.

George's grip was soft, his hand wet with sweat.

"The pleasure is all mine. I really don't believe my eyes," he said more to Adam than to Dani. "I mean, she's here naked and everyone keeps walking by like it's normal."

Adam seemed about to say something, but Dani jumped in first.

"It pretty much is. I've been on campus like this since March, so most people have just gotten used to it."

The three of them had turned and were now walking back toward the science building at a slow pace. Dani was still in the sun without sunscreen, but now that the cameras were off her, she didn't feel the need to act concerned about sunburns since it was still the eight AM hour.

"About fifteen years ago I did some work on *Not Another Teen Movie*," George said to Adam. "You remember that picture?"

"Vaguely," Adam replied.

"It was a take-off on all those teenage dramas and comedies from the 80s and 90s, a total farce. We had this one character, a foreign exchange student, who just goes to high school naked. I mean every scene she's in, she was naked. We even had a scene of her in the principal's office, and he's talking to her and doesn't even mention her lack of clothes. It was totally ridiculous. At least we thought so at the time. But here Danielle is, proving that it wasn't as ridiculous as we thought. Shit, what was that actress's name. Carina or Cerina something. She used to be one of the Power Rangers."

Dani had never seen *Not Another Teen Movie,* but she made a mental note to see if she could find it on Netflix later.

"We were just shooting some filler scenes of Dani going to her first class of the day," Adam said. He explained the situation of being out of sunscreen which sets up the footage that they had already shot.

"Dani here actually came up with the idea of going through the buildings to stay out of the sun since she doesn't have any sunscreen. I thought it was brilliant."

"Yeah," George said as he looked around the campus, although his eyes always kept returning to Dani.

"I think you'll like the episode we put together," Adam continued. "It's light and humorous, and it's got some great stuff from Dani in the studio to intercut between the reality stuff."

"That's great," George said as they stopped just inside the door of the building where Kyle stood watch over the camera equipment. "What kind of restrictions do you have in her contract?"

"Restrictions?"

"Yeah. You know SAG has these nudity riders on everything to spell out what will be shown and for how long and what won't be shown. You know."

"Well, this is a reality show, so since nudity is a part of her life, we didn't put any nudity riders in the contract. Besides that, Dani isn't SAG. At least, not yet."

"So you shoot everything? Even if her labia gets in the shot." As George said this, he bent over and took a good look at Dani's pubic area.

Dani thought he was just talking about the contract to get a good look at her, and her first impulse was to knee him in the face. She thought that would somehow be a terrible idea, so she resisted that urge.

"Um, yeah, but we're not focusing on that area," Adam said, putting a hand on George's shoulder guiding him back up. "I want to focus on the whole person."

"Of course. It's just that they stick out, especially since she's shaved."

"Nobody ever notices unless—," Dani said.

"I don't think this conversation is really appropriate here on the set," Adam said, cutting her off.

They were all silent for a moment that seemed longer than it really was. "Yeah," George said at last. "You're right. I apologize." The last was said to Dani.

She shrugged and looked at Adam. "Shall we continue?"

Adam smiled at her then at George. "We shall. You ready Kyle?"

"Yes sir." Kyle picked up his camera and stalked away further down the hall and away from the entrance.

Dani stepped away from Adam and George and waited just inside the doors.

"Stay behind Kyle and me," Adam said to George, "or you might wind up in the shot. You don't really look like a college professor."

"I guess I don't," George replied and walked down the corridor past the spot where Kyle had set up.

They shot Dani walking at a normal pace through three different buildings and running at an almost sprint in the sunny spaces between those buildings. They shot all the interior shots first before going back and getting those exterior shots just so they wouldn't have to keep adjusting their cameras. Adam kept George behind him during the entire shoot which meant that he was away from Dani. That suited Dani just fine. She got the same vibe from George that she got from her chemistry professor before he tried to sexually assault her while threatening to flunk her out of his class if she didn't cooperate. Luckily, everything he said had been recorded, and Dr. Slater had had him removed from the university. George had the power to kill this show and her rather substantial pay for it, so she knew she would have to avoid any situation where he might be able to use that. Fortunately, Adam seemed to have the same idea about keeping George away from her as he ended the shoot right at the entrance to the building where her class was held.

"This is really amazing," George said after Adam had called a wrap for the morning shoot.

"What time do you get out of classes?" Adam asked her, ignoring George, as he began packing his camera.

"1:50."

"Can you meet me in the studio at 2:15? I want to shoot your comments about this morning."

"Sure."

Dani turned to go, but George moved to block her way into the building.

"I have to say, it was a pleasure meeting you."

"Nice to meet you too," Dani said, hoping that she sounded more sincere than she felt.

"I really hope we get to move forward with a full season."

"I do too."

"If we do, I'm sure we'll see each other again." As he said this, his eyes did their elevator routine, looking at her from head to toe and back up to head.

"I'm sure we will. But if you'll excuse me, I'm going to be late for class." She wasn't close to being late, but she skirted around him and disappeared into the building anyway. Thankfully, he didn't try to follow her.

9

Michael

More than a week had passed since Dave and Debbie's unexpected arrival during Michael's experiment with nudity, but he still hadn't had a chance to talk with Dave about the things that had happened afterward. Michael hadn't even seen Debbie since then, for which he was relieved. He could only imagine that she would try to talk him out of his clothes again. If, that was, he was wearing any. The more he had thought about Dr. Slater's proposal, the more he thought he was going to do it. He sat in his room alone flipping the business card she had given him between his fingers.

When Michael had sat down and written out the pros and cons of participating in Dr. Slater's experiments, the cons had greatly outnumbered the pros. At the top of the list was his mother. He did not want her finding out, but if she did, what could she do other than throw a fit? He was an adult, paying his own way through college through a combination of scholarships and loans. Didn't he have a right to live his own life, make his own decisions? Of course he did. But actually standing up and telling his mother would take a bravery that he had never mustered. After his father died, he and his mother had become everything to each other. It would be difficult risking that if she did find out. And given what had happened with Dani and her family, he fully expected that she would.

The second item on the con side was his relationship with the other guys in the dorm, especially if he was going to become the floor's resident assistant. Dr. Slater had said that she would arrange things with the university housing department so that he could continue as RA, but he wasn't so sure that the other people on the floor would cooperate. In his experience, guys got really defensive when they perceived that another guy showed any interest in the girls they were dating, anything from actual flirting to simple politeness. Exposing one's naked body to such a girl was liable to incur if not the wrath of a lot of boyfriends then at least some heavy suspicion. Michael would have to be understanding of anyone who might feel threatened in this way, especially since he was going to feel defenseless in any physical altercation.

Another con on the list was the constant scrutiny he would be under everywhere he went on campus. And going anywhere off campus was going to be out of the question while he was naked. Places that might be willing to accept a naked Dani were not going to be as welcoming to a naked guy, he thought. Michael already knew there were cameras all over campus. That was how Dr. Slater had seen his previous naked excursion after all. One he started going naked on campus, his image was going to be out there as part of the public record, and he would never be able to take it back.

Most of the pros he listed on his sheet were somewhat frivolous by comparison: the lack of laundry he would have to do each week, the nice tan he would get, and the motivation to keep exercising. The only serious thing on the list was the connection he hoped to form with Dani, and considering that they hardly knew each other, he had no idea how positive that would turn out to be. The cons should have greatly outweighed the pros, but Michael knew he was going to go through with the project anyway. Dr. Slater had asked him, of all the students on campus, to do this. Surely, that had to be an honor of some kind, to be asked to be one's true self to the world, naked in front of everyone. But besides the perceived honor of being asked, Michael was going to do it simply because he wanted to. He had never gotten over how amazing his previous daytime naked excursion had made him feel, the sunshine and warm breeze caressing every inch of his skin. Michael also had the sense that his biggest regrets later in life would be the things he had the chance to do but didn't for whatever reason rather than things he did that he shouldn't have. And when else was he going to get this chance to be naked on campus just like Dani?

Now that he had decided he was going to do it, he had to let Dr. Slater know. He looked at the card, seeing that her office hours included Tuesday from 1:00 to 2:00 PM. It was now 12:52, and even though today was Election Day, he expected her to be in her office. Most people took advantage of the early voting period anyway, and besides, the big race between Hilary Clinton and Donald Trump was expected to go to Clinton easily, especially here in California. Michael slipped out of his shorts and stood in front of the mirror naked like he had the day of his excursion. His message to Dr. Slater had to be both clear and dramatic. He was going to do this. He was going to spend the next several months naked on campus, living here in the dorm, going to classes, eating in the dining hall, everything. There would be no covering up even if, or when, he felt uncomfortable.

Michael took a deep breath, made sure he had his school id and his room key in his hand, and opened the door to his room. The corridor was empty, and he almost turned to take the back stairs down to the ground level. But if he was going to do this, he might as well walk to the elevator and go down like everyone else. Besides, at this time of day, everyone was either in class or eating lunch somewhere. Michael tried to imagine going into the dining hall and eating naked, in close proximity to people from both the male and female dorms that shared that particular cafeteria.

"One step at a time," he whispered to himself when he realized that he was in no way ready for such a thing.

Michael hit the down button and waited for the elevator, feeling awkward. He realized how often he had put his hands in his pockets when having to stand in one spot for any length of time, except now he had no pockets. He let his hands hang at his sides, but that didn't feel right, so he put them behind his back, one fist in his other hand. But that felt too much like he was thrusting his genitals out for display, so he but his hands back at his sides, still thankful that no one was visible in either direction in the corridor. The elevator finally dinged, and the customary five seconds it took for the doors to actually slide open felt like fifty. When they did open, two girls stood inside. Neither of them made any move to step out of the elevator as their eyes widened.

"Whoa," one of them said.

Michael sighed and stepped inside, keeping to the front, close to the closing doors and as far as he could get from them.

"Nice day for a walk," one of them said, a redhead he had seen around over the course of the semester. Michael though she was dating one of the guys up on the fourth floor.

Michael couldn't help but laugh and said, "*The Terminator*."

"What?"

"That line, it's from *The Terminator*. When Arnold Schwarzenegger shows up out of the time bubble naked, and one of the first guys he sees says, 'Nice night for a walk.'"

The girls didn't say anything to that, and Michael felt a bit sheepish that his nerdiness was seeping out. The girls remained silent as the elevator clunked down past the second floor, before one of them started giggling. Michael took a quick glance back and saw that she held her phone in her hand, probably taking a photo or video. He quickly turned back around, glad that they seemed more amused than offended but fearful of any visible arousal that their attention to his naked body might give him. The incident with Dani was still in his mind, and he knew this was something he would have to deal with on an ongoing basis since he was going to commit to this for an entire semester. Michael popped out of the elevator as soon as the doors slid open on the ground level and scurried across the lobby and out into the bright sunshine.

The foot traffic around campus was that of a typical Tuesday, but for Michael, there seemed to be a lot more people out than during his previous naked excursion. He noticed a few of them stop what they were doing and stare at him as he walked by. Others ignored him altogether. Michael didn't know whether to be offended or emboldened by those who did ignore him. If enough people were blasé about his nudity, getting through the next semester might be a lot easier than he anticipated. He kept a brisk walking pace, something Dani did most of the times he had seen her walk across campus, which might have discouraged anyone who might otherwise have stopped to talk to him.

Michael had never been inside Carlisle Hall as it housed mainly departmental offices and hosted only the largest of classes in its first-floor lecture halls, but he knew where it was. The air conditioning caused his skin to break out into goose pimples as soon as he walked inside. Ignoring the few people milling about outside one of those huge lecture halls, Michael bounded up the main stairs to the second floor, finding the sociology department office near the top of the staircase. The receptionist glanced up from her desk at him when he walked in and had barely looked down again before sling-shotting her gaze back at him in a classic double take. Her eyes widened, and her jaw dropped.

"Hi," Michael said, thinking that he was probably blushing.

"Hello," the receptionist replied. "Don't tell me. You want to see Dr. Slater."

"How did you know?" He hoped his voice didn't sound too flirty. On the other hand, the receptionist was pretty even if she was a few years older. As soon as he thought this though, he reminded himself that he needed to stop thinking about how pretty girls were while he had everything on display. Some things were difficult to hide.

"Lucky guess." She pointed to the offices across the reception area from her. "Middle door."

Michael looked and saw that Dr. Slater's door was open. The receptionist went back to typing on her keyboard, so Michael took that as his permission to enter. He took a few steps toward Dr. Slater's office before glancing back at the receptionist to make sure he was still good to go. She was, of course, looking at his naked backside even as she kept typing. She gave him a quick smile before turning back to her monitor.

Michael turned back around, took a deep breath, knowing that this was the moment of commitment—no turning back now—and stepped through the threshold of Dr. Slater's office. She was leaning back in her chair, a Kindle device in her right hand, the index finger of her left poised to turn a page on the screen. She gave him a quick glance in the middle of her reading, but her eyes didn't remain on her Kindle long. Michael supposed that he would be getting a lot of those double takes.

"Mr. Cooley," she said, leaning her chair forward and setting the Kindle on her desk, "what a pleasant surprise."

She stood, her glee evident by the grin on her face, and walked around her desk to him.

"I've been thinking about—," Michael began, but Dr. Slater enveloped him in a hug.

The feel of her blouse was strange against his bare skin. Rather than just stand here, he put his arms around her waist, which was as high has he could reach since his upper arms were pinned to his body by her embrace. He wondered if she had given Dani hugs like this during the original experiment last semester.

It took just a few seconds, but Dr. Slater seemed to catch herself and drew back from Michael.

"Sorry," she said. "I was just so happy you decided— You did decide to do this, right?"

Michael nodded, already missing the feel of her clothed body against his and feeling dirty for it. Dr. Slater was probably older than his mother, although she was still quite attractive.

"Yes," he said.

"Wonderful!" She looked down at his body, her grin widening.

Michael looked down at what she was looking at and was dismayed to see that his penis was almost erect. He moved his hands over his crotch, but he thought it would be bad form and maybe obscene to actually touch himself there.

"Sorry," he said.

"Don't be." She returned to her chair.

"Actually, this was one of my biggest concerns. What should I do when *this* happens?"

Once seated, she motioned to his hands and said, "Not that, whatever you do. Trying to cover it up with your hands only draws attention to it."

Michael moved his hands back to his sides, feeling awkward. Dr. Slater sat looking at his penis as if in a trance. He felt every beat of his heart as the blood continued to pulse into his now full erection.

"Actually," he said, "your staring at it isn't helping."

Dr. Slater turned away, shaking her head just a bit. "No, of course not. Sorry."

Michael put his hand on the back of the chair facing Dr. Slater's desk. He wanted to sit down, but she hadn't invited him to.

"What should I do if this happens again?"

Dr. Slater looked back at him, at his eyes this time. "I think that the best course of action would be to ignore it."

"Ignore it?"

"Yes. It's a part of nature. This whole project is a study of the reactions to human beings in their natural state. You are what, twenty years old?" She continued before he had a chance to answer. "You are at your prime reproductive peak, unlike the women your age who hit it much later. You're expected to get excited at the drop of a hat. So when it happens just ignore it. Flaccid or erect, it's always there, and with your participation in this project, it's always going to be visible. Just let it be however it is."

"But what if certain people make it an issue?" He was thinking of Debbie and her fascination with his public nudity from the week before.

"We have instructions to the university police department regarding any complaints about public nudity."

"I don't mean complaints; I mean people trying to provoke this reaction in me. You know…"

"You mean like my hug just did, apparently?"

Michael shrugged. He hadn't wanted to go that far.

"Here, sit down," she said, pulling a small black hand towel out of a drawer in her desk. "Put this on the chair."

He took it from her, laying it on the chair as he had seen Dani do during the countless times he had watched her *Stossel* TV show appearance. He'd even seen her do it in person on campus a few times. Dr. Slater started speaking as he sat down.

"As you aware from Dani's lack of attire these past several months, simple nudity in public is perfectly legal here. The university police department is aware of this and knows how to record and respond to any complaint calls regarding such nudity. Public lewdness, however, is still illegal. Any such violations will be investigated. In anticipation of having a male for this project, I've had conversations with the chief of the university police about the difference between simple nudity and lewdness. We came to an understanding that an erection while nude does not constitute public lewdness."

"OK," Michael said, mainly just to fill Dr. Slater's pause. "So a naked man walking through the Commons with a hard on is legal?"

"That's right."

"If that's not lewd, what is?"

"Touching oneself or others in a sexual manner or in an attempt to elicit a sexual response. Given that definition, can you see why the best thing you can do when an erection happens is to simply ignore it?"

"Yeah, I guess so." The talk about legalities and law enforcement had caused his own erection to subside, thankfully.

"Don't touch it; don't allow others to touch it; just pretend it isn't there."

"What if others touch it anyway?" Michael was thinking, again, of Debbie.

"If anyone touches you without your permission, they can be charged with sexual assault in addition to public lewdness. If it happened in public, of course."

"I guess Dani was lucky that she didn't have to deal with this."

"Each gender has unique issues to consider when going nude in public like this. Dani had her own obstacles to deal with."

Like how she was blackmailed into this, Michael thought but didn't say out loud.

"I'm not going to lie to you Mr. Cooley," Dr. Slater continued, "women and men are perceived differently by society in general. This is just my hypothesis, but the common perception among a lot of women is that a man welcomes sexual advances from almost any woman, whether in a relationship or not. Men don't have such preconceptions about women, which is why, I think, Dani had so few problems with unwanted touching. I anticipate a lot more aggressive behavior toward you by the opposite sex. It will be up to you to rebuff such advances."

She shrugged and said, "Or not, if you're in a more private place."

Michael wondered how he would handle Debbie in the dorm room. She was so brazen that she might try something even with her boyfriend in the room. For that matter, he wondered how Dave would take his constant nudity. Would he stop bringing Debbie into the dorm altogether?

"Now, the official study won't begin until the start of the spring semester. I'll have a contract ready for you to sign the day before classes start. It will spell out the expectations for you and what you will get in return, i.e. the six semester hours of sociology credit. I just don't have the resources I once had to start the study earlier than that, although you should feel free to be naked whenever and wherever you'd like. I do have an extensive video surveillance system to study reactions to you even now. Unfortunately, when the study starts, I won't have the same resources to record reactions to you that I did with Dani. The university stripped me of some power."

"Stripped?"

"Yes, ironic word choice, I know."

They were silent for an awkward moment before Michael got up enough courage to speak. "What is the goal of this study?"

Dr. Slater's eyebrows raised as she leaned back in her chair. "The goal? The goal would be to demonstrate that a natural human being, without clothes, can be accepted in modern society were it not for the draconian laws against nudity. I guess the main goal is to win freedom for that small percent of the population who would rather be unclad."

"Rather than just study society, you want to change it?"

She smiled at him. "I hope that the results of this study show that society can change, maybe ought to change. But, like everything, the results have to speak for themselves. I started with a female subject because I thought, correctly it turns out, that a female would more easily gain acceptance. But you, a male, are going to be the real test of the feasibility of what I want to demonstrate with this. Women may be aggressive toward you, yes, but in the end, I think they will see you as a novelty. The part I'm worried about is how men will react to you. With Dani, I wondered how other women would react to her, jealousy over boyfriends being the main concern but also insecurities over body image. Would they think Dani was flouting her beauty, and would they judge her harshly for it? Et cetera. But with men and you.... All of that is present, of course, the jealousy and envy, but there is also a current of homophobia that seems to run through many of the college age males I see. Will they refuse to accept you because of the fear of being perceived as homosexual?" She shrugged. "We'll have to see."

Michael hadn't thought about that, but then again, Dr. Slater was paid to think about these things. "So I don't officially start until January?"

"Correct."

"So I can ease myself into this then? I can be naked some of the time but not all the time."

"If you want. Like I said, we have a fantastic video surveillance system throughout the university, so I will get data no matter what you do. But beginning in January, I expect you to be nude 24/7 for the duration of the semester."

Now that he had gone for two naked walks, Michael thought he could do that without any issues. It even felt good, his bare skin in the warm sunshine. But he still had problems imagining himself going into a class naked. What would his professors say? What did they say to Dani the first time she went to class naked? Whatever they said, it probably wouldn't be any worse than what the guys in the dorm would say when he started as a full-time nudist. And he was supposed to be the resident assistant for a floor, which meant that he would have to leave his door open in the late afternoon and early evening so that any residents could feel free to come to him with issues. He wondered how many of them would shy away from him when they would otherwise go to an RA with clothes on.

"Yes ma'am," Michael answered in response to her statement that he should be nude 24/7.

Dr. Slater smiled at him. She pulled a couple more of the black towels from her desk drawer and put them on the desk in front of him. "Here are a couple of spares. When we meet in January, I'll have more for you. And a binder with a Kindle loaded with all of your necessary texts. Another benefit is you won't have to pay for next semester's books."

"Awesome."

"Thank you so much for volunteering for this. I think you are going to learn a lot about yourself while helping us all learn about everyone else."

"I hope so," Michael said.

She glanced at her open door, appeared to see someone, and held up a finger, indicating that she would be done in one minute.

"Well," Michael said, feeling as the interview, such as it was, was at an end. "I guess I'll talk to you in January."

"Yes," she replied, standing to her feet.

Michael took that as his cue to stand as well. Thankfully, all his body parts were in a more relaxed state than they had been when he sat down. Dr. Slater walked around her desk, and Michael was both hoping and fearing that she would hug him again. But she held out a hand, and he shook it.

"Thank you so much for stopping by and committing to the project," she said.

"You're welcome," he replied, feeling awkward at her sudden formality.

He took that as his dismissal, and when he turned to walk out of her office, two girls were standing just outside her door. Their eyes widened almost comically when they saw the frontal view of him, and Michael wondered if he would ever get tired of that look. Whether he did or not, he expected to see a lot of it over the next few months.

10

Adam

Los Angeles was a strange place to be on that Wednesday when Adam took his completed master disc into the Netflix offices. Everywhere he'd gone, people had been subdued, almost in a state of shock, although there had been just a very few who couldn't hide their glee. Donald Trump had somehow defeated Hillary Clinton for the presidency the night before, and while Adam didn't much care for politics and hadn't voted in an election since just after graduating from high school, he knew that most people in Hollywood leaned to the left.

He had spent roughly forty of the previous forty-eight hours cutting the pilot episode together. There was a thrown-together background music track, although it wasn't final. But it would have to do for the meeting. Adam had managed to get the episode down to the standard 23 minutes of a regular network half hour time slot, and since it was so short, the board had agreed to watch the episode during the meeting.

George Blanchard met him in the lobby and accompanied him up in the elevator.

"We can't wait to see what you have," George said as soon as the elevator doors closed. "I've been working on them since I visited you on the set, so everything should go our way."

"I hope so," Adam said.

"We'll get to see all of her right? You didn't do some crazy Austin Powers editing, did you?"

"No, it's all there," Adam said. "Full frontal and everything, just like you saw when you were on campus."

"Great."

"You don't think that will be an issue for the rest of the board?"

"Naw. They talk a good game about not wanting adult content, but they really don't care as long as it increases subscribers. You remember that reality show *Family Business* on Showtime a few years ago, about the porn producer?"

Since Adam had gone into the reality show business, he had made it a point to watch at least one episode of everything that had already been done. "Yeah." As he recalled *Family Business* had shown a lot of nudity and the dialogue was very frank about what they were shooting, but they had stopped short of displaying any of the actual sex on their porn sets.

"The board had talked about bringing that onto Netflix not long ago. They voted it down, but not by much."

The elevator doors opened, and Adam followed George to the same conference room where he had made his original proposal the previous month. An IT guy was there and helped Adam hook his laptop up to the room's projector and then left once he verified that it worked. When all the board members were in and seated, George took charge of the meeting. He re-introduced Adam to the rest of the attendees, and Adam gave his rehearsed intro to the series concept, altered just slightly from the original presentation he had given now that he knew how well Dani's monologues to the camera would go. When he finished, he nodded to George to kill the lights and double-clicked the video file on his desktop. His leg bounced nervously under the table as the episode played, reminding him of an old Robert Klein comedy routine. He kept telling himself that George had put his own money up for the pilot and that as long as he had cut together a watchable show, and Adam knew that he had, George would not allow the board to pass on the full series. Still, he kept watching their reactions. They whispered among themselves, but they all seemed to stop during the sequences where Dani sat and talked to the camera, which were intercut into the scenes of her trying to get across campus without being in the sun and shopping at the grocery store for sunscreen. He had shot her sitting on a stool, her legs crossed, visible to the camera from the knees up so that the viewers never forgot that she was naked.

"My biggest fear," she said at one point as she talked about leaving campus to go to the store, "is not being able to adjust to regular textile life after my time here is over. Because I know that this is finite. I'll be graduating in a little over a year if I keep taking classes at my current pace, and the freedom I have enjoyed here is not available in ninety-nine percent of the rest of the world." She sighed, looking wistful, and Adam heard what sounded to him like approving grunts from the board members. At least, he hoped they were approving.

When the episode ended the room burst into sound; what had been subdued, whispered comments between board members became full conversations. "The stocker at the grocery store had the best reaction," someone said. "I wouldn't have believed it if I didn't just see it," another stated. "That the university would allow it is incredible."

"All right," George said in a booming voice. "Does anyone have any questions for Adam here?"

"Is Ms. Keaton willing to do promotion for the show?" the man who ran the previous meeting asked.

Adam nodded. "Yes, but she's taken a vow to stay naked during her time there at college. She only has one outfit available if she ever does have to go anywhere that requires clothes."

"She took a vow?"

Adam shrugged. "It was a promise she made to the Board of Regents there. Non-binding, of course, but she is going to stick to it."

"According to the story," a middle-aged woman from the far end of the table said, "she was originally coerced into this nudity experiment by a Doctor Slater. Have you approached this professor about participating in the series?"

"I haven't yet since my main focus was on getting this pilot finished, but it is something I plan on doing. I think it's part of Dani's story and needs to be addressed in the show, along with what Dani did for Dr. Slater."

"Her vow, as you put it, was to try to save Dr. Slater's job?"

"In a way. As Dani puts it, it was more to save the research than anything for Dr. Slater personally. She didn't want to have done everything she did for nothing. And it was more of a gesture than any kind of bargain. The impression in the room at the time was that Dr. Slater had basically forced her into the nudity. Her coming into the hearing nude, of her own free will, put a quick end to that impression. It's all in her book."

"When does the book release?"

"I'm not sure the exact date," Adam said, "but I know it's late this month."

"And when will you have a full season ready to air? How can we tie that into the book?"

"I can have a season ready by spring," he replied, hoping that he wasn't biting off more than he could chew, especially considering that he wasn't planning on shooting anything until January, after he had found a roommate to co-star in the show. "That will give some time for the book to generate some buzz."

Questions kept coming at him, and he answered them, feeling like he was repeating the same thing over and over. When the meeting ended, he had been approved unanimously for one season of fifteen half-hour episodes. George Blanchard was to be in charge of the production for Netflix, of course. When the meeting ended, George beckoned Adam to follow him to his office, the walls of which were covered with framed movie posters. George's desk was too large for the small room and was made of an expensive looking reddish wood. It reminded Adam of the Resolute Desk in the Oval Office of the White House.

"Sit down," George said, motioning to one of the two chairs in front of his desk. The chairs were plain, too plain for such an ornate desk, with wood frames and green upholstered seats.

Adam sat, and George settled into his large leather chair which was much more of a match for his desk.

"I can't tell you how much I appreciate your help in getting this through," Adam said.

George held up a hand. "You don't have to thank me. You made a great pilot. And that girl, Dani. She can be a star if she wants to be. With this show, she'll be a star whether she wants to be or not."

"Yeah, she's great. I wasn't sure how she'd be when I approached her with this idea, but I think I got lucky."

"We all did. We got lucky when that crazy professor made her go naked all that time. She ought to win a fucking medal."

Adam nodded but remained silent.

"I'm going to try to visit the set as much as I can, but that's a ways out there."

"That's all right," Adam said, wishing he wouldn't bother to show up at all.

"So you're going to start shooting right before the spring semester starts?"

"That's the plan."

"Good. And until then, you'll be auditioning for the roommate position?"

"Yeah."

"Good. Keep me in the loop with the resumes and headshots of the top contenders."

"Sure."

"All right." George leaned back in his chair, a satisfied grin on his face.

"Well," Adam said after a moment, "I had better get to work. I need to put the call out for a roommate, scout positions on campus and off. All that."

"Sure," George said.

Adam stood, but before he could turn to leave, George said, "I'd like to have a meeting with Dani. One on one, just to talk to her about her future, her aspirations."

Adam stood in front of the desk, silent.

"You can't keep her all to yourself," George said.

Yes I can, Adam thought. "No. I'll talk to her, try to set something up."

"Good deal," George said, standing up and offering his hand across the desk for Adam to shake.

With hesitation and feeling like he was cementing a promise to get George his one-on-one with Dani, Adam shook George's hand.

"All right then," George said with a grin.

The first thing Adam did when he got to his car was call Dani although he thought he should probably be calling Audrey, her agent, first.

"You're kidding!" Dani said when he told her that the full season had been green lit.

"What, you didn't think it would get picked up?"

"Well, I didn't know."

"Did you watch the episode?" He had sent her a link to the final edit as an unlisted and private YouTube video.

"I watched part of it," she said with hesitation. "It's weird watching myself. Especially when I'm naked."

"But you're not naked," Adam replied. "You said it yourself. You're free of clothes and nude, but not naked."

"Yeah, I know. But it was still jarring to see myself on video. And my voice. I don't sound the way I think I sound to myself when I'm talking, if you know what I mean."

"Yeah, I think I do."

"So what do we do now? When do we start shooting for real?"

"I'm going to be in Palm Desert tomorrow to find some temporary lodging for myself and a small crew. I'll also be putting out a casting call for a roommate for you. It'll have to be someone who's already a student at CVU."

"Really?" Dani asked in a less than enthusiastic voice.

"Yeah, we need more of a regular cast than just you. And you having a roommate who doesn't necessarily agree with your nudist lifestyle was one of the selling points of the show."

"I know. But I did enjoy having a room all to myself this semester. Just don't pick Diane."

Adam started to ask who that was before remembering her previous roommate as described in her book. "She's not a theater major, is she?"

"No."

"Then she'll probably never see the casting call. Still, that kind of conflict would be good for the show and would tie in nicely with the book."

"No," Dani said with more emphasis.

"Think about it," Adam said. "If she's good on camera, she could be a great asset to the show."

"No, she would be a poison to the show. And remember, this is my life when the cameras aren't running."

"All right. I'll cross Diane off the list then."

"Thank you."

When Dani asked other questions about the show, mainly about how and when she would be paid, he had to refer her to her agent. "I should have called her first," Adam confessed, "but I was just so excited to tell you myself."

"I'm glad you did."

"In fact, let me call her now. I'm heading to the office to get some documents ready to email her, so I want to give her a heads up."

"OK. Thank you Adam. For everything."

He felt something like butterflies in his stomach at the sound of her voice saying his first name. *What am I, in high school?* he asked himself before saying anything more.

"Thank you for going along with me Dani. We still have a long way

to go yet."
"I know. It's exciting."

11

Dani

Dani didn't have much to do with the TV show production throughout the rest of the fall semester except to sign the contracts and paperwork that Audrey brought to her two days after her call from Adam. Her book was to be released the Tuesday after Thanksgiving, and the university bookstore had scheduled her for a book signing that evening. With some amusement, Dani thought back to the days when she used to claim that she hated being the center of attention. She had been nothing but the center of attention since walking nude out of Dr. Slater's office last March, and, she had no choice but to admit now, she loved it. With this TV show, being the center of attention was something she had to get used to.

Early in the morning on the day before Thanksgiving, Dani stood in front of her open closet looking at the only thing hanging there, her sleeveless yellow dress. She had worn it on the plane ride from Texas back in June so that she'd have it on at the hearing of the University Board of Regents that was to decide the fate of Dr. Slater. She had taken it off while waiting to go into that hearing and, outside of footwear, had not worn a stitch of clothing since. She had accidentally left her luggage in the trunk of Samantha's car at the Dallas-Fort Worth airport, so the yellow dress was the only clothing she had on campus. Dani removed the dress from the wire hanger and laid it front down on her bed. She unzipped the zipper but let the dress lie there a while longer. Her flight back home was scheduled to leave the Palm Springs airport at 9:45 AM. It was not quite 7:00 now, so she had time. Taking a deep breath, she lifted the dress, held it over her head, and let it fall over her, making sure that her arms went into the correct holes. It was a light dress, designed to be worn in summer, but it still felt heavy. The fabric was scratchy against her deeply tanned skin. Her arms didn't want to bend at the necessary angles to get the zipper up. Dani had worn this dress several times before and hadn't ever had any trouble zipping it up. She finally managed to get the zipper all the way to the top although she felt like her arms were twisted into pretzels while doing it. Dani lowered her arms and shut the closet door to look at herself in the full-length mirror there.

The image looking back at her seemed to be a different person. Her shoulders were slumped, and she wore a frown on her face. Dani raised her shoulders and tried to smile, but that smile looked forced in the image. She thought about that moment at the end of Dr. Slater's two-month study when she had first put clothes on again. At the time, she had viewed it as the end of something that she had always thought of as an ordeal, something to endure. It was the wearing of clothes for the time between the end of the spring semester and the start of the summer sessions that showed her what the public nudity had meant to her. The putting on of clothes now, with her full knowledge and recognition of how the nudity had fulfilled and defined her, was far worse than dressing last May. But still, she was flying home to Texas today, and they wouldn't very well let her on the plane nude.

Dani hadn't spoken to her father since coming back to Coachella Valley University in June. He was usually at work during the times that she and her mother spoke on the phone. She and Daddy had liked each other's Facebook posts and had exchanged a comment or two. That was all. Dani herself didn't post much on social media. She couldn't very well post pictures of her day-to-day life since Facebook and Instagram would ban someone for posting anything with nudity, but she did have a Twitter account which was a bit more open. Her parents, as far as she knew, weren't on Twitter. She knew from her dad's Facebook posts that he was almost gleeful over the results of the Presidential election, not so much that Donald Trump had won but that Hillary Clinton had lost. She hoped that his good spirits would somehow extend to her and his feelings on her public nudity at school.

Dani sighed and grabbed her large purse which contained what little she was taking home with her. It seemed strange to be leaving for four days and not even have an overnight bag, but then again, every other article of clothing she owned was in her bedroom back home. Slinging the purse over her shoulder, she opened her door and looked up and down the corridor. Walking out with clothes on, for her, was probably how most people would feel about walking out nude. It was early enough in the day and late enough in Thanksgiving week that the hall was empty. She walked quickly after pausing to make sure she had her room key somewhere within the unfamiliar bulk of the purse and to make sure the door was locked. The fabric of her dress rubbing against her skin as she walked was both constraining and stimulating. Looking down at herself, she saw that her nipples pressed prominently against the dress. Perhaps she should have bought a bra from the university store before embarking on this trip, she thought, but she immediately dismissed the idea, not wanting her body to be any more constrained than it already was.

It occurred to her as she walked to the parking lot and the old Ford Crown Victoria she had used for her trip to the grocery store that in a year and a half or less she would have her Bachelor's degree and would have to move back into the world of the constantly clothed. The thought both filled her with dread of how she would cope with it and determination to enjoy the rest of her time at CVU. Maybe her time at Coachella Valley, her book, and the reality show would all help to make what she experienced here possible in other places. As she approached the car, she realized that she was pulling at the neck of the dress, trying to hold it away from her body. She let go of the dress and pulled the car keys from the purse.

The drive to the Palm Springs Airport didn't take long, and Dani parked in the ten dollar a day long term parking lot. An Uber would have been cheaper, but after Audrey had gone over the contract she had brought, Dani didn't worry about money much anymore. Besides, she'd had the idea of driving nude to the airport and getting dressed in the parking lot before dismissing it as the actions of someone who had gone crazy. How could she have developed such a deep aversion to clothes in such a short time?

The flight to DFW seemed shorter than it actually was. As Dani stepped off the plane, the air seeping into the jet bridge from outside felt cold and heavy, even though the pilot had said the temperature here was sixty-three degrees. She had felt temperatures in the morning in Palm Desert get down into the fifties in the past weeks but had never felt uncomfortable outside even without clothes. Dani walked into the terminal and followed the signs to the baggage claim where she expected her mom to be waiting. Both parents were there, much to her surprise since her father had not been at the airport to pick her up when she came home last summer. Daddy greeted her first, with a hug, but was silent.

"It's so wonderful to see you," her mother said as Daddy released her from the hug.

Dani hadn't planned on feeling this emotional at seeing her parents, and she was so close to tears that she choked up when she tried to say something.

"How was your flight?" Daddy asked, because it was what he always asked when she got off a plane.

"Fine," she managed to say as she received a hug from Mom.

"Oh, I brought your sweater," Mom said as she pulled away, and Dani saw her old white sweater draped over her arm.

"Thank you," Dani said.

She was still cold and put the sweater on without even thinking about it. Once she did think about it, she wondered if her aversion to clothing only extended to the Coachella Valley. Ever since she had first gone away to college, being back home in Texas had always felt like being on a different planet from Southern California, probably because the parents she had grown up under were here. The recent difference in her state of dress in each place only added to that feeling.

Since Dani had no luggage to wait for, her father seemed to feel no need to stand around the baggage claim area and ushered them all out to the car.

"So, tell me about this TV show," Dani's mom said as soon as the car got through the parking toll booths on the way out of the airport.

"Deborah," Daddy said in a warning tone.

"James," Mom said back to him. "I want to hear about it. This is a big deal in her life."

"Well, it all came about because of my book."

"A Hollywood producer read your book before it was even out," Mom said. "You hear that, James?"

In the back seat, Dani cringed and sank down in her seat. Her parents were the last two people on the planet she wanted reading her book. Going naked before the world was one thing; publishing the secrets of one's heart in prose was something else. She wished she had given more thought to it rather than following advice from her agent and editor, both of whom probably had dollar signs occluding their vision.

"I thought we agreed not to talk about it," Daddy said.

"I know, but now that she's here, it's hard not to talk about it. I mean, our daughter is famous!"

"Or infamous."

"Not from her point of view."

"I'm fine with not talking about it," Dani said. "I mean, it's all I ever have to talk about with anyone at school anyway."

"See," Daddy said, "she doesn't want to talk about it."

"I think she should. We are her family."

"Really, I'd rather not. I'd rather go back to life like it used to be, at least for a little while." As Dani said this, she texted her friend Samantha to tell her that he was back in town and already needed rescuing from her parents.

"U wanna come over?" Samantha texted back.

"Yes and no. I don't want to hurt their feelings."

"How about I come over there?"

"That would be awesome!"

The ride to her parents' house took almost an hour with all the slow moving traffic. Her mom asked about her classes and her grades. Dani gave her an update on each of her courses, the assignments she'd had to do, and the grades she had earned for each of them. She had more B's than A's which she attributed to the distractions from the media attention, but none of her grades had dipped into C territory.

Walking back into the house after so many months away was, again, like stepping back in time. Her high school years suddenly seemed like they were mere months ago rather than years. Dani hadn't realized how much she missed home. She took off the sweater and hung it up on the coat tree by the front door.

"Make yourself at home," her mom said, as though she was a guest.

Her room was as she had left it in June. This was still her official residence even though she had been living in the dorm at Coachella Valley University for over two years, and her parents had told her time after time that she would always have a room here. Her first impulse once she was alone in the room was to remove the stupid dress. The previous hours of wearing it hadn't gotten her used to wearing anything, and it still felt heavy hanging off her shoulders. Dani had as much trouble unzipping it as she'd had zipping it up, but she finally got it down far enough so that she could pull it off over her head. The laundry hamper was in the corner as it had been throughout her high school years, but it was empty now. Dani threw the dress into it and looked into her closet. Her suitcase was on the shelf above the clothes, but she could see that everything she had packed back in June had been hung back up or, she assumed, put back into her bureau drawers.

Someone walked past the open door of her room, and she heard a heavy sigh from her father as he headed toward her parents' room.

"Sorry," she said, rushing over to close her door.

As much as she wished she could just be her regular nude self all the time, even here, she also wanted a Thanksgiving as free of conflict as possible. She resolved that she would only be nude here, in her room, and with the door closed. Staying cooped up in her room was not an option since it would cause almost as much conflict as walking downstairs in the nude would. If she had to wear something, she might as well put on something comfortable, she thought as she pulled on a pair of plain gray sweatpants and a Texas Rangers baseball t-shirt from her bureau.

The doorbell rang just as she opened her bedroom door and walked out. Dani bounded down the stairs and beat her mother to the front door.

"I got it. It's probably Sam."

"OK," Mom said and turned back toward the kitchen.

Dani looked through the peep hole just to make sure and opened the door. Samantha glared at her.

"What's wrong?" Dani said.

Samantha held up one of the advance copies of her book *The "Volunteer"*. "What the hell, Dani?"

"Where did you get that?"

"Ebay, where else?"

Dani stood there a moment, not knowing what to say. Finally, she stepped aside and motioned for Samantha to come in.

"I was wondering why I had to go online to find the book that my best friend wrote rather than getting one directly from her," Samantha said as she walked into the living room. "Now I know why."

"The book's not even out yet. That's just an advance, and it's not supposed to be for resale. I was going to give you a signed copy of the final book."

Samantha sat on the couch. "Do I look as much like an asshole in the final book as I do in the advance copy?"

Dani sighed and sat beside her. "I thought I told you that you came out looking a little like a bad guy, thanks to my editor."

"You did. But still, it was rough reading it for myself."

"I know. I'm sorry. They just thought it would make for a more interesting story if there was someone pushing me into being naked in public at home, and not doing it because I wanted to. And I tried to show how much of a help you were afterward: the trip to the nudist camp and driving me to the airport. Did you read that far?"

"No. I stopped when I took you to see Chris and told you I wouldn't let you get your clothes out of the trunk until after you'd seen him."

Dani slumped her shoulders, remembering that it was actually her idea all along and that Samantha, fearing her best friend's arrest, had tried to talk her out of walking into Chris's workplace, a Comfort Inn, without clothes.

"I'm sorry Sam. I should have been stronger. But they've been in publishing for so long, and I was afraid they'd void the contract and not publish the book if I didn't go along with them."

"Isn't this a non-fiction memoir? They should know not to put fiction into non-fiction. I mean, really. Saying I locked your clothes in the trunk?"

"Well, technically, you did."

"Only because *you* told me to! I mean seriously, didn't you feel bad making me out to look like a total jerk?"

"Yes, I did. That's what I'm telling you." Dani held out her hand. "Let me see the book."

"Why?"

"I want to show you something."

"What?"

"Something I did. A message, mainly to you but also to anyone reading the book. I'm just glad the editors never said anything about it."

Samantha handed the book to Dani who thumbed through the first chapter. "Here. The last paragraph that starts on page 14."

Dani handed the book back to Samantha who started reading it to herself. It was a long paragraph about skinny dipping in the swimming pool of an apartment complex the summer after their freshman year in high school.

"See, this is bullshit too," Samantha said while she was still reading. "Skinny-dipping that night was totally your idea. And you so wanted to jump out and flash this drunk guy who showed up."

"I know." Dani held out her hand again, and Samantha handed the book back to her. This time, Dani looked toward the end of the book. "If you read up to going to see Chris, you should have seen this."

Dani gave the book back to Samantha, her finger marking a paragraph on page 197. It was dialogue between Samantha and Dani, with Samantha speaking on the line that Dani had pointed to.

"'Ah, so you admit you are now'" Samantha read aloud. "'You were then too. You were just scared of getting caught, like now. That whole skinny dipping thing was your idea. And when that drunk guy came by, I had to hold you into the pool and shush you to be quiet. You had wanted to flash him. "He's not going to call the cops; he's drunk," you said.'"

"Keep reading," Dani said.

"'I did not.'

"'Did too.'

"'That's not the way I remember it.'

"'Then your memory is faulty,' Samantha said.'"

Samantha looked up from the book and at Dani.

"So what is that supposed to mean?"

"Like I said, it's a message that people shouldn't trust every word. I mean, the whole time I was writing it, I kept having to imagine how every conversation went. I don't remember everything word for word. I had to get creative. But I still wanted to tell people not to trust everything in the book. Making myself seem just a little bit unreliable was the only way I could think of to do that."

Samantha looked back down at the book, thumbing through the last pages.

"You still mad at me?" Dani asked.

Samantha shook her head.

"Good. So let me make it up to you. Come to Coachella for a few days after Christmas and be on an episode of my show."

"I can't do that. I've got my own classes to go to."

"Come in January, before your classes start. I have to go back early anyway for the show prep. I can talk to Adam about taping some segments with you in them. I mean, way more people are going to watch the show than read the book, and I want people to know you're my best friend."

Samantha sighed, shaking her head, but Dani could tell that she really wanted to come.

"Palm trees and warm weather in early January. Doesn't that sound nice?"

"I couldn't afford the airfare."

"Don't worry about that. If I can't get it added to the show budget, I'll pay for it myself."

Samantha smiled and then laughed. "I guess we won't be going to very many places if you'll be naked the whole time."

Dani smiled back at her and said, "You'd be surprised."

12

Michael

Although Thanksgiving dinner with Mom, Uncle Randy, Aunt Cindy, and four of his cousins had been a good time of reminiscing, Michael was anxious to leave and get back to school. It had been the sixth Thanksgiving without his father. Thanksgiving had been his father's favorite holiday. "Football and food and no worries about gifts," he had always said. "What's not to love about that."

Michael left home early Saturday, much to the dismay of his mother who had expected him to remain with her until Sunday, and he arrived back at his dorm room before one PM. Thankfully, his mother had not followed him back to CVU as she had for the start of the semester. Now that he had experienced freedom to truly be himself here at school, he just couldn't feel comfortable at home with the relatives he had known all his life. Michael couldn't say or express what he really felt, especially around his mother. And actually, he didn't really care much what the other relatives thought. It was his mother that caused him the discomfort. Something had changed in her since his dad's death.

Now, back in his dorm room, he could breathe again. His first impulse was to take his clothes off. Dave wasn't expected back until late tomorrow night. The two of them hadn't talked much in the past month, but they had imparted their Thanksgiving plans to each other. And if Michael was going to spend the next semester nude on campus, he might as well get comfortable in his own skin.

Once his clothes were off, he looked out his window at the nearly empty campus. It was, as usual in the Coachella Valley, a warm sunny day. Why not go for a walk in the sunshine and get further acclimated to what he would be doing all of next semester? Michael still couldn't believe he had signed up for constant nudity. Hell, he couldn't believe that it had even been asked of him. He slipped into his sandals and walked out of his room.

The dorm was empty enough that Michael felt comfortable taking the elevator. The thought of having to be in such close quarters with people while he was nude was still uncomfortable to him, but no one was on the elevators on this Saturday afternoon. As expected, the elevator took him all the way to the ground level without stopping. Even though this wasn't his first nude outing, it was the first time he had entered the ground floor common area in his birthday suit. The game room and lounge were both empty, so Michael stopped and just stood, feeling the breeze from the air conditioning vents. He tried to imagine standing like this on a typical night when at least a dozen people were here socializing. In none of the scenarios he envisioned did people just carry on as if he were fully clothed. This was a male dorm, but at least as many girls as guys were here on a typical night. The scariest images Michael came up with involved guys wanting him to cover up around their girlfriends and being quite angry about it. How would he deal with that if something happened during Dr. Slater's experiment, when he had to stay naked per the contract?

Michael shook his head, pulling himself out of his imagined difficulties, and walked out the front door. The sun was bright, but there was a coolness in the air that wasn't present here most of the year, even though the temperature was supposedly in the mid-eighties. After 115 to 120 during the summer months, Michael supposed that the eighties would feel cool to anyone. The dorm was at the edge of campus, facing a fairly busy street that saw regular non-university traffic, and Michael heard a car honk at him as he walked up the sidewalk toward the main part of campus. He waved at the driver who honked at him, trying to project an image of friendly normalcy. It occurred to him that most people had never been naked outside in the daytime. He wondered what the percentage was. 50%? 80%? How could anyone tell? That clothing was such a part of society, that no matter where you were, you were expected to be dressed, made going against that, being nude and free in places where nobody expected it, an act of courage. Would Michael have the courage to finish Dr. Slater's experiment, finish the spring semester having never worn clothes?

The street he walked alongside was known as dorm row. Holcombe Hall, the female dorm where Dani lived, was close to his dorm. As he passed it, he couldn't help but feel another surge of admiration for Dani, her courage for being naked twenty-four hours a day for months at a time, no matter what people said or thought about it. He supposed she also had had to get dressed to go home for the Thanksgiving holiday, and he wondered how she was handling such a return to societal expectations. Knowing her, she probably got naked the first chance she got. But then he had to stop his thoughts. Michael really didn't know Dani. He'd had two conversations with her, had seen her around campus many times, and had seen her on TV on the *Stossel* show. He couldn't say he really knew her. But he hoped to change that now that he was an official part of Dr. Slater's study.

A Honda Odyssey van pulled up to the curb in the loading zone in front of Holcombe Hall, and Michael braced for some kind of verbal attack. Instead, he heard a "Woohoo!" as the passenger side door opened.

"Hi there," a girl with brown hair and braces in her teeth that made her look too young to be at a university said as she stepped out of the van.

"Hi," Michael replied and started to walk away.

"Michael, wait," a familiar voice said from the other side of the van.

He stopped at the mention of his name. The girl with the braces was staring at his pelvic region, and Michael fought the urge to cover himself with his hands. Was she old enough to be seeing this? Debbie walked around the front of the van, smiling so big she was almost laughing, and stood beside the girl with the braces. Their resemblance to each other was striking.

"I don't believe it," Braces said, shaking her head but still fixing her gaze on the parts of Michael that would normally be covered.

"I fucking told you," Debbie replied. She addressed Michael. "Out for a stroll again?"

"Yeah. Something like that."

Debbie was gazing at him too, and his body was responding to such blatant looks from the two young women.

"I should probably get going," he said.

Debbie took a step toward him. "As long as you're here, can you carry my suitcase up to my room? It's one of those really old ones and doesn't have wheels on it."

"I don't know. I don't think Dave would react well if he found out I had been naked in your room."

Debbie laughed. "Dave? Did he not tell you? We broke up just before the break. I am free and single."

The girl with braces laughed. Michael looked at her and then back at Debbie.

"Oh, this is my sister Julie," Debbie said.

Julie stepped toward him and held out her hand. Michael shook it out of habit, although he had to note that she had stopped her hand precariously close to his rapidly rising penis. Debbie failed to suppress a giggle which made Julie giggle.

"Do you go to school here?" Michael asked Julie, mainly to try to end the awkward silence that followed the giggles.

"No."

"Julie's in tenth grade," Debbie said. "She wanted to hang with me for a little while and see what it's like on the big campus. What do you think so far Julie?"

"It's awesome," Julie replied, her eyes scanning Michael up and down.

"Anyway," Debbie said, sliding the side door of the van open, "the suitcase is here."

Michael saw a pea green vintage Samsonite hard back suitcase. It looked like something from the 1970s, with one handle and no wheels. With a sigh, Michael grabbed the handle and swung it out of the van and onto the sidewalk. It was heavier than it looked.

"Thank you so much," Debbie said, throwing the side door of the van closed.

"No problem."

Michael lifted the suitcase again and held it against his thigh. He stepped awkwardly, wishing he could have had another suitcase for the other hand to balance the weight as he walked. The eyes of the girl at the check-in desk widened when she saw Michael walk in behind Debbie and Julie. Michael moved the heavy suitcase in front of him so that it was covering him from his waist down to his knees. This only forced him to shorten his steps as his knees kept hitting the suitcase.

"He's just helping us with our bags," Debbie told the check-in girl.

"But he's naked."

"I know. Isn't it awesome!"

"I don't know if he's allowed in like that."

"Why not? He was walking outside like this. And we have a resident here who hasn't worn clothes in almost a year."

"Yeah, but she's a girl. And she's part of some study."

"I am too," Michael said.

"What?"

"The study. I'm a part of it." Michael thought he could talk about the study since he hadn't officially started in it. He was also tired of Debbie and the check-in girl talking about him like he wasn't there.

"You're part of the study?" Debbie asked. "No way!"

Michael nodded, now thinking that he shouldn't have told someone he knows.

Debbie's eyes widened, as if an idea had just occurred to her. "So you're going to be naked all the time now, like Dani?"

"Yeah. Next semester though."

Debbie and Julie held the inner doors open for him and he lugged the suitcase through, still holding it in front of himself but aware that the girl behind the check-in desk could now see his bare backside.

"So what, this was just a test run?" Debbie asked.

"Yeah, kind of."

"And what do you think of it so far? I mean, if you have to do what Dani did, you have to be naked all the time wherever you go. In your classes, at your meals, when you go out on dates even."

Michael wanted to ask why Debbie would mention dating to him, but he remained silent. He set the heavy suitcase down and waited with them for the elevator while Debbie kept on talking.

"And there will be pictures of you taken everywhere. You can't stop it, you know. Everyone carries a camera on their phone. Not to mention all the security cameras all over campus. Everyone you know will see them eventually. Just like with Dani. And what are you going to do when you get excited? Guys can't exactly hide that like us girls can."

"I actually talked about that with Dr. Slater," Michael interjected, but he didn't think Debbie heard him.

"What are you going to do when you're at a job interview, and the person you're talking to, the person you hope will give you a job, pulls out your naked pictures and asks about them? I mean, did you really think about all the ramifications of what you are about to do. An entire semester, naked?"

The elevator dinged, and the doors opened. Michael heaved the suitcase back up against his side and staggered into the elevator with it.

"And what are you going to do when your mother sees one of those photos?" Debbie continued as she and her sister followed him into the elevator. "Dani never thought her parents would find out what she was doing, but lo and behold, there they were not even two weeks after she started. I heard they even flew all the way out here from Texas to see for themselves."

"I don't want my mother to find out what I'm doing," Michael said as Debbie hit the button for the fourth floor as the doors closed. "But if she does, I don't know what I'm going to do about it. This is just something I want to do. I wanted to be a part of it somehow that first day I saw Dani naked outside on campus."

"And what if you suddenly meet Ms. Right, and she doesn't want you running around naked in front of every other woman in the world."

"If she were really Ms. Right, for me at least, she wouldn't mind because she would know it was something I wanted to do."

Debbie stopped talking as the elevator doors opened onto the fourth floor. Michael was surprised at himself. For the first time he could remember, he'd been able to articulate the perfect answer to an argument without having it come to him hours too late. Debbie and Julie stepped into the hall and held open the elevator doors for Michael and the suitcase. He heard the voices before he got out. At least five young women were in the corridor, two of them on step ladders, putting up Christmas decorations. Michael heard one squeal and a couple of others say, "What the hell?"

"Everyone, this is Michael," Debbie said. "He was out walking and working on his tan when he graciously offered to carry my suitcase for me."

Michael moved the suitcase to cover himself, holding the handle with both hands.

"Hi Michael," a busty brunette on one of the step ladders said.

Michael smiled and nodded toward her, too shy to say anything. Debbie and Julie walked past the Christmas decoration crew. Michael had to turn the suitcase and carry it at his hip again to be able to get past them in the narrow corridor. He felt something brush his butt, but he didn't know if it was accidental or if one of the girls had tried to cop a feel. And honestly, did it matter to him? If it were something intentional, he would only feel flattered even though he felt like he shouldn't be.

"Here we are," Debbie said, using her card key to open the door to room 431.

She dropped her purse on the bed closest to the door. Michael was happy to swing the suitcase onto the bed and be done with it.

"There you go," he said and turned to leave.

"Wait," Debbie said. "Don't go."

"I really ought to."

Michael felt flush as he caught Debbie looking down at his package. He'd already been stimulated enough, and he didn't need her prolonged gaze to make it almost unbearable. And having her little sister in the room was both embarrassing and inappropriate.

"It's just that…"

"What?" Michael asked when Debbie paused.

"I like looking at you. I mean, talking to you."

Michael noticed Julie slinking away. She sat down at the desk on the other side of the room.

"You were my roommate's — my best friend's — girlfriend."

Debbie shrugged as if it was no big deal. "But that's over now. We broke up."

"And whose idea was that?"

"Why does that matter?"

"It matters to me."

"Yeah, but why."

"Because he's my friend, and I can't be seen moving in on his girl as soon as they're apart. Appearances matter."

"Well, you're already naked in my room."

Debbie was exasperating! "That was not my intention," he said.

"No, it wasn't. But you can't leave like that."

Michael still felt flush, and he had an idea of what Debbie was driving at. He just didn't want to believe it.

"Like what?" he said.

"Like that," Debbie replied, pointing to his erection.

Despite what Dr. Slater had told him about ignoring any public erections, he tended to agree with Debbie. But he also knew that he had to get out of this room before something happened that he would regret later.

"You can take care of it, if you want. We wouldn't mind, would we Julie?"

"Nope. Wouldn't mind at all." Julie sat back in the chair, her eyes glued to Michael.

For a couple of seconds, Michael considered it. But he shook his head. "It wouldn't be appropriate."

"It would be more appropriate than walking out there and letting everyone else see it. And really, doing that might jeopardize the study. Wouldn't it?"

"No, I doubt it."

Michael stepped back and opened the door, looking out into the hallway. The five girls were gone, presumably having moved on to another floor.

"Well, thank you for helping with the suitcase." Debbie put a hand on his arm. "Really."

"Any time," Michael replied and hurried down the hall to the stairwell.

He thought about taking the elevator but didn't want to risk having to share such a small space in his current condition. Once in the stairwell, he skipped down one flight and stopped on the landing. He took deep breaths, trying to will his penis back under control, but he couldn't get the way Debbie had looked at him out of his mind. His hand found its way to it. Relief wouldn't take very long, and then he could get back to normal. Hoping there wasn't a camera in the stairwell, he stroked himself just a few times and ejaculated in the corner, his knees almost buckling with the spasm of pure pleasure.

Afterward, as he continued walking down the stairs, careful not to let that part of his anatomy bounce and spring back to life, he was filled with a powerful regret and self-loathing. How could he go without clothes for an entire semester, especially with girls like Debbie running around? The answer was obvious: he couldn't. He would have to march into Dr. Slater's office and back out of the whole thing. This was just crazy.

Once he got back outside and into the waning sunshine, he stopped beside the building to catch his breath. He still had to walk naked back to his dorm. The sun felt so good on his shoulders as he walked out of the building's shadow, and there were so few people out and about that Michael decided to extend his walk. If he were going to back out of the project, at least he could enjoy being naked outside while he still could. Instead of heading back to his dorm, he walked across the commons and all the way around the edge of the campus.

Despite the lack of activity at the university, he was stopped twice to pose for photos with people. By the time he got back to the dorm, having had no issues with his male anatomy, he was feeling better about the project. Perhaps, if he "took care" of himself, as Debbie had put it, each morning, he would be fine for the rest of the day. He was willing to try, especially as walking naked across campus with sunshine and a nice breeze felt so good.

13

Adam

December was a frustrating month. Adam wanted to shoot some footage of Dani that he might be able to use in the series, but she was busy studying for final exams. As attractive as Dani was, Adam couldn't use much footage of her sitting at her desk studying. So he busied himself auditioning girls to play her roommate. He had narrowed them down to two, but he wasn't thrilled about either one of them. Maybe he should just nix the roommate idea and let Dani keep her private room. This last audition was thirty minutes of tedium. The girl had no camera presence, didn't seem to ever know where the camera was even though it was sitting on a tripod. And whenever she said that she didn't agree with Dani's public nudity, she never portrayed a sense of sincerity. In fact, she seemed rather starstruck about sharing a room with Dani.

Maybe she would be good with a script, but this was supposed to be a reality show, as much as was possible anyway. Dani's roommate would have to be able to improv, and none of the girls who had applied for the part seemed to be any good at that. Adam still didn't know what he was going to do. He wanted someone to play off Dani, didn't want her to be solo every episode. She had told him that her friend Samantha was visiting in January and that she would be willing to be in the show. But she was only going to be here for a week, and that was before classes even started. He'd only get one episode at most with Samantha.

These thoughts ran through his head as he walked from the RATV building back to his production motorhome, which was, once again, parked behind Dani's dorm. Adam was about halfway to the trailer when he spotted a naked man walking toward him. He was slim and fit with reddish brown hair and skin that glowed red on his chest and shoulders.

"That looks like it will hurt later," Adam said as the man approached.

"What?" They stopped near each other.
"The sunburn."
The man looked down at himself. "Oh crap, I forgot the sunscreen."
"Do you do this often? Go for walks in the altogether, I mean."
"A few times."
The man was looking around as if he were looking for an escape.
"Here," Adam said, motioning toward the nearest building, "let's step over in the shade."
"I should get going. I don't like staying in one spot when I'm on one of these walks."
"I want to talk to you though. It won't take long. I'm working with Danielle Keaton. You know her, right?"
"Yeah, everybody knows her."
Adam had taken a couple of steps toward the shady spot and was glad to see that the naked man was following him.
"You're not that producer, are you?" the young naked man asked.
"I am. Adam Munch." Adam turned once he got well into the shade and held out his hand.
"Michael. Michael Cooley." They shook hands.
"So how many times have you done this?"
"What, walk around naked?"
"Yeah."
"Five or six times, I guess."
"And what made you start doing it?"
Michael shrugged. "I guess I wanted to experience just a little bit of what Dani did, what she felt. You know?"
"Yeah, it is an unusual situation."
"You can say that again."
Adam glanced around at the people, mostly students, watching them. "Do you know Dani personally?"
"I guess so," Michael said with some hesitation. "I mean, we've talked. It's kind of funny. We talked the first day she was naked and again the first time I was naked outside."
"Oh really? You just ran into each other on campus?"
"Well, she saw me from a distance and came to talk to me."
"And what did you talk about?"
Michael laughed. "Since we were both naked, we talked about being naked. How awesome it was, you know. I think I asked her why she kept doing it when she didn't have to anymore."
"She didn't seem upset that you were naked? Like you were trying to steal her thunder?"
"No. She seemed really friendly."
Adam nodded. He took another look at Michael's body, thinking about how it would look on camera. He didn't know how Netflix would feel about male frontal nudity on the show, but they seemed perfectly fine with Naked Dani. "I am producing a reality series around Dani, portraying her naked life here on campus."

"Yeah, she told me something about that."

"How would you like to be in a few episodes?"

"Me?" He looked incredulous.

"Yeah, you. I can't have Dani by herself every episode. I need a friend of hers to play off her. You'd be paid, of course. And it wouldn't be every episode." Unless Michael was a hit with the audience and the network, Adam added to himself.

"Oh, I don't know. I mean, I'm going to be like this all next semester."

"What? You mean naked?"

"Yeah."

"Why is that?"

"I don't know if I should say."

"I can keep a secret."

Michael looked around at the meandering onlookers. None of them were within earshot. "You know that study that Dani was in?"

Adam nodded.

"Well, I'm in it next semester. Dr. Slater — she doesn't have the resources she had with Dani, but she still wants me to, you know, stay naked all the time for the next semester."

"I see. Are you part of the study now?"

"No, it doesn't start until next semester. But I've been trying to get myself ready for it."

"By doing these little walks?"

"Yeah."

"Did you apply to be part of this study?"

"No, Dr. Slater saw video of one of my walks and kind of recruited me for it."

"I see."

"So, I don't know if I should be on your show if I'm supposed to be in Dr. Slater's study."

"We can make it work," Adam said, thinking about how this crazy sociologist's study could be incorporated into the show. There was no way around it; he was going to have to go talk to this sociology professor sooner rather than later.

"You still want me on the show even if I'm naked all the time."

"Absolutely. I mean, Dani's naked all the time too, right?"

"Yeah."

The kid still seemed hesitant though. "Where is this show going to be on?"

"Netflix."

"Netflix. Wow. Everyone has that."

"A lot of people do. If you were on the show, you'd be seen by a lot of Hollywood folks. You might even be able to turn that into a career in the entertainment business."

"Yeah, but I'd be naked the whole time."

"But you won't be the only one, and you will get a lot of notice."

"I never thought about a career in entertainment."

"You're in Southern California. Don't say the idea never crossed your mind."

"Well yeah, but I'm working on an engineering degree."

"So keep working on it. Keep all your options open. This may lead to things not in front of the camera. You ever see a movie called *Vanishing Point*?"

Michael shook his head. "No, never heard of it."

"Came out in the early seventies. It's basically a cross-country car chase movie. But at one of the stops the hero makes on the way, there's this girl riding a motorcycle completely naked. She gets four or five minutes of screen time, gets off the motorcycle and has a conversation with the hero, but we never see her with anything on at all. That girl was played by Gilda Texter who later worked in Hollywood for decades as — get this — a wardrobe and costume designer."

"That's funny."

"It's true. Ironic, but true. You never know what opportunities will open up. But you have to take them when they come."

Adam could tell that Michael wanted to charge ahead, but something was holding him back. Probably people whom he didn't want to know that he was into public nudity.

"Can I think about it?" he said.

"Sure. We won't start shooting any new content until January, but I'll need to have some scenarios worked out before then. I'd like you to be a part of some of them. Maybe you could even be some kind of love interest for Dani."

Michael's eyes widened, and his jaw dropped open. "What?"

"It's just a possibility. And it's all up to Dani. But hey, you two already dress alike." Adam laughed at his own joke which got a smile from Michael.

"That would be cool."

Adam could see the wheels turning in the kid's mind. And he also had an idea why Michael wanted to go naked in public in the first place and then just happened to run into Dani his first time out.

"Do you know where the Radio and Television building is?"

"Yeah."

"Can you meet me there tomorrow morning, room 210? Say nine o'clock? I want to get you on camera. Call it a screen test."

"OK. But how long will it take? I have a class at eleven."

"Oh, we'll be done long before then."

Michael nodded. "Ok."

"Good." Adam instinctively held his hand out, and they shook again.

"See you tomorrow," Michael said.

"Yeah."

Adam watched Michael walk away, wishing he was close to that toned and had a sudden misgiving about suggesting that Michael become Dani's love interest. Why would he suggest such a thing? And why should it even matter to him? Anyway, it was up to Dani to decide.

And even if she agreed to it for the show, that didn't mean he would become a love interest in real life. After all, "reality show" didn't mean reality.

Dani would be thrilled about keeping her private room. If, that was, Adam nixed the roommate plan. He was going to wait and see how Michael did on camera before he made that decision. And he was sure he would wait until the decision was made before he told Dani anything. He just wished he didn't have such misgivings about inviting Michael onto the show.

14

Dani

After Dani's flight from DFW landed at the Palm Springs airport after Thanksgiving break, she grabbed her small carry-on bag from under the seat in front of her, waited her turn to stand and disembark, which seemed to take hours since she was at the back of the plane, marched through the terminal and out into the sunny parking lot, found where she had parked the Crown Victoria that the university had either loaned or given her, threw her carry-on bag into the passenger seat, and stripped out of her t-shirt and jeans while standing beside the driver's side door, right in the airport parking lot. She didn't care if anyone saw her or if there were cameras pointed her way. She'd been nude for over 95% of the past eight months, and she was finding clothes more and more uncomfortable during those few times when she had to wear them. Underwear, both bras and panties, were now intolerable, and she had stopped wearing them altogether even when she did have to wear clothes. Only when she was comfortably unclad did she get in the car and drive back to the CVU campus. The parking attendant stuttered wishing her a good morning when she stopped at the booth to pay the parking fee.

Dani hadn't spent a whole lot of time thinking about what her life would be like after college. She had written in her book, which was being released to the world within days, that she planned on going to law school after she earned her bachelor's degree, and that still was her plan. But while being home with family and being generally uncomfortable in whatever she had been wearing for most of that time, she really began to think about what her life would be like. Lawyers generally had to dress nice when meeting with clients and even nicer whenever they had to appear in court. In Dani's experience, the "nicer" the clothes were, the more uncomfortable they felt. Is that really the future she was working toward here in the total freedom of Coachella

Valley?

A certain notoriety was always going to follow her because of her time here, thanks to the news stories and the *Stossel* appearance. But if this reality series is even a small hit, that notoriety was going to be multiplied exponentially, especially with Netflix's tendency to leave shows produced in-house on the network in perpetuity. If the show was a big hit, both Adam and Netflix would want additional seasons. If Dani took classes over the summer, which was her intention, she could be finished with her degree by the next December, just a little over a year away. CVU didn't have a law school, so she couldn't continue her studies here unless she decided to pursue a graduate degree in something else, something CVU did offer.

Dani knew she couldn't keep going to school forever, especially at CVU which was so far away from home. But this freedom she had here, freedom that had come to define her now, was such a treasure to her that she knew that seeing it end was going to be devastating. "Just live in the now," she told herself as she drove to campus.

She didn't have to tell herself that over the following three weeks as she was kept busy with papers, assignments, and studying for exams and with a book signing and three radio interviews to promote her book. She had taken a heavy course load this semester, trying to accelerate her graduation in spite of her desire to remain at CVU longer. Of course, when she had registered for this semester, she hadn't realized what her nudity vow would come to mean to her. She had only registered for twelve hours for next semester, the minimum number to be considered a full-time student, in anticipation of the show shooting keeping her busy. Perhaps she should just keep taking the minimum to draw out her time at Coachella Valley. If the show was a success, that's probably what she would do. She might even add a major or two just to keep going. With the money she would be making from the TV series, she wouldn't need the scholarship, so she could just keep going to school and paying for it herself.

Adam was busy with show prep, spending his time between the production motorhome and the Radio and Television Building. She only saw him twice in the three weeks between Thanksgiving break and the end of the semester. The first time was on the day classes resumed. Dani knocked on the trailer door to tell Adam about Samantha's visit in early January.

He seemed irritated when he opened the door, so much so that Dani wondered how often he was disturbed while working in the trailer, but his face relaxed when he saw that it was Dani. "Oh, hey."

"Hi."

"You want to come in?"

Dani looked past Adam and didn't see anyone else inside. While she was developing trust with Adam, and even liked him, she'd had a rule since the incident with her former chemistry professor to never be alone in a room with a man. "No, I have to get to class. I just wanted to tell you that my friend Samantha will be visiting in January, before classes start."

"OK."

"I kind of told her she could be on the show."

"You 'kind of' told her?"

"Okay, I flat out told her she could be on it."

"How will she look on camera?" Adam asked. "Can she send me a demo tape?"

"She'll be fine on camera. And she really ought to be in the show at some point since she was in my book."

Adam seemed to think for a moment. "OK. But if she's flat or boring she won't make the final cut."

"Fine."

Adam scratched his head. His eyes were puffy and red, and Dani wondered how much sleep he was getting.

"I'm going to be working behind the scenes for a while, looking for a roommate for you."

"Do you have to?" Dani said, hoping it didn't sound like a whine.

"I think, with the right person, it would make the show so much better."

Dani was more concerned about her day-to-day life than the show, but she just shrugged.

"So you may not see much of me over the next couple of weeks," he added.

"That's fine. Finals are coming up."

Dani detected a slight slump in his shoulders. Was he disappointed that she seemed fine with not seeing him for a couple of weeks? Or was that just her imagination? They stood in silence for an awkward moment, looking toward but not at each other.

"Well," Dani finally said, "I better get to class."

"Yeah. Good luck on your finals."

Ultimately, it was Dani who turned away, heading across campus to her British lit class. Life returned to her pre-Adam normal, not that anything had been normal since Dr. Slater's nudity project had begun. She completed her assignments and studied for the exams that she had to take. Thankfully, she had done well enough that she had exempted herself from the final exam in two of her classes.

The second time she saw Adam, he had texted her on the last day of regular classes, two days before finals were to begin.

"Can you come to a meeting?" the text read.

"Sure," she replied.

"3:00 PM today, room 210, Carlisle Hall?"

Dani's jaw dropped when she saw the location, but she typed, "I'll be there."

Three o'clock was ten minutes after Dani's last class of the day was scheduled to end. She shouldn't be surprised; Adam knew her schedule better than she did. Her professor seemed to cooperate by dismissing everyone about fifteen minutes early. It was, though, the last regular session, and there wasn't much left to discuss. Dani wandered over to Carlisle Hall and reached room 210, the Sociology Department office, ten minutes before three. She couldn't help but relive that fateful day last March, remember the sheer terror she had felt at walking naked through these hallways and outside into the world. She was a much different person now. The receptionist was the same lady who had been there on Dani's first day of nudity.

"You're back," she said when Dani walked in.

"Hi. I was invited to a meeting here."

"Yes, it's in Dr. Slater's office. Mr. Munch isn't here yet, but you can go right in."

Dani smiled at her. "Thank you."

She shuffled over to Dr. Slater's open door, not so eager to be alone with her for any length of time, but she couldn't say why. Although Dani made Dr. Slater out to be the villain in her book, she did owe her for making the last several amazing months possible, her book deal and a reality series, along with the large sums of money she would receive from both of those. Dr. Slater was at her desk, engrossed in whatever was on her computer screen. Dani stood at the threshold of the office, expecting Dr. Slater to look up. When she didn't, Dani began to feel awkward just standing there. Only when she tapped on the open door did Dr. Slater look up from her screen.

"Ms. Keaton! Please, come in."

"Hi Dr. Slater." Dani's pause to drop one of her seat towels into the chair before sitting down was barely perceptible.

"I was just reading some things Mr. Munch sent me. This TV series in an interesting development, isn't it?"

"Yeah, it is."

"I never anticipated such a whirlwind when we started this. I mean, I knew there would be media coverage, but this—"

"I have you to thank for it."

Dr. Slater shook her head. "No. It was you who performed your tasks so admirably. It was you who continued even after our agreement had ended. It was you who wrote the book that attracted a television adaptation even before the publication date."

"But without you and your research, none of that would have been possible."

Dr. Slater shrugged. "Pfft, my research was going nowhere until you came along."

"I can see I'm late," Adam said from the doorway. "And I thought I was early."

Dr. Slater stood, and Dani followed suit.

"Adam Munch, I presume," Dr. Slater said.

"Adam, please." They shook hands across her desk.

"And you can call me Lorraine. Please, sit."

Adam gave a nod and a brief greeting to Dani as they both sat down.

"So what can I do for you?" Dr. Slater asked when everyone was settled.

"You know why I'm on campus?"

She nodded.

"Lorraine, I'd like you to be part of the show. Let's say a recurring character. And I'd like to shoot some footage inside your classroom. Dani is taking one of your courses next semester, right?"

"I am," Dani said. "Advanced topics. Community based research."

"Ah. I'm so glad you'll be in that class." She turned back to Adam. "Of course you can shoot in my class, especially with Dani there."

"Good. There will be some sort of remuneration for appearing in the show in more than a non-speaking role."

"That's not necessary. I'm happy to help produce and promote your show. Anything, really, that has to do with Ms. Keaton here."

"That's wonderful, but it is built into the show's budget. If you'd like, I can work with Sylvia about putting your pay back into the university or anywhere else you wish."

"The university student scholarship fund will be fine."

"OK, I'll tell Sylvia that. And you'll be willing to sit in the studio for direct to camera commentary?"

"Sure. Whatever you need."

"Awesome. Thank you." Adam paused. He seemed to be searching for the right way to ask his next question. "Now, Lorraine, I met a young man on campus the other day. He was undressed, like Dani here. I stopped and talked to him, and I'd like to put him in several episodes of the show. He said I should talk to you about that."

Dr. Slater was nodding. "Is his name Michael Cooley?"

"It is."

"Mr. Cooley is the next phase of the research project. We will be monitoring and recording his interactions over the next semester as he goes about his daily life without clothing. How did you picture his involvement in the TV show?"

"A recurring role. Not in every episode, but in most of them. Maybe even a love interest for Dani."

Just when Dani was wondering why she had been invited to this meeting, Adam says something unbelievable. "A what?"

"A love interest. Just for the show."

"I barely even know him. You want to throw us together just because he's naked everywhere now?"

Adam sighed. "At this beginning stage, we have to build our viewership. And look, he's extremely fit and not bad looking. We are going to have a built-in male audience with you. With him, we may draw more women in."

"I'd be interested to see the actual viewer numbers once he's introduced," Dr. Slater said.

Dani started to object more, but thinking about all the staging that went into this supposed "reality" show helped her hold her tongue.

"Unfortunately, the entire first season will be done before anything airs, but we can measure viewership episode by episode when they start to air. What Michael was concerned about was his involvement in your study. Last semester, you told Dani to keep the study a secret."

"I did," Dr. Slater admitted. "My concern was that if the people actually being observed knew they were being studied, they would alter their behavior. Now that the cat's out of the bag with all the hubbub over Dani's portion of the study, that secrecy becomes a bit moot now. Of course, Dani's portion was supposed to have lasted an entire semester and then have ended before we moved to a male nude. We only had two months with Dani, but she remained nude so that we could continue observations throughout the summer and fall semesters. That observation will now shift to Mr. Cooley's interactions. Although I would prefer him to be the only full-time nude student on campus for our studies, I thought it was better to go ahead and start that part of the study rather than wait for Ms. Keaton to graduate."

"So," Adam said, drawing out the word, "you're okay with him being in the show?"

"Of course. Media was always an expected part of this project. Dani was on the news an awful lot."

"And she wrote a book," Adam added.

"I heard."

"Have you read it?"

"Not yet. But I hear I'm more or less the villain in it."

"I didn't mean it to come out that way," Dani explained.

Dr. Slater held up her hand and made a brushing away motion. "It's all right, of course. I understand how you were feeling at the time. But I didn't want to lose you."

"Lose her?" Adam asked.

Dr. Slater took a deep breath and looked away for a moment. "I haven't talked with anyone outside the department about this." She looked back at Adam and Dani. "Every incoming freshman takes a personality test for the psychology department."

"I remember that," Dani said. "It took forever."

"Eight hundred questions," Dr. Slater said. "We made our selections for the nude female from the results of those tests. Ms. Keaton here was one of the three candidates we identified. We had tried two young women whom we had ranked slightly higher, but they backed out rather quickly for one reason or another."

"So the two girls who got academic probation named in the hearing last summer—" Dani began.

"Had nothing to do with the study," Dr. Slater finished. "We had given up on the study for the spring semester and were going to wait for fall, starting with Ms. Keaton. But then she got into a bit of trouble, and we faced the possibility of starting in the fall with no candidates. So we did an abbreviated study with Ms. Keaton here. I confess I did make it seem like her participation was in exchange for having her probation revoked."

"Was it?" Adam asked.

"Well, yes. But if she wasn't going to participate, I didn't care whether she was here at CVU or not."

"That sounds harsh," Adam said.

"Sorry. But it's the truth. And that was before I learned how wonderful Ms. Keaton—Dani— was for this. I never envisioned someone going to the lengths that she went to."

Everything about the project flashed through Dani's mind, the call from the president of the university, Dr. Slater's proposal and her immediate demand to either accept it and strip right then or accept probation, that first day naked on campus, and every day thereafter. She had only ever seen it from her point of view, never from anyone else's. She snapped out of her reverie when she realized that the room was quiet, and Adam and Dr. Slater were looking at her.

"Sorry," she said. "I was thinking how I need to change some of the things in my book."

"Don't worry about that," Dr. Slater said. "You wrote of your experiences based on what you knew at the time. No one is going to fault you for that. And besides, no one needs to know about my selection methods."

"You don't want to mention that on the show?" Adam asked. "Tell your side of the story, outside of Dani's book?"

Dr. Slater shrugged. "How the world views me doesn't really concern me. It's the research that matters, and I will talk about that, both in the scenes you shoot in class and the — what did you call it? — direct to camera commentary."

Adam nodded. "That'll be great. I want the show to explore the philosophy behind what Dani is doing."

"Good."

Adam talked for most of the rest of the meeting, detailing when he wanted to shoot (throughout January and February beginning long before the first day of classes), the time he needed for editing and post-production, and when he hoped the show would premiere. "I'm hoping it's before the end of the spring semester. That way, if it's a hit, we can shoot a second season over the summer or in September when the fall classes start up."

Later, after Dr. Slater ended the meeting by claiming to be busy grading final papers and preparing for the exams, Dani and Adam walked down the stairs and out into the afternoon sun.

"A love interest?" Dani said to him as soon as they were out of earshot of anyone. "When were you going to tell me about this?"

"Today."

"Today? In front of Dr. Slater?"

"It's a recent development," Adam said.

"How so? Did he apply to play the part of my roommate?"

"No, I ran into him on campus. He was just taking a naked walk like he was doing a few weeks ago when you ran into him. I think he has a crush on you. He said he started doing it to know what you were feeling, to experience what you experienced. He spilled the beans about being in Dr. Slater's next phase, and I knew then that I had to get him and Dr. Slater in the show."

The two of them were walking fast, and Dani realized she was the one setting the pace, making herself active because she was angry.

"He said he talked to you," Adam said.

"He did. And he's nice and all, but I don't need to be dating someone just for the show. And especially someone just because he happens to be a public nudist too."

Adam stopped, but Dani took a couple of steps before stopping herself and turning to face him.

"A public nudist too? Is that the problem you're having, that you might not be the center of attention anymore?"

"No. I don't need you playing matchmaker so you can get high ratings for this show. My dating life should be MY dating life."

"I never said you had to date him. I said he could be a possible love interest. We put him on the show and see how the two of you interact. That's all."

Dani shook her head. "You're picking my roommate and setting me up on a date, and you don't think that's going a bit too far?"

"I'm not picking your roommate."

"How are you not picking my roommate? You're holding auditions for it."

"And those auditions are not going well. So much so that I decided to scrap the whole thing."

"So you're saying I can keep my private room next semester?"

"As far as I'm concerned, you can."

Dani had to resist an urge to hug him which wasn't that difficult since she was still angry about the dating Michael for the show thing.

"I thought you'd like that," Adam said and then resumed walking back toward the production trailer. "I also have another meeting later this month with Donald Haddon."

"Who's that?" Dani asked, walking beside him now.

"He is the new university chaplain taking over in January."

"What about?"

"What do you think? You and the show. I remembered the part in your book about trying to go to church services. I really want to shoot something like that. So I found this guy's number and called him."

"And?"

"And we'll see."

Dani thought about that service she attended the previous spring, how much she had wanted to be accepted and how unwelcome she had felt, especially when the minister started talking about modesty. She had wondered if he hadn't seen her enter — she had arrived late — and changed his sermon.

"Is that okay?" Adam asked when she hadn't said anything.
"Yeah, that's fine."
"That is the kind of message you want to convey, right? That Christianity and nudity are not incompatible?"
"Yeah."
"Good. It might also be controversial enough to stir up even more publicity."
"Is that a good thing?"
"Anything that makes people watch is a good thing."
Dani started to comment that it was a gimmick, like the entire show, but she didn't. She had tests to study for, and Adam had his work to do. They reached the back of the dorm and stopped just outside of the production trailer door.
"Well, thanks for coming to the meeting," Adam said.
"Sure."
"And good luck on your finals."
"Thanks. I'll see you later."
Dani walked to the back door of the dorm wondering why Adam seemed so hesitant to part ways. When she glanced back as she went into the door, Adam was still standing by the door of the motorhome looking her way. She waved, and he started as if coming out of a trance. He waved back, and Dani went inside.

15

Michael

After Michael's encounter with Debbie on the Saturday after Thanksgiving, it took him six days to muster the courage to try another naked excursion outside of his dorm room. Dave had returned from the Thanksgiving break on Sunday night. Michael didn't know if Dave still talked with Debbie, so he thought he should tell him about that encounter before she did.

"Oh, I saw Debbie yesterday," he casually inserted into a conversation that Sunday night.

"Yeah?"

"Yeah. She told me you two broke up."

"Man, I got so tired of her shit."

"So you broke up with her?"

"Hell yeah, I broke up with her."

Dave seemed angry about the whole thing, so Michael didn't press him on why he had cut it off with her. Michael had just assumed that Debbie had been the one to end the relationship since Dave was so quiet around women and had told him before how few girlfriends he'd had in high school. Debbie had also seemed so matter of fact about the breakup. If Dave had broken up with her, she didn't seem very upset about it. But Michael felt some relief that he hadn't crossed a line with Debbie just as Dave was hoping to win her back. He still decided against telling Dave that he had been naked in her room with her.

When Michael left his room on his next naked excursion, a Friday, Dave had already left to go home for the weekend. Michael didn't have any arousal issues like he'd had the previous time in spite of there being many more people out and about on campus. But he also didn't run into Debbie. He did run into the producer of Dani's reality series who invited him to a screen test for the show the following morning. Michael spent that evening trying to decide what to wear, if anything, to this screen test. In the end, he decided to go naked again. That was how he would be for the duration of the next semester and, therefore, for all of his appearances on the show, if he got on. In the back of his mind, he still worried about his mother seeing him, but he figured he would cross that bridge when he came to it. And he was sure he would come to it. After all, Dani's parents found out about her public nudity early on, and she'd only been on the local TV news at that point. The thought of his mother seeing him on Netflix without him telling her ahead of time was not pleasant, and Michael realized with some trepidation that he would have to tell her about the whole thing before the show aired. He almost hoped that Adam Munch wouldn't want him for the show.

It was only after he left his room that Saturday morning that he realized he had never gotten dressed after the previous day's outing. Maybe he was getting used to this. The screen test itself was uneventful. Mr. Munch had a girl with short spiky blonde hair put a bit of makeup on him. Then Michael stood in front of a green screen and answered the questions that Mr. Munch asked, the first one of which was whether he enjoyed walking out in public nude and if so, why.

"It's very freeing," Michael had replied, reminding himself to use his hands as he talked and not to slouch. "I spent a night at my cousin's house a year or two ago. Their twins were two and a half at the time. After dinner, my cousin took them to the back of the house to give them a bath. About twenty minutes later, these two wet, naked toddlers come running through the house with my cousin chasing them with a towel. It was so funny and so cute. Little kids like to run around naked. Then they're taught somewhere along the way that being naked is inappropriate at best and downright wrong at worst. Here at CVU, I have the opportunity to return to that little kid feeling. So I'm taking it."

The rest of the questions were similar: why did he agree to participate in Dr. Slater's research; why did he want to be on Dani's reality series, etc. At the end, Mr. Munch seemed pleased with his answers. Michael walked back to the dorm with a sense of nervous excitement. He was going to be in a major Netflix series, but he was going to be naked for the duration of it. Would the millions of people watching see him as brave or as just strange? After all, he was just following in Dani's footsteps. She was the brave one. He was just a copycat. And what would the people who knew him, family and family friends, think? What would they say to him the next time they saw him? And how would he answer them? It was overwhelming to think about, so he tried to shove those thoughts aside.

Michael spent the next week finishing his semester projects and assignments. He had one more thing he wanted to try before the semester ended, before he would be bound by Dr. Slater's research project. He wanted to go to a class nude, just to see what it would be like — before he went to every single class next semester that way. The prospect still scared him, and he wound up putting it off until the last day of regular classes. He only had two classes on the schedule, chemistry at nine AM and the other, his United States history class, at two PM. There was no chemistry lab that day, and the lecture hall was so large and so sparsely occupied for that session that he could get in, sit in the back, and probably not even be noticed even by the professor, Dr. Hays.

Following what he had seen Dani do when sitting in public, Michael found a hand towel to carry with him to sit on. During all his previous naked outings, he had only walked or stood; he had never had occasion to sit down. He had bought all his textbooks on Kindle, so he only had to carry his iPad, which he also used to take notes. His body erupted in goose pimples as soon as he stepped outside. It was much cooler that morning than he had felt in the Coachella Valley since he had been going to school there, and of course, that coolness had to come on the day when he was determined to attend a class in the nude. Once he started walking the blood started flowing, and the low temperature began to feel invigorating.

Michael ignored the comments from the people he passed about it being too chilly for his attire, or lack thereof, and arrived at the lecture hall right before nine o'clock. It felt strange walking naked into a building that wasn't his dorm, and he reminded himself that he had gone into a women's dorm a couple of weeks earlier. He entered the lecture hall at the back. The seats descended in semi-circular rows down to the professor's desk below. Michael sat on the back row, not wanting to draw any attention to himself. He felt somewhat hidden by the desk over his lap. He set his iPad on the desk and opened his Kindle and Notes apps. A couple of latecomers to class gave him the classic double take as they hurried down the aisle to seats two rows ahead of him, but no one else seemed to notice him, especially not the elderly Dr. Hays giving his semester review lecture down below.

Class ended early, and Michael, sitting on the back row, was the first out the door. He heard the scattered giggles as he exited the building, but he was used to hearing them on his outdoor walks. It was warmer out than it had been this morning, but it still qualified as a cool day by Coachella Valley standards. Michael was comfortable when a gust of wind wasn't hitting him. The wind, at this temperature, was abrasive, and Michael ducked into the Student Union building to warm up. He wondered how Dani was handling the low temperatures, and he wished he could run into her again. In all his naked outings, he had only ever seen her that first time. He seemed to catch glimpses of her all the time when he was out and about in his clothes. Sometimes life didn't seem fair, especially now when he had so much to ask her about the TV show.

The Student Union building was more crowded than he expected. It seemed that most eyes turned toward him when he walked inside. The seating area for the bistro was next to the door he used, and he felt more on display than he had ever felt. It was one thing to meet passersby outside, when everyone including himself was walking one way or the other, but these people were all sitting still, just looking at him. He hurried into the climate-controlled building, not sure where he was heading. He thought about eating at the bistro since his debit card was in the pocket of his iPad cover. But that would mean sitting with all those people now giving him the strange looks. He was hungry though. Maybe he would get something to eat and take it somewhere else within the building. There were all sorts of spaces where one could sit and lounge, study, or eat. The line at the bistro was three people deep, and Michael didn't care for standing stationary in line to order. He had based all his previous nude outings on keeping mobile, until today in chemistry class, that was. But Michael had also seen Dani standing in that very line wearing nothing but a pair of sandals on at least three occasions over the past nine months, and he couldn't very well stay mobile for all of next semester. The growling in his stomach was the clincher. Michael took a deep breath and got in line behind a tall brown-haired girl in her high school's letterman's jacket with three volleyball patches on the sleeve. She turned to look at who had stopped behind her before whipping her head back to look toward the order counter again.

"Aren't you cold?" she said after a few seconds, without looking back at him.

"Not anymore."

"But you were outside."

"Yeah. But it wasn't that bad. It's kind of weird. If I had been in a t-shirt and shorts, I would have felt colder than I did like this. It's like the body is self-regulating or something when you don't cover it up."

The girl turned and looked at him, but Michael thought she was trying to be careful and not let her eyes drop below his waist. "Can I ask you why you're doing this? Going naked, especially when it's this cold outside."

"It's not really that cold outside. It just feels cold because we've been roasting all year."

The girl gave him an exasperated look. "But, naked?"

Dani was so much better at defending her actions. Michael tried to think of what she would say, had said, in these situations. He was just about to speak when he heard a familiar voice behind him.

"Oh my God! 58 degrees outside, and you're still naked!"

Michael turned to see Debbie gazing at him with the corner of her mouth turned so that Michael couldn't tell if she was smiling or leering. He felt the need to say something, but the only thing he could come up with was "58? That's what it is?"

"That's what our high is supposed to be. It's probably colder than that right now." Debbie looked to the girl with the volleyball letter jacket. "Making new friends, I see."

"Just casual conversation in line," Michael said, trying to figure out if he detected a hint of jealousy in Debbie's voice. Before he could follow up with anything, he was interrupted again.

"Excuse me," a middle-aged man in a white shirt said. His name tag read Lawrence. "I'm going to have to ask you to either comply with our dress code or leave."

"What dress code?" Debbie said before Michael could reply.

Lawrence stiffened and said, "All customers must wear shirt, shoes, and either pants, shorts, or skirt."

"Bullshit," Debbie shot back. "Do you know how many times I've seen Dani Keaton here, standing in line, ordering food, and eating at one of your tables wearing nothing but a smile?"

"I cannot speak about other customers or what other managers have allowed."

"What other managers?"

"There are two assistant managers who work various shifts."

"But you're the main manager?"

"Yes, I am the store manager."

"How long have you been the store manager here?" Debbie asked.

"That's not relevant," Lawrence began.

"You just made it relevant by invoking other managers. Now how long have you been the store manager here?"

"Two years."

"Two years! And you've never seen Dani Keaton in here over the past nine months? Not even one time?"

"Well, I, uh," Lawrence stuttered. "This is different."

The girl with the volleyball letter jacket stepped up to the counter and started ordering her lunch. Michael wanted to say something on his own behalf, but Debbie again spoke before he could get anything out.

"Different, how?"

"I have to protect my female staff."

"Protect them from what? Did you worry about your male staff when Dani was in here? Do you think we can't handle seeing a dick? Most of us spend our whole lives dealing with dicks."

"It shouldn't be—" Lawrence seemed lost, trying to find what to say. Michael almost laughed as Debbie's insult sailed right over his head.

"Have you ever been sued for gender discrimination?" Debbie continued. "Because that's what this is. You just can't make up a policy whenever someone you don't like walks in, and you can't just selectively enforce a policy to favor one group over another."

The volleyball jacket girl finished ordering, swiped her card on the reader on the counter, and took her receipt from the cashier. That cashier looked at Michael, so Michael stepped up. The cashier glanced from Michael to Lawrence even as Debbie talked.

"If you had refused service to Dani Keaton during any of her visits here, we wouldn't be having this trouble."

The cashier looked back at Michael. He didn't see if Lawrence had given her any look of approval or reproach.

"I'll have a number two with chips and a drink," Michael said.

The cashier rang it up and give him a total. Michael swiped his debit card and waited for his receipt, pulling a bag of sea salt and vinegar flavored chips from the rack.

"Thank you," the cashier said when she gave the receipt and an empty cup to him. "You're number 43. Try to stay warm."

"I will," Michael replied.

Lawrence had backed away during Debbie's onslaught, and he finally just turned and retreated past the counter, heading into the kitchen. Debbie, by tilting her head, motioned Michael over to a table near the exit. The plastic chair surface looked cold which reminded him to pull his towel out of his iPad case and drape it over the seat. Debbie sat down on the other side of the table. Michael set his chips down and took his cup to the drink fountain. The place seemed eerily silent until the noise of the ice dispenser dropped several cubes into his cup. He finished getting his Diet Coke, grabbed a straw and lid, and scurried back to the table, feeling every bit on display.

"You were amazing," he said to Debbie once he sat down and got the lid and straw together on his cup.

"What?"

"The way you handled that guy."

"Oh. My dad was a lawyer, so I'm used to getting into arguments like that."

"*Was* a lawyer?"

"I guess he still is, but lately he's been busy as a state senator."

"A state senator. Here? In California, I mean."

Debbie shook her head. "In Arizona."

"Is that what you plan on doing? Being a lawyer or a politician?"

She shook her head again. "No. No way."

"I could see you being good at it," Michael said. "I mean, you just called that guy a dick, and he didn't even realize you were calling him a dick."

Debbie giggled, and Michael thought her eyes almost twinkled. "I don't think I meant to call him a dick."

"But that's what you were thinking, right?"

Debbie shrugged. "Well. Yeah."

The girl at the pick-up counter called his number. When Michael got up to get his order, he was dismayed that the problem he'd had the day he carried Debbie's suitcase up to her room was trying to return. He wasn't erect, but he was swinging lower than usual. This hadn't been close to a problem on his previous three naked outings, but then again, he wasn't out walking the campus this time; he was standing and sitting still where people could get a good look at him. As he picked up his tray, the girl behind the counter did just that with a half-smile.

"Enjoy," she said to him.

"Thanks."

He hurried back to the table with his tray, sitting down and using the table for cover.

"Mmmm," Debbie said, watching him sit.

"What?" And then he realized that the common denominator with this outing and the last one when he'd had the problem was Debbie. She had that gleam in her eye again as she watched him.

"Just enjoying the view," she said.

Michael smiled, feeling flush. He was probably blushing. He wanted her to stop saying things like that, but he also didn't want her to stop saying things like that.

"So, what do you want to do?" he asked to try to change the subject.

"I want to sit here and watch you eat lunch."

"No," Michael replied around the first bite of his sandwich. He waited to swallow before adding, "I mean with your life. If you don't want to be a lawyer, what do you want to do?"

"A veterinarian."

"A veterinarian? Why?"

"I've loved animals since I was a kid, and I've just always wanted to be a vet."

Michael took another bite of his sandwich. "I've heard that vets have to have more school than a regular human doctor. Is that true?"

"Well, you have to know the anatomy of a bunch of different animals. So, yeah."

"And yet, you still want to pursue that?"

"Oh yeah."

"That takes a lot of dedication."

Debbie nodded. "It does."

Michael ate in silence as Debbie sat across from him, looking either at her phone or at him. She spent enough time on her phone that Michael wasn't too uncomfortable being watched by her, although he did see a few people in the bistro looking his way and sneaking photos with their own phones. He supposed it was part of the territory of participating in Dr. Slater's experiment. There were certainly enough photos and videos of Dani Keaton floating around online now. What Michael didn't think Dani had to deal with was the unwelcome reception he had just gotten from the bistro manager. Dani seemed to be welcomed everywhere she went on campus. A naked girl seemed to be perceived as someone vulnerable, someone to be protected. Today's experience made Michael feel like a naked guy was someone to be feared, someone to be protected from. He wondered what Dr. Slater would make of today. He glanced around the ceiling, looking for the security cameras, and made a mental note to email Dr. Slater about the incident. There were what looked like three cameras in the bistro area.

"So, are you going to be naked all day today,?" Debbie asked as Michael finished his sandwich.

"Thinking about it. I have a history class at 2:00."

"And you're going to be naked everywhere next semester?"

"That's the plan."

"Then you need someone to look after you. Like I just did here."

"Someone?"

Debbie lifted an eyebrow. "OK, me. You need me to look after you."
"How would that work? Would you follow me around everywhere?"
"Something like that. What's your class schedule like next semester?"
Michael pulled it up on his phone and passed it over to her.
"Yeah," she mused. "I could walk with you to and from four classes. I'm booked up for your Tuesday-Thursday engineering class though."
"I ought to be able to stand up for myself," Michael said.
"But it helps to have someone else as an advocate. Just think about it."
Michael didn't relish the thought of having Debbie with him all the time given the problems he'd had being naked around her so far. But maybe if he got used to being with her, that problem wouldn't pop up again.
"Yeah, maybe," he said. "But I don't want you to feel like you're stuck with me."
"Don't worry about that."
"Maybe you can be on the Naked Dani reality show with me."
Debbie eyes shot up to his. "What?"
"They are shooting a reality show with Dani next semester. I ran into the producer the other day, and he wants me to be in a few episodes."
"Oh." Debbie paused a moment as Michael finished the last of his potato chips. "I can't be on that show."
"Why not?"
Debbie took a deep breath. "Because opponents of my father could use the fact that his daughter is cavorting with naked people on a TV show against him."
"Oh."
Michael must have looked disappointed. Debbie reached across the table and took his hand.
"We can still hang out and walk together. I just won't be on camera."
"OK."
She smiled at him, and Michael felt a fluttering in his gut. What was he getting himself into with his roommate's ex-girlfriend?

16

Adam

Coachella Valley University was a ghost town on New Year's Eve. Adam used the quiet to scout campus locations and shoot background shots to use for scene transitions. He considered this the first day of principal photography for the series, except for the pilot which he would insert somewhere into the first season. The new chaplain would be on campus for the first time today before beginning his official duties in January. Adam had a meeting in his new office scheduled for one o'clock.

The production trailer had been moved during finals week to accommodate the students who had to move into the dorm at the beginning of the semester. Even though it was a rented motorhome, Adam still thought of it as "the trailer". It would be back behind the dorm the day classes started. In the meantime, Adam had set up shop in the Radio and Television Building. As he walked, he found an outdoor sculpture garden near the art building, and he made a mental note to find and talk to the drawing teacher. Adam knew that Dani modeled for classes here, and he would love to shoot an outdoor session here in the garden. Perhaps they could do an entire episode on nudity in art. He was sure Dani would have a lot to say about the subject during the studio narration sessions. And perhaps Adam could work with the art department to have a special exhibit of nude figures in one of the galleries.

Adam shot the sculpture garden from various angles, only a few seconds from each spot, and checked his watch. It was almost time for his meeting, so he made his way to the Student Union building. The chaplain's office was on the second floor, near the large meeting hall where the services were held. Adam looked inside the hall and saw nothing but chairs arranged in rows. It was too dark inside to see all the way to the front. He thought about going in and trying to find the light switch so he could take a few seconds of video but decided against it. Perhaps the new chaplain would show him around.

Adam found the chaplain's office after walking a lap around the second floor of the Student Union and wondered how he had passed it the first time. A tall man with graying reddish hair was hanging photos and diplomas on the wall to the left of the desk. He didn't seem to notice anyone there until Adam tapped on the door frame.

"Yes?" he said, turning toward Adam.

"Hi, I'm Adam Munch." He wanted to ask the man's name, but he couldn't remember the name he had been given, which wasn't normally like him as remembering people's names was part of his business. "From Munchie Productions."

"Ah yes." He set the photo he had been trying to hang onto the corner of the desk and stepped forward. "I'm Don Haddon, the new Christian chaplain here."

Adam shook his offered hand. "Pleased to meet you. Should I call you Father or Reverend?" Adam cringed as he felt the question came out much too awkwardly.

"You can call me Don."

"All right. And you can call me Adam."

"Good deal, Adam. Please sit down."

"Thank you." Adam sat in one of the chairs across from the big desk.

Don took the big chair, leaned back, and laced his hands across his chest. "Now what can I do for you Adam?"

"I told you on the phone that I am a television producer."

Don nodded. "I remember."

"I am shooting a reality show centered around a particular student here."

Don held up a hand. "Let me guess. Danielle Keaton."

"Yes." Adam cringed in anticipation of a negative response.

"I have a confession to make. When I saw this job opening and realized it was where Ms. Keaton had been attending classes in the nude, I applied immediately."

"Why is that?" Adam asked, thinking he might be on some mission to convert Dani back into clothes.

"Because I saw her on *Stossel* stand up, literally naked to the world, and proudly state that she was a Christian. That was very powerful."

"Yeah, it was," Adam said, thinking back to the first time he watched it. "Is that a good thing?"

The minister laughed out loud. "Yes. Yes, it is."

"That seems unusual, coming from a preacher."

"Unfortunately, it is unusual. But it shouldn't be."

Adam sat there nodding, not knowing what to say.

"Tell me," Don said, "have you ever heard of Imago Dei?"

Adam wasn't sure he heard him correctly, so he just shook his head no.

"It's Latin for 'Image of God'. Genesis says that we, human beings, were created in that image of God. When God was almost finished with creation, he called it 'good'. Then he made us human beings. And he called that 'very good'. We were made in the image of God, and it was that image that upgraded creation from good to very good. So when we humans call the nude body obscene, call ourselves obscene in fact, we are also calling that image of God obscene. I cannot abide that, especially in this day and age when the Internet has given us an epidemic of pornography."

"Pornography?"

"Yes. A pandemic of it."

Adam scratched his head. "You know, a lot of people called Dani's *Stossel* episode pornographic."

"And therein lies the problem. When people, and especially those within the church, take a pornographic or sexualized view of the body, they become unable to distinguish between what God has called very good and what Satan has used for lies."

"So you are anti-pornography?"

"Oh yes. Absolutely. Pornography is one big lie. It's addictive and destructive, both of those who make it and those who consume it."

"But you don't think what I'm trying to do is pornography?"

"What is it you're trying to do?"

That was a good question, Adam thought. When he launched the project, he was just trying to make something that would get him noticed by entertainment executives. Had that changed?

"I want to give the world an accurate portrayal of Dani," he said. "What she believes and what she's doing here. And, hopefully, create a show that entertains while it informs. When I pitched it to Netflix, I called it *Duck Dynasty* meets *Girls Gone Wild*, but that's not close to accurate, given Dani's personality. I've never seen her try to be sexy or provocative. She's just herself."

"If what you say is true and the comparison to *Girls Gone Wild* isn't accurate, then I don't think it sounds pornographic to me."

"It's not. It won't be. The only reason people would think that it was is because Dani will be unclothed throughout."

"I think that's what the world needs right now."

"So Dani would be welcome at your services just as she is?"

"Oh absolutely!"

"And can we shoot some footage of her at a service? For the show?"

Don leaned back in his chair and slowly nodded. "I think so. As long as you include at least some part of the message."

"If it's important to Dani, then it will be included. If I can make it fit into the time limits of the episode."

"And how intrusive will the shoot be? Cameras, lights, and all that?"

"It will probably just be me with a camera. We may have one more cameraman, but if we shoot when I really want to, he won't be here."

"When is that?"

"The 15th. The Sunday before classes start." Monday the 16th was a holiday, so classes wouldn't start until Tuesday. Adam hoped there would be enough people on campus to attend the service given that extra day for students to arrive and get settled, but that was a risk he would have to take. He needed to shoot footage fast so he could start editing episodes.

"That will be my first service here."

Adam tried and failed to get a read on whether Don thought shooting during his first service was good or bad. Adam made a mental note to never play poker with Don. "We could shoot on another Sunday if you'd rather."

"No, the 15th is fine. What about lighting?"

"There is a light built onto the cameras, and we try to shoot in natural light as often as possible. How is the light in the hall where the service is held."

Don seemed to muse a minute, then stood up. "I'll show you."

Adam followed him out of the office and into the large room where the service was to be held. There were some stage lights, but they were all fixed and pointed toward the front. Adam wanted to get as many shots of Dani walking in and interacting with the other attendees as he could. The house lights were a mix of florescent lights in the ceiling and incandescent lights on the walls in fixtures that looked almost Art Deco in style. Adam took few shots with the camera he still had with him, and he hoped they would be suitable when he looked at them later. They looked fine on his viewfinder, but he couldn't really trust that.

Adam went over how he thought the shot would go. He would enter before Dani and set up so that he got her entrance. He'd then move behind her, still shooting, so that he got the reactions of the people already there. Dani would have to arrive early, so everyone is not already seated and facing the front. She might object to that given her experience at the service described in her book. He also didn't want to tell her anything about this new minister so that their first meeting could be shot on video for the show. Her reaction when she learns that this preacher is actually a fan of hers should make for a very interesting scene.

"You won't be walking around during the sermon, will you?" Don asked as Adam switched his camera off.

"I will be standing up and moving around a bit, but I'll be along the walls using the zoom. Trying to be as unobtrusive as possible. Is that okay?"

"Yes, that'll be fine."

They both walked back toward the exit, and as Don was shutting the lights off in the hall, Adam felt a text hit his phone. He glanced at it while Don wasn't looking at him. It was Dani. "Plane just landed. R U at CVU?" Adam typed "Yes" and hit send. He thanked Don for his time and said that he looked forward to the 15th, but he declined the invitation to go back into the office and continue the conversation. Dani would be arriving back at her dorm, and Adam wanted to talk with her.

At least, that's what he told himself, but he wasn't entirely comfortable talking about God while he was trying to figure out how to make a show centered around a naked girl as entertaining as possible.

Adam handed Don his business card. "If you have any other questions or concerns, please don't hesitate to ask."

Don looked at the card before slipping it into his front pocket. "I'll do that."

They shook hands, and Adam left without a real sense of the man. But then, Adam's dealings with clergy had been almost non-existent. He walked toward Dani's dorm and arrived just in time to see the Crown Victoria turn into the parking lot where his production trailer would soon sit. Dani stepped out of the car, naked already.

"You didn't strip on the plane, did you?" Adam asked before Dani had even seen him approach.

Dani laughed. "No, but I thought about it. Back in DFW waiting in line to get through security, I kept thinking about how much easier this would be if everyone was naked."

It was Adam's turn to laugh. "You did make it out of the airport though?"

"Yeah. I took everything off before I got into the car." She sighed as she grabbed her dress and overcoat from the passenger seat and threw them over her shoulder. She then took her overnight bag out of the back seat of the car, and looked at Adam. "How am I going to be able to assimilate back into regular society after I leave here? I mean, if it's not cold, I almost can't stand to have clothes on."

"Hopefully, you can change the world enough while you're here that you won't have to assimilate too much."

"You think so?" Dani had started walking toward her dorm, and Adam walked alongside her.

Adam held his hand out, offering to carry Dani's bag, but she ignored the gesture.

"I can hope," he said. "If our show is successful, it's got to have some kind of effect."

Dani stopped and looked up at him. "Our show? Not your show?"

"It's always been our show. We don't have a writer, and you are the star. Thanks for coming back early, by the way." He had asked her to return to campus two weeks early so they could brainstorm shooting locations and scenarios. Her friend Samantha would be arriving in three days, and he wanted to be ready to shoot as soon as she got there.

"Of course. Maybe I'll stay through the summer, Thanksgiving, and Christmas and never have to wear clothes for the entire year."

"That would be something," Adam said.

Dani continued walking toward the back door of the dorm. Adam walked with her, not wanting to let her get away but, for some reason, hesitant to ask anything that might be misconstrued. He watched her swipe her card key and heard the door click.

"Do you have any plans for tonight?" Adam asked as she pulled it open.

She stopped and held the door open with her back. "I was just going to go up and crash in my room."

"It is New Years Eve, you know."

"I know. But I doubt I'll make it to midnight. What is twelve o'clock to you will feel like two o'clock to me."

"I didn't think of that. Jet lag."

Dani shrugged, started to go into the dorm, and then stopped. "What are you doing tonight?"

"Some of the local Radio and TV students are having a party at The Spot. I thought I might go and have a couple of beers and people watch." The Spot was a small night club at the edge of the campus. It was also one of the off-campus locations that said it would be okay with Dani's nudity.

"People watch?"

"Yeah. You can learn a lot about human behavior just by people watching."

"If I show up there with you, I think we'll be the ones being watched."

"Is that such a bad thing?"

Dani smiled. "You know I don't mind it. The question is, can you manage to sit there with me and not feel the need to start shooting footage?"

"I'll leave the camera and equipment behind."

"All right. I'm going to take a little nap first. You want to meet there at 9:00?"

"Sounds good to me." He hoped his newfound feeling of elation wasn't detectable in his voice.

"I'll see you then."

"Have a good nap."

Adam watched the door shut before turning and heading back toward the RATV building. He found himself humming "Singin' in the Rain" under a cloudless sky as he walked.

17

Dani

Dani sat in the Crown Victoria the university had loaned her and watched the planes land at the Palm Springs International Airport. She was in the parking lot of a Fiesta Market & Liquor at the corner of Vista Chino and Gene Autry Trail. On her phone was the flight status of Samantha's plane, American Airlines Flight 2307 from Dallas-Fort Worth. According to the display, the plane should be touching down any minute. As each plane approached the runway and disappeared from her sight, Dani wondered if that one was Samantha's. It was now too dark to see each plane's markings. All she could see were lights, so she couldn't tell the American Airlines planes from those of any other airline. Her phone screen, which had just gone dark, lit up again with the text from Samantha: "Just landed. Waiting to get off the plane."

Dani hit the button to dial Adam's number. He was set up at the exit to the airport terminal. She wondered if this was how everything was going to be for the next few months, nothing spontaneous, everything planned ahead of time so that Adam can get his shot of it. That would get old quickly.

"Hey," Adam answered.

"Plane just landed. She's waiting to get off."

"OK. Text me just before you start driving over here." Adam ended the call.

Dani hated to be critical of Adam. He was making her famous on her terms, putting her message out, one of personal empowerment, not exploitation. And she liked him. She really did. The two of them had gone to a club on New Year's Eve. Dani had been exhausted from her flight back out and had resolved to herself that she would leave the club by ten o'clock that night, which would have been midnight at home. She wound up staying until after midnight, Pacific time, talking and dancing with Adam. He made her feel safe, which was important in that setting. Although there weren't a whole lot of people there, being in a night club next to a university campus that was still mostly deserted, being the only naked person in said night club, where people were drinking and having a good time, was a lot different than being naked on a college campus where everyone was going about their business. Early in the evening there had been a trio of guys who kept walking by close to their table and staring at her as they sat and talked.

"Are they bothering you?" Adam asked.

Dani shrugged. "I'm used to it by now."

Adam stood up and started walking to their table. Before he got there, all three of them got up and left the club. Adam stood where he was until they got out the door and then returned to Dani.

"I'll bet you never thought you could be that intimidating," Dani said with a giggle when Adam returned.

"I was just going to buy them a round of drinks and shoot the shit."

"Sure you were." But Dani couldn't erase her smile.

"Small minded people," Adam said and took a sip of his beer.

Their conversation that night had been a nice respite from the constant talk about show ideas. Adam opened up to her about his background, growing up in the Denver area and graduating from the now famous, or infamous, Columbine High School.

"That must have been weird," Dani said.

Adam shook his head. "I only went there my senior year. We lived in Aurora before that. And I graduated in 2004, so all the students who were there during the shooting would have all graduated and moved on by the time I arrived."

"I'll bet you had some teachers who were there that day though."

"A few. And the ones who had been there long enough to have experienced that day had other things to talk about."

Dani got a sense that Adam didn't want to talk about Columbine and had decided to change the subject when he volunteered another tidbit about his past.

"You remember that theater shooting in Aurora?"

"Yeah, I think so," she replied.

"I had tickets to go see *The Dark Knight Rises* that night. I was living in LA by then, but I was back in Colorado visiting my parents that week. Our tickets were for a later showing at that theater. We had just gotten in the car to go when we heard the news of the shooting on the radio." He was silent for a moment, and Dani reached out and touched his hand, wrapping hers around his as he held his bottle of Coors Light. "That near miss bothers me a lot more than just having graduated from Columbine. I've still never seen *The Dark Knight Rises*." He paused again and then said with a laugh, "And I love Christopher Nolan."

Dani wasn't sure who Christopher Nolan was, but she didn't want to ask and reveal that little bit of ignorance. "Wow. I guess it's a good thing you don't live in Colorado anymore." She let go of his hand.

Adam smiled at her and took a drink of his beer. "Those things could happen anywhere. Except Texas maybe. If something like that theater shooting had happened where you live, the guy would have been gunned down pretty quick."

"Now you sound like my father."

"Oh? Is he a big Second Amendment guy?"

"Huge."

Adam shrugged. "It just makes sense. When only the bad guys have guns, the good guys are in trouble."

"How do you live in Hollywood?"

"I don't talk politics."

"But you just did," Dani said.

"But you're a real person, not part of Hollywood." Adam took another drink of beer. "I really don't follow politics. I haven't voted in I don't know when. It's just that contemplating being the victim of a mass shooting made me wish I had a gun of my own, to shoot back."

"My dad would say 'if you don't follow politics, politics will follow you.'"

"I know. And I should get more informed and vote. I just can't stand any of the politicians I see." Adam took another drink of his beer. "They're all a bunch of lying crooks."

The rest of the conversation that night had been about light topics, movies and music foremost among them. Dani was just glad to talk about something other than her constant nudity or the reality show production, although she suspected that Adam was making a concentrated effort to not talk about either of those things. More than a couple of times, she saw him start to say something, stop, and catch himself. That effort, if that's what it really was, made Dani like him even more.

Now though, Adam was all business. Her phone dinged again, and Dani saw a text from Samantha: "Just got my bag off the carousel." That was the pre-arranged signal. Dani texted Adam, "Driving out now," put the car into gear, and drove toward the main entrance of the Palm Springs International Airport. Adam and Dani had had a video conference call with Samantha the day before, so he should be able to spot her and get long range video of Dani picking her up. The cameras and microphones in the Crown Victoria would pick up their conversation on the way to the university, with Adam following them in his Corvette.

Dani turned and drove through the main entrance of the airport. She spotted Samantha approaching the curb in the arrivals pick up area, her black suitcase rolling behind her, and passed Adam with his camera just before she stopped to pick her up. After popping the release for the trunk, Dani's first impulse was to get out of the car and help Samantha load her bag. She was about to do just that when she realized she was naked and not on the CVU campus. Looking around, she saw a whole bunch of people not paying any attention to them, so she shrugged and got out anyway. If anything, it will make for an interesting scene for the show. Samantha had already retracted the handle and heaved the suitcase into the trunk.

"Oh my God!" Samantha said when she saw Dani. "What are you doing?"

"Picking up a friend at the airport," Dani said and gave her a quick hug.

Samantha was wearing a lot of makeup, just as Adam had told her to do, even though, as he said, it wasn't theatrical makeup. Dani had sat in Mandy's make up chair before heading toward the airport

"Let's go before you get into trouble," Samantha said.

She shooed Dani back toward the driver's side of the car, and Dani noticed people looking at her now, some of them with mouths open and others with phones pointed her direction.

"It's Naked Dani," she heard someone say.

She wondered if she would ever get used to the idea of celebrity as she slid back behind the wheel of the big Crown Victoria. Samantha got into the front seat next to her, and Dani drove away as quickly as she could before some prude complained and got the airport police involved.

"It's so nice here," Samantha said. "It's cold back home."

"Yeah, the weather here is great. How was your flight?"

Samantha shrugged. "Fine, I guess."

"That's right. You'd never flown before."

"Nope. Dad was always big on long road trips in the car or the van, so we never got to fly anywhere."

Samantha looked around the car, into the corners and behind them in the back seat. "Are we really being recorded now?"

"Yep."

"I'm probably not supposed to talk about that, huh?"

"Adam will just edit it out."

Dani took the long way around the airport parking lot so that Adam could have time to catch up with them after stowing his camera in his Corvette. When she spotted him behind them, she sped up and headed toward CVU.

"So when you landed last Saturday, how long did it take you to get naked?" Samantha asked.

"I got to the airport parking lot."

"Geez Dani. So you haven't worn clothes at all since the new year started."

"Nope."

"Are you going to try to make it through the whole year?"

Dani shrugged. "The thought had occurred to me. But it would mean missing Thanksgiving and Christmas at home. Plus, there's not much to do on campus in May after the spring semester ends. And the regular summer sessions don't start until the first week of June."

"I think you should try. I could get away from my family and come out here in December, just so you wouldn't be alone for Christmas."

"You'd do that for me?"

"Absolutely."

Dani reached over and squeezed Samantha's hand. "Thanks. You're the best."

"Now, can we talk about some of the people back home?"

"Sure. Like I said, Adam will edit out what doesn't need to be on the show. And actually, he will use very little. They're only going to be thirty-minute episodes. Which will really only be like twenty-three minutes or something like that."

"Why so short?"

"Commercial breaks, I guess. Although if they're on Netflix, they won't be showing commercials."

"Syndication, maybe?"

"Maybe."

Samantha spent the rest of the drive updating Dani on who was dating whom, who had quit school, who was working where, and who had just turned up pregnant. By the time they got to the dorm, Dani figured that Adam would be able to use less than five minutes of their conversation, which was probably all he would have been able to put into the show anyway.

Sylvia had arranged for another bed to be moved into Dani's single room, so it looked more like the typical college dorm room. When they walked in, followed closely by Adam with his camera stabilization gear on, it was obvious which bed was the new, unused one, and Samantha went straight there and heaved her suitcase onto it.

"All the drawers except the top one are empty," Dani told her, "so you don't have to live out of the suitcase."

Samantha went straight to the closet on Dani's side of the room and opened it up. Her yellow dress and the long winter coat she had worn onto the plane at a chilly DFW Airport after the Christmas break were the only things hanging there.

"You really didn't bring any clothes with you, did you?"

Adam turned the camera away from Samantha and toward Dani. Dani held her arms out as if presenting herself. "Why would I?"

Samantha nodded. "You *do* look good."

"I look free. Because I am free."

"That's one word for it."

"All right, let's cut there," Adam said. "That was good."

"But?" Dani said.

"I want to be in the room and get a shot of you coming in. So, Samantha, could you take your suitcase and go out in the hall with Dani?"

Samantha looked at Dani who just shrugged as if to say, *this is my life now.*

18

Michael

Unlike his trip in August, Michael drove to Coachella Valley University to begin the spring semester in January without his mother tailing him. He'd had to leave early in order to move from his double room on the third floor up to the single RA room on the fourth and to attend his Resident Assistant training. So he had left on a Sunday, more than a full week before classes started. Michael had made a show of rolling his suitcase to his car, opening the hatchback, and putting it inside. What he didn't tell his mother was that the suitcase was empty. His toiletries were in the backpack in the front passenger seat next to him. Michael would be going to CVU with only the clothes he had on. There was no backing out of Dr. Slater's project now without a long trip home and back to get more clothes. Not that he anticipated any backing out. What Dr. Slater and Dani had already done was historic, and he wanted to be a part of it.

When he parked in the empty lot next to his dorm, he got out of his Prius, leaving the driver's side door open. He removed his keys and wallet from his pockets, put them in the driver's seat, and walked around to the back of the car. The temperature was in the low seventies, typical for a January afternoon in Coachella Valley. Michael opened the hatchback and then unzipped the main compartment of his suitcase. He looked around at what little of the campus he could see from this spot. Three people were walking along the edge of the Commons far in the distance. Michael saw no one else. Taking a deep breath, he pulled his t-shirt off over his head, folded it, and put it in the open suitcase. He lifted his foot while bending down to lean on the back of the Prius and took one shoe off and then the other, leaving them on the concrete of the parking lot. The socks came next. After putting them in the suitcase, Michael stood up straight again and unbuttoned and unzipped his jeans.

Pausing a moment, he took another look around. Once he got the pants off, that was it. He would be naked until the end of the semester. He'd be naked everywhere, in all his classes, in his dorm, during the fifteen hours each week he had to work on RA tasks in the dorm, at the dining hall, in the library, and in all the other places he couldn't even think of at the moment, from now in early to mid-January all the way to early May, four entire months, close to 120 days. Could he handle all the reactions he would get? He'd already had the bistro manager try to deny him service because of his nudity even before he started on Dr. Slater's project. He was thankful that Debbie had been there then. She had promised to stay close this semester and to back him up if he ever needed it, but how often was she going to be available? She couldn't be with him all the time. And would he want her with him all the time? Surprisingly, the answer to that question was not no. He wouldn't mind having her with him whenever possible. Knowing that Dave had broken up with her helped to assuage any guilt he thought he should have felt over wanting to spend time with her. With a sigh, he pushed his pants down and stepped out of them. Knowing that he would be removing his clothes as soon as he got to campus, Michael had not worn underwear. Now he was standing in the parking lot stark naked. And stark naked he would remain. He folded his jeans and put them into the suitcase on top of his shirt and socks and zipped it shut. After closing the hatchback, Michael slipped his tennis shoes back onto his feet, returned to the driver's door, reached across and grabbed his backpack, moving his keys and wallet from the driver's seat to one of the side pockets of said backpack, and headed up to his room.

The first thing Michael did when he got to the room and dropped the backpack on his bed was take his shoes off. They didn't feel right without socks, and they certainly didn't feel right being the only thing he was wearing. His new phone case had spots for the cards in his wallet, and he transferred them over, glad that the university used cards for dorm room keys like hotels. He had everything he needed to carry in his phone case as he went back out and headed for the student housing office to get the key to his new room.

He had left his sandals in the room over the break, but he decided to walk barefoot to the student housing office. The concrete sidewalk felt warm and hard under the sun despite the cooler temperatures, so he moved a little to his right and walked in the cool grass. He stopped after a few steps, curling his toes into the grass, with a sense of being one with the natural world. *Why did society look so down upon being in one's natural state?* Michael took a deep breath and kept walking, staying in the mowed and manicured grass. His footfalls made barely a sound until he got close to his destination and was forced to switch to walking on the concrete where the slap, slap, slap of his feet seemed jarring after the cool quiet grass. That sound became a bit higher pitched after he entered the building and walked on the linoleum floor. Michael had to smile at himself. When was the last time he ever thought about what type of surface he was walking on?

The housing office was on the first floor, so Michael didn't have to choose between the stairs or the elevator. He didn't see anyone in the building until he walked through the glass doors. The eyes of the girl at the reception counter widened when she saw him.

"Ummm," she said, unable to come up with the standard greeting.

The carpet of the student housing office was a welcome change from the hard linoleum of the hallway. Michael smiled at the girl at the counter as he stepped forward, trying to exude friendliness and normalcy. He imagined that this was a slow day for her, so his appearance here had to be a highlight.

"Hi," Michael said when he got to the counter. He stood close to it, so the girl could no longer see him from the waist down.

She seemed to snap out of a daze. "How can I help you?"

"My name is Michael Cooley, and I am supposed to pick up a room key and an RA packet here."

"OK."

She turned and pulled open the top drawer of the filing cabinet behind her. As she thumbed through the folders, a tall, forty-ish woman wearing a white blouse and plaid skirt walked out from the back and seemed to study Michael with a frown on her face. He recognized her as the person he interviewed with for the RA job back in October, but he couldn't remember her name.

"Mr. Cooley. A little casual today, aren't we?"

Michael looked down at himself and felt himself blush. At least the counter was blocking her view of him.

"Yes, you could say that," he said.

"Is this going to be standard for you this semester?"

Michael smiled, not sure how to respond. "Well, it is comfortable."

"I'm sure it is, for you. For those around you, I don't know."

Michael shrugged. "People seem to have gotten used to Dani Keaton."

"Yes. And I was told by our sociology department that a member of our RA training class would be emulating Miss Keaton. We have a small class this semester, being in the middle of the academic year, four women and one man. I never thought it would be the man."

Michael shrugged and held out his arms as if to say *here I am*.

"I guess it's the next logical step for whatever it is that that woman is trying to prove," the housing manager continued. "But once you're out of her clutches, whenever that is, I expect you to be fully clothed while performing your RA duties."

"Yes ma'am," Michael replied.

The girl at the filing cabinet pulled out a flat, brown 9 by 12 envelope. Michael could see his name written in Sharpie on the top of it. The girl brought it to counter and handed it to Michael. He opened it and found his card key for the new room along with the packet for a beginning Resident Assistant.

"Training is at 9:00 AM on Wednesday in room 112 of this building," the manager was saying as Michael examined his packet. "We will break for lunch at 12:00 and be done by 4:00. And you will be paid for the day."

"OK. Thank you."

The two women stood there, waiting for him to leave. Michael figured they wanted a show, so he decided to give them one. He turned and walked away, giving them both their first look at his full backside. He stopped at the door and turned, giving the manager her first full frontal view of him. Her eyes seemed to widen, and her mouth curled into a smirk.

"On Wednesday, will it be a full hour for lunch?"

"It will."

Michael gave her his best smile and said, "Cool. See you Wednesday," and walked out. He didn't look back as he walked down the corridor toward the building exit, but he could almost feel them both watching him. Being a normal guy, he liked the female attention, but he was afraid that he had put himself under closer scrutiny in his new RA job. There was nothing he could do about that, however. This constant nudity was his life for the next few months, and he would just have to adjust to whatever came about because of it, just like Dani had done the previous spring.

As he walked outside, back in the grass again, thinking about Dani, he saw her in a distant parking lot getting out of a large white car. Another girl, blonde and wearing a yellow t-shirt and khaki shorts, got out of the passenger side. Michael sped up as fast as he could without breaking into a run, heading in their direction. Then he saw Adam, the TV producer, get out of the red Corvette next to the white car. He walked around the Corvette to the passenger door and began donning his camera gear. When he seemed to notice Michael coming their way, he started working faster. Michael did his best to ignore him, thinking that that's what Adam would want him to do. And then it hit Michael that he was about to be naked on video, maybe for a TV series that would be seen by millions of people. He slowed his walking. Dani and the other girl were standing by the big white car talking. Since they didn't seem to be going anywhere, Michael slowed down to a normal walking pace.

"Hey Michael," Dani said when he got close.

The other girl looked at him, giggled, and looked away before looking back at him again and shaking her head. Michael felt a surge of happiness that Dani remembered his name until he realized that he was carrying an envelope with his full name on it in large letters.

"Hey Dani."

Adam had moved away and to the side of them, so he could get all three of them in the shot. Michael willed himself to look at the two girls and not at the camera.

"This is my friend from Texas, Samantha."

Michael smiled at her. "Nice to meet you." He held out his hand. "I'm Michael."

Samantha shook his hand while looking somewhere above him. "Nice to meet you too."

Michael could see a small microphone clipped to her collar. The wire seemed to go under her shirt and to a little black box clipped to the belt she wore. Dani wore the same necklace she usually had on, and Michael wondered if it had a microphone in it. Adam couldn't very well have wired her for sound like he'd done Samantha. Michael had to smile at that thought. After an awkward moment of silence during which Samantha and Dani were probably wondering what Michael was grinning about, Adam motioned for them to do or say something.

"Nice car," Michael said. "Looks like the police cars back home."

"Yeah, it's like driving a tank."

"Where did you go?" Michael thought the question might be forward, so he added, "I mean, I thought you had to stay on campus because..." he motioned to her body, her nudity.

"There are certain places I have special permission to go. We just got back from the mall, actually."

Samantha gave a little laugh, probably at Michael's facial expression.

"You went to the mall like that? I mean, they let you?"

"Yeah. There were only a few stores we could go into, but mall management was fine with me there."

"Until some people ruined it," Samantha said.

"Yeah, there were apparently a couple of people who complained, so a police officer asked us to leave."

"A police officer asked you to leave? He didn't write you a ticket or want to arrest you or anything?"

Dani laughed. "No. Like I said, mall management was okay with it. Until they weren't."

"Wow. I don't think I could do that. It's all I can do to be naked here on campus where I know it's okay. Supposedly."

"Supposedly?"

"Yeah, well, the manager at the Bistro a few weeks ago didn't want to serve me. Have you ever had any issues there?"

Dani shook her head. "Nope. And I've eaten there a lot over the past few months." She looked from Adam to Samantha. "In fact, we were headed there now. You want to join us?"

Michael looked at Adam who gave him a big nod.

"Sure."

They all started walking, Adam behind them for a moment before telling them to stop so that he could move in front and get a shot of them head on.

"I think it's safe to say I wouldn't even have gotten to the front door of the mall before someone came and asked me to leave," Michael said to Dani once they started walking again with Adam leading the way, walking backward and shooting.

"Maybe you're not big enough of a celebrity yet."

"I don't think that's it."

"You think it's because you're a guy."

"I do."

Dani shrugged. "Maybe."

Michael was silent for a few seconds as he tried to think about what he was trying to say. "Think about it. In our culture, women are to be desired. Men are the ones doing the desiring. Men are supposed to ask the women on dates, to propose marriage, and all that. At the wedding, it is the woman who is given away. No one gives the groom away. And since it's women who are desired, a naked woman is more easily accepted than a naked man."

"Maybe," Dani repeated.

"And your reproductive organs are all internal for the most part. Mine are not. I think that intimidates people, especially other men."

"Why do you think it intimidates other men? Homophobia?"

Michael shrugged. Remembering what the Bistro manager said to him, he tried to answer Dani's question. "I think some guys—" He paused and started again. "Men have been hardwired throughout history to be the provider and the protector of their families. Some of them take their role of protector just a bit too far."

"What do you mean?" Samantha, who had been following the conversation closely, although silently until now, asked.

"I mean that society has programmed them into seeing another naked man as some kind of threat that they should protect women from. Somehow. I don't know."

"And what makes you say that?" Dani asked.

"That Bistro manager. When he said he wasn't going to serve me, he said that he had to protect his female employees or some such bullshit."

"Hmmm. Interesting," Dani mused.

They had reached the Student Union building, and Adam called, "Cut," and then lowered his camera. "That was good. Fascinating discussion."

"Dr. Slater would probably be interested in it too," Dani said.

"That seems to be the point of this whole thing," Michael added.

"Do you think her idea was to study how people react to nudity or to change it?" Adam asked as he checked some settings on his camera.

It was Dani who answered. "Knowing her, both."

Adam finished with the camera and started inside the building. "Give me about thirty seconds to set up and then walk inside. Go past me and into the Bistro but stop before you order."

He disappeared into the building. Michael looked at Dani and Samantha. Samantha seemed to have lost her shyness about looking at him. "How long have you been shooting stuff?"

"All week," Samantha replied. "From the moment I got to the airport to now."

"A lot of starts and stops," Dani added as she looked at the closed doors in front of them.

Samantha looked at Dani. "Ready?"

Dani nodded, and the trio started forward, allowing the automatic doors to slide open in front of them. The Bistro was just to the left of this entrance, so they filed past Adam and his camera, stopping about ten feet from the counter and looking up at the menu display above.

"Cut," Adam said and moved into the Bistro.

Michael started to ask why he said "cut" when he was also the cameraman before realizing that he was just giving a message to Dani and Samantha that he had paused recording. Adam positioned himself in front of the counter and got down on one knee to get a low shot of them looking at the menu.

"Go," Adam said.

"What do you usually get here," Samantha asked as if they had just walked up.

As Dani was about to reply, Lawrence, the Bistro manager, came out and stood ready to take their order. Michael looked around at the dining area as Dani answered something that he didn't even register. Only one table was occupied, by a couple of university maintenance workers. Of course Lawrence had to work the counter; there were barely any students on campus, including his normal work-study staff. Lawrence seemed to see Dani first, and he started to smile until his eyes found Michael's. His smile melted away.

"How can I help you?" he finally said.

"I'll have the number two with chips and a drink," Michael said, repeating his order from the last time he saw Lawrence.

Michael selected his chips from the rack and set it next to the empty cup Lawrence had put on the counter.

Once Dani and Samantha ordered, Adam called "Cut," and stood up to order something for himself and to pay for all four lunches. Lawrence seemed to be extra friendly with Dani and Samantha as he handed them their cups. Michael ignored him and filled his drink.

"Where do we want to sit?" he asked Adam.

"Right over there. I'll sit at the table next to you and shoot your lunch conversation."

When Michael got to the table Adam had indicated, he realized he had a dilemma. When he'd left his room, he hadn't planned on sitting down anywhere until he got back, so he now had nothing to put between his bare bottom and the chair. He looked at the brown envelope in his hand and decided to use it, taking his stapled packet and card key out and putting them on the table before he laid it in the chair.

Michael felt like a third wheel once Dani and Samantha sat down with their drinks and chips. They talked about the places they'd been to during the week and Samantha's impending flight home the following Thursday. Michael sat crunching his chips and sipping his Diet Coke until Lawrence brought all four sandwiches out on a round tray. He seemed to take a good look at Dani as he sat her sandwich in front of her.

"I guess it's all right for me to be in here today," Michael said as Lawrence got around to him with his sandwich.

"I'm sorry?" Lawrence said.

"I mean, you don't have any of your female staff here today. So it's all right for me to be here like this, right?"

"Oh, is this the guy?" Dani asked.

Lawrence's head snapped around toward her. Michael guessed that being the subject of prior conversation shocked him.

"That's him."

"Look," Lawrence said, "I'm sorry about that. It's just shocking, you know."

"Why was it shocking to see me after so many months of seeing Dani here?"

"I don't— I mean, well— I don't know. She doesn't have what you have."

"You mean male genitalia," Dani said.

"Yeah. Look, I'm sorry about last time. I should have handled it better. If they say it's all right for Dani here to go naked, then I guess it's all right for anyone else too. I just— It's different."

"Okay," Michael said.

"Okay?"

"Yeah." Michael took a bite of his sandwich as he looked away from Lawrence and back to Dani and Samantha.

Lawrence stood there a moment before he seemed to get the message and walked away, placing Adam's sandwich on his table as Adam continued to shoot.

Dani reached out and took Michael's hand. "I know how hard it is the first few weeks," she said. "It'll probably be harder for you."

Michael smiled at her. "Thanks. At least you paved the way for me."

As if to break the moment of levity, Dani pulled her hand back and said, "That I did!"

19

Adam

Adam was glad that Mandy had been available to do hair and makeup for Dani and Samantha for at least a couple of days of shooting the week that Samantha was in Coachella Valley, but shooting as a one-man crew was wearing on him. He was, at the last minute, able to hire a couple of local high school students to follow him and get signed releases from the members of the public they encountered so he wouldn't have to blur so many faces in post-productions. The outings the two of them had made should fill at least two full episodes, from the mall trip to eating at Denny's and hiking through Joshua Tree National Park. He was glad that Dani had had a clothed companion who could be wired for sound just in case the camera microphone didn't pick everything up.

Samantha had wanted to do her own nude walk across campus with Dani, but she was adamant that it not be taped for the show. In fact, they didn't even want Adam in the vicinity while they did it, on Samantha's last full day at CVU. Adam had read about Samantha's trip with Dani to the nudist resort in Texas in Dani's book, so he thought she would be open to a little public nudity herself, if for nothing else to experience just a taste of what her friend was experiencing. When Samantha was in the studio talking to the camera about the week's experiences, what Dani referred to as "stool sessions", Adam had tried to convince her to walk naked with Dani for the show. But she had remained steadfast in her refusal to be nude on camera.

Adam was in the Radio and Television Building mixing video and audio while Samantha did her walk with Dani, although he did see them while on the way to get some lunch. When Samantha recognized him, she squealed and tried to hide behind Dani. Adam could only laugh. She seemed fine being nude in front of strangers (what few there were that day) but not in front of anyone she knew (with the exception of Dani, of course). What Samantha didn't realize, and what Adam didn't have the heart to tell her, was that Sylvia Smith had been saving video files of Dani on campus from the university's UHD video security cameras spread around campus onto a shared Dropbox folder. Sure enough, those video files were in the folder the following morning. Adam wasn't going to use them for the show, but it was interesting to see someone experiencing public nudity for the first time next to someone who was used to it. In what little video he had looked at, Samantha was almost bouncing on her heels while Dani seemed so nonchalant about everything.

Running into Michael after the mall trip was a stroke of luck. With Samantha visiting before almost every other student returned to campus, Adam figured the entire week would just be Dani and Samantha. Seeing Michael on campus and already naked per Dr. Slater's project made for a great scene at the Bistro followed by great stool sessions from each of them. He figured he got enough footage for at least two full episodes, and the semester hadn't even started yet. If things worked out with today's church service, he could have three full episodes before the first day of classes.

Samantha's visit with Dani had provided her a companion to talk with. The more Adam thought about it, the more he wanted someone with her when she went to the service and met with the new minister Donald Haddon. But the only person he could ask was Michael who would also be naked. Adam had very mixed feelings about this. Yes, he had told Dani that Michael would be in the show as sort of a fake love interest. The only problem with that was that Dani was a very feeling, caring, and honest person. When she reached out at the table in the Bistro and took Michael's hand, she wasn't acting. There was nothing fake about her. Intellectually, there shouldn't be any issue with Dani's and Michael's fake relationship becoming real. In fact, it ought to help with the show. So why did Adam have misgivings? He tried to tell himself that he and this television project should not be the catalyst for a real romance for Dani. But he suspected that the real reason was jealousy. He grew more and more fond of Dani with each passing day, her courage to be her pure self, her conviction that what she was doing, continuing Dr. Slater's study on her own when it was no longer required of her, was not only right but important for the world to see and understand. And she was beautiful. Adam couldn't discount that. Dani's beauty was innate. She didn't need clothes or makeup to be beautiful; she just was. Yes, he had Mandy put theatrical make up on her so she would look her best on video which always brings out every flaw. But there were a couple of days during Samantha's visit that Mandy hadn't been there. Adam had told both Samantha and Dani to put on a liberal amount of their regular make up, but he wasn't sure Dani had. In fact, he wasn't sure if she even owned any make up. And yet, she still looked stunning in the footage he had reviewed.

Still, Michael had been the only option for a companion to the church service, so after he shot his stool session after their lunch at the Bistro,

Adam pulled him aside.

"How do you feel about going to church?"

"What?" Michael had asked, seemingly dumbfounded.

"A church service. On campus."

Michael laughed and motioned down at his body. "I doubt they'll let me in."

Adam laughed. "I wouldn't count on that. We've already been given the go ahead."

"I've never gone to church much," Michael confessed. "Just Christmas and Easter, although if you ever talked to my mother, you'd swear she was there every Sunday."

Adam laughed. "This will be a new experience for you. And you'd be going with Dani."

Michael hadn't needed much time to think about it. "Well, all right then."

Adam went to the Student Union early that morning and shot a few minutes of test footage in the ballroom where the service was to be held. The lighting looked good, and there wasn't an echo on the audio recorded on the camera. He would get the audio recording of the sermon to mix in with the video after today's shoot. Adam walked back to the Radio and Television Building just in time to see Dani and Michael emerge. Their hair had been styled, and they both wore a decent amount of theatrical makeup but not enough to make the skin tone of their faces mismatch that of the rest of their bodies. Dani carried her zippered Kindle case. Adam knew that it contained her Kindle with all her textbooks loaded on it, her wallet with various IDs, and her little hand towels to sit on. He was surprised to see that Michael carried an identical case. Adam figured that Michael must have had his pre-project meeting with Dr. Slater.

"Good morning," Adam said. "You both look great. Are you warm enough?" He was looking at Dani as he asked the question, but he meant it for both of them. It was a cool morning, not yet sixty degrees.

Dani nodded.

"Yeah," Michael said. "It feels fine out here."

Dani wore a necklace with a crucifix on it, the first time Adam had seen her wear anything besides the one she wore during Dr. Slater's study. She noticed Adam looking at it and put her hand up to it.

"I dressed up for church," she said with a laugh.

"I see that," Adam replied. "You'll have to remember that when we do some pick up shots later."

"Pick up shots?"

"Yeah, I want to get a shot of you meeting up with Michael on the way from your dorm to the service. But we don't have time for that at the moment, so we'll get it afterward."

While they walked, Adam felt a text hit his phone. He had no intention of answering it, but he peeked at his Home Screen just to see who had sent it. Sighing when he saw George Blanchard's name, he read, "Want to schedule a couple of set visits over the next two weeks. Call me."

"Everything all right?" Dani asked as he slipped the phone back into his pocket.

"Yeah," Adam said, not wanting to talk about it.

He knew what George wanted, of course, and he was only going to get it over Adam's dead body. He was not going to allow Dani to be exploited. And if people thought this reality series was exploitative, then they missed the point. As for George, he knew what a guy like him could promise a young actress. But Adam didn't think Dani would fall for his promises. She wasn't an actress for one thing. And being constantly naked around all kinds of people had taught her to keep her guard up. Adam had warned her about George, and he would do so again before any set visits. He was confident that she would be just fine.

Before Adam could even question himself as to why he felt so protective of Dani, they turned a corner and found themselves just outside the Student Union building.

"Let's go around to the other entrance," Adam said.

Michael and Dani gave him a questioning look.

"That's the door you'd go in if you were coming from your dorms."

"Oh," Dani said.

Once they got around to the other side, Adam stood right in front of the door and got a shot of Dani and Michael approaching. They walked at least a full yard away from each other.

"Don't you think you should walk closer together?" Adam asked when they got to him.

Dani and Michael looked at each other and shrugged.

"You think we should hold hands?" Michael asked.

"No." Adam hoped his answer didn't seem too abrupt. "This episode will air early, so we've got to make it look like the two of you just met."

"OK," Michael said.

The two of them walked toward the dorms about fifty yards before Adam called for them to stop. They walked toward the Student Union closer together this time, both of them carrying their Kindle cases in their left hands. It almost looked like they were carrying Bibles, which was appropriate considering where they were going. They both wore neutral expressions and didn't speak.

"Cut," Adam said when they got within a few yards of the doors. "How about you go back and do it again, except this time, look happy to be here."

Dani sighed, but Michael said, "Sorry. It's just, I don't know what to expect in there."

"It's all right," Adam said. "Don't worry about it."

The third shot of them approaching the building was better. Adam had them stop at the threshold and wait for him to get set up inside. The people around them, the majority of them faculty and staff as the students were still arriving on campus, didn't seem to know what to do.

Many of them just stopped and looked at the two naked people. Adam wished there was a more organic way to get the shots he wanted, but when he was a one-man crew, this was the way it had to be. Seeing all the people standing around outside through the glass, Adam stalked back out and told Dani and Michael to back up a few hundred feet and do the walk again just so the crowd would disperse, either by entering the building or by going on their merry ways. Adam watched Dani and Michael walk to a point about a hundred feet away and stop. They stayed there for a moment until most of the crowd around the door finally walked into the building and streamed past Adam and his camera. A few of them turned into the Bistro which was open for coffee and donuts. Most of the rest of them continued toward the ballroom where the church service was to be held. He checked his phone and saw that they only had five minutes left until the service was scheduled to start. So much for getting there early like he'd planned.

20

Dani

Although Dani had stopped caring what others thought of her and her constant nudity months ago, she still had trepidations about walking naked into a church service after her experience last April. The man who was minister then seemed to have changed his message on the fly in order to single her out and to make her feel like being there in her natural state was one of the worst things she could have done. She knew, of course, that the university had a new Christian chaplain and that the minister from last spring would be somewhere else now. Dani had been alone when she walked into that previous service. Would walking in next to a naked man draw even more criticism? Would the churchgoers assume they were fornicating, since seemingly everyone associated nudity with sex? That previous service had been in the evening, with sparse attendance. This was a Sunday morning, and she expected a bigger crowd even if all the students hadn't yet made it back to campus for the new semester. She had left that previous service early, without talking to a single person. Dani had no idea how long Adam would want them to stay today after the service ended.

"I want to get the reactions of people," Adam told her, "so when we get there, I want you to just walk right on in. I'll be behind you with the camera. There will be two seats reserved for you down the middle aisle, third row from the front on your right."

They were already inside the Student Union Building, standing at the foot of the large stairwell that led up to the second floor.

"Why so close to the front?" Michael asked.

Adam shrugged. "That's just where they're putting you."

"Do you remember that first shoot we did?" Dani asked. "At the grocery store. And then at the mall with Sam. You had assistants going around getting people to sign releases."

"We don't need to do that on campus," Adam replied as he made some adjustments to his camera. "If they are affiliated with the university, either faculty, staff, or student, then they've already signed a release."

Dani had asked the question, hoping to get Adam to reconsider his "getting people's reactions" idea, but she had seen enough shoots on campus so far to know that he hadn't had anyone here sign a release.

"But how do you know everyone in the service is affiliated with the university?"

"Because they'd go to a real church if they weren't." Adam checked the time on his phone and looked back up at them. "Let's go."

Dani sighed and walked up the stairs with Michael beside her. The ballroom doors were propped open when they arrived. The service hadn't started yet, and large groups were standing around in various areas of the ballroom, talking and socializing. The chatter of the group nearest the doors came to an abrupt stop as soon and Dani and Michael walked in. The eyes of the ones facing the doorway widened, and the heads of the people facing away turned to look at them. The expressions on their faces gave Dani the impression that they were all thinking, *What are THEY doing here?* It was the same way she felt last spring when she walked into this room, although that time, she had arrived late, sat at the back, and left early, so that the total number of people who had seen her had been smaller than the group now gawking at her and Michael.

"Just keep walking," Michael whispered to her.

It was only then that she realized she had stopped. Taking a deep breath, she walked forward down the center aisle created by the rows of interlocking chairs that served as pews in this makeshift church and toward the raised platform at the far end of the ballroom. Various musical instruments were set up on the stage, including a keyboard, a drum set within a glass enclosure, and two guitars, along with an array of amplifiers and speakers on each side. The volume of the conversation throughout the ballroom lowered to a whisper as the other clusters of people began to notice the naked couple. Dani and Michael found the two chairs with the tent-folded Reserved signs on the seats. Moving those to the floor beneath the chairs, they spread their small black towels on the seats and sat down. Dani crossed her legs and arms, although her crossed arms only served to push her breasts up higher. She wanted to hide, but she also wanted to be defiant. The defiance soon won out, and Dani dropped her arms to her sides, hands on her thighs. Michael seemed calm, but then again, he hadn't grown up in church and had no experience with how judgmental the people could seem.

Soft organ music began playing, and Dani noticed that a young woman had snuck onto the stage and sat at the keyboard. The small clusters throughout the ballroom began to break up as people went to find their seats. Three college aged guys walked onto the stage and took up their instruments. Once everyone was seated, the one with the lead guitar walked up to the microphone, introduced himself as Roger, welcomed everyone to the CVU non-denomination service, and invited everyone to stand. *Of course, they want us to stand,* Dani thought.

They sang three songs that Dani had never heard before in all her years of churchgoing, with the lyrics projected onto a blank area of the wall above the stage. Dani watched Adam walk around the ballroom as she and Michael mouthed the words to the songs, getting shots from every angle he could. Adam stepped up onto a corner of the stage at one point which drew a strange look from the guy playing the drums. The tempo of the third song was slow, one of those quiet, contemplative songs, and Roger finished it with a prayer. The rest of the band set their instruments down and meandered off stage as Roger prayed. When Roger said "Amen," he left the stage, taking the microphone stand with him, and everyone sat back down. A tall, thin man with graying hair stepped up onto the platform from the front row once Roger had completely vacated the stage.

"Thank you worship team," he said motioning to where Roger had disappeared with the Bible in his hand. A small microphone was clipped over his ear and around his cheek. "They're pretty good for only having rehearsed once together, right?"

There were murmurs of agreement from the crowd.

"I'd like to welcome everyone to the service this morning. My name is Don Haddon, and I am very happy to be here. Today is a beginning, and beginnings are exciting. A new semester is about to start. We just started a new calendar year a couple of weeks ago." He paused between each sentence, so the murmurs of approval and even an amen here and there were heard. "A new presidential administration is about to begin later this week." The murmur decreased, but the ones that remained were louder. "And, of course, today is the first Sunday service here in my tenure as the Christian chaplain here at Coachella Valley University. It's a fresh slate for all of us. Like they say about Opening Day of baseball season, every team is tied for first place. Everyone has high hopes at the beginning of any undertaking. So this morning, we are going to look at the beginning of all things and the hopes that God had when he created everything we see around us, including ourselves. If you have your Bibles, please turn to Genesis chapter one. The word Genesis means beginning, and you will find it at the beginning of your Bible. Verse one starts with 'In the beginning…'"

Dani's Kindle had come loaded with a copy of the ESV translation of the Bible when Dr. Slater had given it to her the previous spring. She had read from it occasionally, but not as often as she should. Of course, "not as often as she should" was the answer she always gave whenever she talked about reading the Bible.

The pastor read through parts of the first chapter of Genesis, summarizing the parts he didn't read. "'And God made the beasts of the earth according to their kinds and the livestock according to their kinds, and everything that creeps on the ground according to its kind. And God saw that it was good.' Verse 26, 'Then God said, "Let us make man in our image, after our likeness. And let them have dominion over the fish of the sea and over the birds of the heavens and over the livestock and over all the earth and over every creeping thing that creeps on the earth."' Verse 27, 'So God created man in his own image, in the image of God he created him, male and female he created them.'"

The pastor paused there for effect. "'In the image of God.' 'Let us make man in our image, after our likeness.' This may be the most significant passage in the Bible. We, you and me, are not just another species of animal somehow gifted with intelligence. We are created by God in his image. You might say that we are self-portraits of God, and we were given dominion over the rest of creation. This is the basis of our relationship with God, a relationship that is detailed throughout the rest of the Bible. Continuing on to verse 31, 'And God saw everything that he had made, and behold, it was very good.' You'll notice that back in verse 25, before God created man, he saw that what he created was good. It was only after man and woman were created that it became '*very* good'."

The pastor continued onto chapter two where, he said, the narrative backtracks to give a more descriptive account of the creation of both man and woman. As he talked, Dani scanned down to the end of the chapter and saw the last verse: "And the man and his wife were both naked and were not ashamed." What was the pastor going to say when he got to that verse? Thankfully, he associated the nakedness of Adam and Eve with creation being "very good" and that that nakedness was very important in the relationship between man and wife and God, but he didn't call any attention to her or Michael. Adam was still moving around with his camera always running, getting different shots of the pastor and of Dani and Michael sitting in the crowd.

"Moving on to Chapter Three," the pastor said.

He read the paragraph about Eve's encounter with the serpent, eating the fruit from the Tree of Knowledge, and sharing that fruit with Adam without much comment.

"Verse 7, 'Then the eyes of both were opened, and they knew that they were naked. And they sewed fig leaves together and made themselves loincloths.' They knew they they were naked. I've often contemplated this passage. They knew that they were naked. When they made themselves loincloths, who were they hiding themselves from? They were so used to one another's company, that I don't think they were hiding from each other. The text says that they acted together to make those loincloths. There was no one else there. Except God. God was there. And as we will see from verse 8, he often walked in the garden and visited with them. I've often wondered about this knowledge or awareness of being naked when the concept of clothing hadn't even been thought of yet. That knowledge could only have been the shame of eating the forbidden fruit, shame that made them want to hide in every way they could hide. Hide from God. But they couldn't hide from God.

"Verse 8, 'And they heard the sound of the Lord God walking in the garden in the cool of the day, and the man and his wife hid themselves from the presence of the Lord God among the trees of the garden.' I want to go back to the beginning of this verse: 'they heard the sound of the Lord God walking in the garden in the cool of the day.' I want you to understand the gravity of that. Lord God, the creator of the universe, walked in the garden, talking with the man and the woman. Adam and Eve. Our ancestors. Us. Human beings that were created to have communion with the God of the universe.

"Now let's turn our attention to the next book in the Bible, the book of Exodus, chapter 33."

He paused to give everyone a chance to find that chapter before explaining the background, that God had just commanded Moses to take the Israelites out of Sinai. The pastor read some of the latter verses of the chapter, talking about how God had talked to Moses through a burning bush, a cloud, or a pillar of fire. But Moses wanted to see God face to face.

"Verse 20, 'But, he said, you cannot see my face, for man shall not see me and live.' Verse 21, 'And the Lord said, Behold, there is a place by me where you shall stand on the rock, and while my glory passes by I will put you in a cleft of the rock, and I will cover you with my hand until I have passed by. Then I will take away my hand, and you shall see my back, but my face shall not be seen.'"

The pastor paused. "We went from walking and talking with God in the garden to not being able to even look at his face. And this wasn't just any man; this was Moses, who had found favor with God. Not even Moses could look at God's glory and live. The original sin in the Garden of Eden, and all the subsequent sin that resulted from that, has separated us from God in a way that he never intended in the beginning. And yet, we, all of us, still carry that image of God. It's almost as if the clothes we all wear, covering that image of God, symbolize that separation.

"But God sent His son, Jesus Christ, to earth to bridge that separation. He came and lived a sinless life and then offered himself as a sacrifice to atone for our sins. When he died in what was one of the most painful and humiliating ways ever conceived, the Bible says he was naked. When he conquered death and rose again, the Bible says he left the grave clothes behind in the tomb, which means, of course, that he emerged naked.

"We were made in the image of God. The image and likeness of God. And we spend our lives covering that image. And if we don't cover that image, in whatever context, we are labeled deviants or perverts or worse by people from all sides of society."

The pastor stopped and looked straight at Dani and Michael. "When I heard about the opening for a Christian chaplain here at Coachella Valley University, I immediately knew that this was where God wanted me to be at this time. I was already looking for a new position, and I knew that this was the place where society's views on always covering the image of God were being challenged by a very brave person. Two brave persons now.

"Society, of course, is objecting. I've heard that first brave young woman called a brazen exhibitionist, a harlot, and a prostitute by both secular and Christian sources. It reminds me of what young Joseph and Mary must have gone through. Joseph, betrothed to Mary but not yet allowed to consummate their relationship, and Mary, now suddenly with child. Mary was in trouble either way. Either she had broken the betrothal customs with Joseph, or she had been with another man. And Joseph, caught between a rock and a hard place. If he insisted that he had maintained the custom and not had sexual intercourse with Mary, then she had been unfaithful and why was Joseph still standing by her? People gossiped and judged without knowing the full picture."

He took a long pause, looking out at everyone in the makeshift pews. "I'm going to be honest with you. We have a pornography epidemic. And I'm not talking about in the world; I'm talking about within the church. And not just within the church membership. Within the clergy."

He paused again, as if to let what he had just said sink in.

"In one survey I've seen, 63 percent of pastors confirmed that they are struggling with secret sexual addiction or compulsion, including, but not limited to, the use of pornography. 63 percent. And what does it tell us that 63 percent of the people who are supposed to be guiding us have a problem with pornography? First, what is pornography? What is its essence? Pornography is a lie. A lie from Satan. It lies about how people look, how people act, how one can achieve pleasure with no responsibility, no consequences, no sacrifice, no patience, no kindness, no love. And how do you counter lies?"

He paused, and Dani heard a few people mumble "Truth."

"Truth," the pastor said, holding up a Bible. "Truth. Truth is not found in the rules of society, in legalism. Truth is found here, in the word of God. Over the next several weeks, we are going to look at that truth and explore a way to rob pornography of its allure. You may be surprised at what we find."

As the pastor closed the sermon by finishing the story of the fall of man, how Adam and Eve witnessed the killing of an animal to make skins to cover themselves as the first death that resulted from the eating of the forbidden fruit, thus setting the stage for generations of animal sacrifices to atone for sin, and the expulsion from the Garden of Eden, Dani was surprised to find a knot in her throat when she tried to swallow. Tears came to her eyes, and she had to fight from letting them roll down her cheeks. The sudden emotion surprised her, but the more she thought about it, the more it made sense to her. She had expected rejection when she arrived at the service and had instead found acceptance and understanding from the man she thought would be leading that rejection. He had even called her brave.

The pastor ended his sermon with a prayer in which he called for a return to God's original intention, fellowship with men and women, all of whom bear his image and likeness. The band returned to the stage during that prayer. The pastor then invited anyone who wanted to talk about surrendering or re-surrendering their lives to Christ to come talk to him in front of the stage. He stepped down, and the band played a hymn that Dani recognized, "Jesus, I Come". No one went to the front to talk to the pastor, so the service ended as soon as the song ended, with the worship leader wishing everyone a wonderful afternoon.

Dani was probably the first to stand up to leave, thankful that she and Michael had been given aisle seats. Adam had rushed from the side to the front of the stage and was now coming up the aisle, intent on following Dani and Michael. Dani got about halfway to the exit before she was stopped by a middle-aged man she had seen on campus before, probably a professor somewhere.

"I'm very happy to see you here," he said, offering his hand.

"Thank you," Dani replied, shaking his hand automatically.

"And you too," the maybe-professor said to Michael.

"Thanks."

The aisle was filling in now, making a quick getaway impossible. Dani noticed that a line had formed in front of her with people wanting to say a quick word to the pastor who had stationed himself right by the main exit. Dani wanted to be away from here, but she also wanted to thank the pastor. She reluctantly stopped at the back of the line and waited. Michael stopped with her.

"What are we doing?" he whispered.

She looked back and saw that he had his hands grasped together in front of his pelvic area, making him look awkward and embarrassed.

"I want to talk to the preacher," she whispered back to him. "You can go outside if you want."

"No, I'll stay with you." He dropped his hands to his sides and seemed to try to relax.

"Just act normal," Dani told him as people passed by them toward the exit.

Most of the people seemed to ignore the two naked people which suited Dani just fine. She saw a couple of ladies look at them and then quickly turn away. The looks from most of the men seemed to linger, especially on Dani. Those men ignored Michael for the most part.

Thankfully, the line moved quickly, and Dani saw the pastor shake hands quickly, exchanging very few words with each person as they passed out into the Student Union's main corridor. His smile widened when he made eye contact with Dani.

"Good morning," he said, extending his hand. "Don Haddon. You must be Danielle Keaton."

"I am." She shook his hand as she noticed that he maintained eye contact. "I wanted to thank you for the sermon."

"Well, I wanted to thank you for being here and say that you are welcome each and every Sunday. I hope to see you here again next week. I think you'll appreciate the sermon series."

"I'm going to try to be here."

"Good. And my door is always open. My office is just next door." Pastor Haddon pointed past Dani.

"Thank you."

Dani walked into the hall as Pastor Haddon introduced himself to Michael and told him the same things he had told her. Adam stood just past them, shooting the exchange at close range. She tried to ignore the various looks that the exiting churchgoers gave her. Some of them looked like they wanted to approach her and say something, but she turned away before they could make a move, walking toward the stairs and picking up speed when Michael caught up to her. The two of them scurried down to the ground floor, reaching the bottom just as Adam appeared at the top. He rushed down so fast that Dani was afraid he would trip and fall and crush his expensive camera.

"Let's head to the studio," he said. "I want to record your thoughts on the service while they're still fresh."

21

Michael

Monday, Martin Luther King Day, was busy for the resident assistants as it seemed that everyone took advantage of the holiday to get moved back into their dorm rooms. Because this was the middle of the academic year, Michael only had two brand new students moving onto his floor. He issued them their room keys and meal cards and gave them the tour and the orientation.

"Dude, why are you naked?" the second student, an athletic looking guy named Brandon, asked when he arrived at the RA's room. The first, a short lad with glasses and dark brown hair named Ethan, had been dumbfounded into silence.

"That's a good question," Michael said, trying to maintain a friendly rapport. "I'm part of a special program here at Coachella Valley University. He left it at that, and the two new students didn't offer any follow up questions.

During the tour, Michael noticed that neither student would look at him. He showed them the facilities on the floor and took them down the elevator to the lobby.

"Jesus, put some pants on," a guy waiting for the elevator on the ground floor said when they stepped out.

Michael wanted to tell the guy that he wasn't Jesus, but he ignored the comment and continued the tour, showing the new students the lounge, the TV room, and walking them out the back exit to walk across the courtyard toward the dining hall.

"You can go outside like that?" Brandon asked.

"Yeah. CVU is a very progressive school." Michael didn't know what else to say.

"Woo hoo!" a female voice called as they entered the dining hall.

Michael had to struggle to keep his mind on the task at hand, but he showed the new students everything he had been trained to show them.

"How does it feel?" the first student, Ethan, asked him when the tour was finished.

"Very liberating," Michael replied, although he knew he was lying. He was prohibited from wearing clothes under the terms of Dr. Slater's project, so the forced nudity took that aspect of liberation away. He knew that being the only naked guy on a floor full of guys would be difficult, and he had been getting scowls and frowns everywhere he went in the dorm.

He carried his Kindle case with him everywhere he went now since he could put his phone and seat towel inside. When he got back to his room after the tour, he opened his case to find a text message on his phone.

"How's it going Nudie?" Debbie had typed.

Michael thought about giving the standard reply and telling her everything was fine, but this was the girl who had promised to stand up for him. He really had no one else to confide in. Dani had done all this before and might commiserate with his difficult feelings. But then again, she might not. She seemed to love being perpetually naked and might just tell him to let everything go and just enjoy the moment. Debbie, however, had been with him when he had been challenged by the Bistro manager. If she hadn't been, he probably would have just meekly walked away.

"I don't know if I can do this all semester," he typed back to her.

"What, the RA stuff or the naked stuff?" Debbie typed back.

"Naked."

"What's ur room #?"

Michael typed and sent it, and she replied with, "I'll be right there."

He thought about texting back, telling her not to come, but just as he was about to do so, a guy came to his door, which he was required to keep open for the time being to make himself available for any assistance as the RA, saw him sitting at his desk, and abruptly turned and walked away. Maybe the guy didn't need any assistance. Maybe he was told that the floor RA was naked and had just come by to see for himself. But if someone from his floor went to an RA on another floor for help, how badly would that reflect on him? Michael jumped up and went to his door, but the guy was already gone. He thought about just walking the floor to make himself more available, but instead, he went back to his desk and his web browser.

He surfed Wikipedia mindlessly, starting with an article on naturism and clicking one link after another, skimming articles on various nudist resorts in California, Texas, Florida, and France. He went on to nudes in art and was in the middle of a short biography of the sculptor Bernini when Debbie walked in. He minimized his browser right away.

"What were you looking at?" she said with a smirk.

"Nothing."

"Yeah, right." She looked down at his lap. "I guess I'd be able to tell if you were looking at porn."

Michael looked down at himself, relieved to see that he was in no way aroused, and crossed his legs.

"I'm sorry," Debbie said. "It's just too easy to make you blush."

"Well, I'm already half embarrassed all the time anyway."

"Then why did you sign up for this?"

Michael shrugged. He had been asking himself that same question since his return to campus. He'd gone naked that first time just to see how it had felt for Dani and wound up running into her. His subsequent naked outings had been done in hopes of running into Dani again. When Dr. Slater tagged him for her project, once again, he agreed mainly to see how it had felt for Dani. And he'd be lying if he said he hadn't had romantic notions about Dani. But after seeing her with Adam as they filmed the show, he was beginning to think that Dani was still out of his league even if he was one of Dr. Slater's subjects just as she had been. How was he ever going to compete with a Hollywood television producer? And considering that Debbie was right here, why would he want to try?

"I thought it would be fun," Michael said to Debbie.

She smiled. "Then let's make it fun."

"How do we do that?"

"Well…. What's making it not fun?"

"People's reactions." He stopped and thought for a second. All the really negative reactions he'd experienced had come from either the manager at the Bistro or the guys here at the dorm. And all of them were male. "Guy's reactions."

"Just the guys?"

Michael nodded. "Yeah, so far."

Debbie walked further into the room and sat on the edge of his bed. "And why do you think it's the guys reacting so strongly?"

Michael shrugged.

"You're naked in a guys' dorm, so they probably think you're naked for reasons that you're not, right?"

"They think I'm gay?"

"Could be."

"But I'm not!"

"I know that. But *they* don't."

"Well, what do I do about that? I can't just issue a proclamation that I'm straight. And I have to keep my door open for two hours each evening as part of my job as an RA. So I can't really hide."

"You could make it obvious that you're not gay."

"How do I do that?"

Debbie held her arms up as if to say, here I am. "I am willing to volunteer two hours of my day to help them see that you are straight."

"You'd do that?"

"Sure. I can't think of a better place to study every evening. And I could bring some of my girlfriends over as chaperones. When these guys come by and see you with two or three hot babes in your room with you, they may start going naked themselves. And personally, I don't see any problem whatsoever with a college where all the guys are naked all the time."

"No, I guess you wouldn't."

Debbie smiled and stood up. "Then it's settled." She walked over to Michael, pushed his crossed leg off the other one, and sat down on his lap. "Since classes haven't started yet, I don't have anything to study."

"What are you going to do here for two hours then?" Michael asked.

Debbie put her arms around Michael and leaned toward him. "You like me, right?"

"Yeah."

"I like you too. And not just because you're naked all the time, although that is a bonus. I like you because you're not pretending to be someone else. What you see is what you get. Especially now."

"And the thing with Dave?" Michael asked, wanting to be loyal to his former roommate. "It's really over?"

"Oh yeah. We were never very serious to begin with, you know."

Michael nodded, recalling his conversation with Dave, about how he said he had been the one to break off the relationship and how angry he had seemed to be about the whole thing. He wondered what the real story was and if he would ever find out.

Debbie leaned in and kissed him, long and hard with an open mouth. Michael, realizing he was naked with an open door and couldn't handle this much stimulation, finally and reluctantly pulled away. They smiled at each other.

"Something seems to be poking me," Debbie said.

"You've had that effect on me from the start," Michael confessed.

"I noticed."

She looked at Michael's desk, found an old *Fangoria* magazine, and handed it to him. He used it to cover his lap after she got up, not without sneaking a peek at what she had caused. Walking to the window, she looked out onto the darkening campus.

"Oh my God!" she said.

"What?"

She motioned him over, so Michael stood up, still holding the magazine in front of him, and walked to the window. Outside was a naked guy walking away from the dorm toward the Commons. He had dark hair and glasses, and when he turned his head to look back at the dorm, Michael was surprised to see who it was.

"Ethan," he said.

"Who?"

"He was one of my new students today. Really shy and quiet." Michael did remember him asking what it felt like to go nude on campus. It looked like his curiosity wasn't quite satisfied by Michael's answer.

"See, you're inspiring people already." Debbie put her arm around Michael's shoulders.

22

Adam

Once the semester was underway, with all the students moved back into their dorms, Adam was finally able to get the production trailer / motorhome parked back in the lot behind Holcombe Hall, Dani's dorm. That was good for quick hair and makeup sessions on Dani as soon as she woke up and headed out for the day. They shot a lot of footage of Dani walking across campus and visits to the campus bookstore and the parking office. Even though she already had all her books loaded on her Kindle and she didn't need a parking sticker since the car she was driving was owned by the university, Adam had wanted the show to reflect typical college life as much as possible. Dani, of course, commented on how unreal their so-called reality show was, but Adam just shrugged off her complaints and continued with his pre-planned shoots.

Today, Thursday of week two of the semester, Adam and Cliff, another cameraman he had hired when Kyle was unavailable, were prepping a shoot in the outdoor sculpture garden next to the art building. Art students were carting their easels from the studio and setting them up in the large open area between the sculptures and the Commons. There just happened to be a two-foot-high pedestal near this open area, presumably for some future sculpture. Dani was stretching next to the pedestal in preparation of climbing up and posing.

Adam, not wanting to ask the art teacher to take time out of his day to come to the studio later, had asked him to talk on camera for a bit before the class started.

"What do I need to say?" the instructor asked as Mandy did a quick brush through of his hair.

"Just introduce yourself and talk about figure drawing in general and about taking the class outside. Whatever you feel. We'll edit it if you stumble over words or anything."

Mandy finished and nodded to Adam. Adam lifted the camera, started recording, and pointed to the teacher.

"Hi, my name is Matt Roth, and I'm a drawing and painting instructor here at Coachella Valley University, and this is my figure drawing class. Figure drawing is, 99.9 percent of the time, done in a closed studio, with access limited to only the instructor and the students enrolled in the class to protect the, what do you call it — dignity, I guess, of the model. Because the model is usually nude. Normally, the model always wears a robe when not posing on the stand. That's the standard protocol. But with Dani, who is nude everywhere she goes, things are a bit different. There's no need for a robe. I mean, why enforce standard protocols in the art studio when the model isn't following those protocols outside the studio? And with the weather here in Coachella Valley in January, why not just take the class outdoors before we heat up for the long summer. It's a very rare opportunity to draw a nude model outdoors, especially on campus like this. I'm sure we'll get our share of lookie-lou's, but Dani is used to that by now, I'm sure. And I expect everyone to respect the artists' views of the model and not break into our semi-circle here. This opportunity also gives the students a chance to work with a slowly moving light source, with the sun not staying stationary. I'll have to remind them all of that as they work on shading and capturing the cast shadows. Although with the short poses we are doing today, they may not get to shading. This is the first day this semester that we are drawing from the model."

He stopped and looked at Adam with eyebrows raised. Adam stopped recording and lowered the camera.

"That's great. Matt, did you say?"

"Yes."

"All right." Adam motioned to one of the RATV students he had hired as production assistants. "Jennifer here will have a form for you to fill out, just so we spell your name right on the show."

Adam checked the time on his phone. 11:06. Class was six minutes late getting started, which wasn't bad considering that the students had had to bring their easels outside and set up here. Matt had the form filled out in less than a minute and was urging his students to get out their newsprint pads for the warmup gestures. Adam was happy to see that Cliff was shooting everything. He lifted his own camera to his shoulder and started recording as well.

"Once you get set up," Matt was saying in a loud voice, "come gather behind me while I demo the first couple of poses."

The students, all seventeen of them, gathered around behind the easel where Matt had stationed himself.

"What I want you to see," he told them, "is how I capture the weight and gesture of the pose. My proportions will probably be close to correct since I've done this so long, but that's not what I want you to concentrate on for these fast gestures. I want your arms to get loose with big, broad strokes. I want you to see the model, where her weight is. Is it mostly on one foot, or is it more evenly distributed? Pay attention to the relationships between the feet, the pelvis, which way it's leaning, and the shoulders, which way they are leaning. Okay?"

The students nodded and murmured.

"All right Dani, let's do three one-minute poses. Since I'm drawing, can you just count sixty seconds each pose."

"Sure," she said and stepped up onto the pedestal.

"First pose."

Dani took a pose with most of her weight on her left foot, her right arm in the air with the hand flat like she was a waitress holding a tray. Matt talked while he drew, telling the students about every mark he was making. Unfortunately, Adam couldn't get a shot of the drawing pad with all the students gathered around, so he had to settle for a shot of the group of them with an elevated Dani in the background.

When Matt finally paused long enough to take a breath, Dani said, "That's been a minute and a half."

"Sorry. I talk slower than I draw. Next pose."

After the third pose, Matt told the students to all disperse to their easels, and Adam could get a shot of the page where the instructor had been drawing. All three figures were on the same page, side by side. He got a shot of it, figuring he might intercut the finished drawings with Dani's poses (anything was possible this early in production). Once the students were back at their easels, Matt timed Dani's poses, which started out at one minute each and then went down to thirty seconds. She took a variety of athletic poses that reminded Adam of speed skaters, javelin and discus throwers, baseball or softball players, and mixed martial arts fighters.

After about fifteen minutes of gesture poses which must have been like a cardio workout for Dani, Matt announced that they were moving into a twenty-minute pose. Dani took a simple standing pose with her weight slightly shifted to her right leg, her left hand on her hip and her right hand against her thigh.

"You should spend the first minute of this pose drawing it like you just did for the short poses. Capture the gesture. I'll tell you when the first minute is up, and by then you should have the entire figure rendered. Then you can go back in and refine it."

The drawing began, the sound of charcoal on paper drowned out by the sounds of being outside. Matt announced when the first minute was over and then began going around to each student offering suggestions and comments. Adam and Cliff kept shooting even though the whole class seemed rather dull for those not participating. He took shots of the passersby, many of whom stopped and watched the class for a minute or two. Dani seemed comfortable with the attention. She kept her gaze on a nearby palm tree and didn't seem to look away from it even when the onlookers numbered at least twice the number of artists drawing her. Adam shot so much footage that he probably wouldn't use that he was glad his camera was digital rather than one that shot on expensive film stock. But he kept shooting. He never could tell whether a particular shot might work well with whatever Dani said during the "stool session" about the class later that afternoon.

During the last pose of the class, a thirty minute one with Dani sitting on a stool that was perched on top of the pedestal, Matt approached Adam and said, "This is really amazing."

"What is?" Adam asked, pointing the camera at him.

"That we can get figure drawing out of the studio and out in the open. That people not in the class can see how it is conducted. See those two girls over there drawing in sketch books? They're not even in the class. I've never seen them before, so I don't even know if they're in the art program here. But there they are, drawing away. And it's all because of Dani. We wouldn't be outside the studio without her."

Matt walked away without saying anything else, to resume talking to his students. Adam paused recording and lowered his camera for a moment. Cliff was still shooting the passersby, many of whom just stopped and watched. But a few of them had their phones out, taking photos or videos of their own. Adam was about to raise his camera and resume shooting when he saw an unexpected, and unwelcome, sight. George Blanchard walked out the door of the art building, his eyes lighting up when he saw Dani on top of the pedestal. He stopped there, his gaze lingering on Dani for a long moment before scanning the rest of the scene and finding Adam.

"Shit," Adam said under his breath.

George lumbered toward him, and Adam kept his camera down even though he was tempted to raise it to his shoulder and resume shooting.

"Adam," George said, "how goes it?"

"Great."

George stopped at Adam's terse one word answer. "Sorry for the surprise visit, but I saw art class on the call sheet, and, well, I took a few art classes back in the day. So I thought I would drop in. I have to say, I never had a class like this."

George had asked Adam to submit call sheets with locations so he could keep up with the shooting schedule. Adam had been doing so, although half the time, they broke off and did something on the fly.

"Few have," Adam said.

The urge to mount the camera on his shoulder and start shooting, thus ignoring George, was almost overwhelming. Adam had to remind himself that George was the reason he even had this gig, so he needed to be respectful.

"So how is our star?" George said, turning to leer—look—at Dani.

"She is amazing," Adam replied, surprising himself with the word he had used. He had just meant to say she was fine. How did "amazing" jump out of his mouth?

George looked at him with what Adam could only describe as a shit-eating grin.

"Amazing, huh?"

"Not like that. I mean, she's a trooper. Does everything asked of her. For the show, I mean." Adam really needed to learn how to talk to George and people of his ilk.

"So we're going to have a hit on our hands?"

"If we don't, it won't be Dani's fault." And now he was throwing himself under the bus. He really needed to shut up.

Matt called out to the students, "Two minutes left on this pose."

Adam raised his camera, telling George, "I need to shoot the end of class."

"Go right ahead," George said, stepping behind Adam so he wouldn't be in the frame.

When the alarm on Matt's phone sounded, Matt silenced it and said, "Thank you Dani!"

Most of the students voiced some form of thanks, and some of them even applauded.

"Now, we are stopping here a bit early so each of you can take your easel and whatever else needs to go back in the studio. We'll have Dani back on Tuesday, but with a forecast high of only sixty-three, I think we'll stay inside."

The students packed away their drawing pads into their portfolios and started carrying their easels or drawing horses back into the building. Some of them left their portfolios leaning against the pedestal Dani had posed on while others tried to carry everything at the same time. Adam turned his camera's attention to Dani who had climbed down from the pedestal and was shaking her hand at the wrist. She seemed to be limping as she walked around the pedestal.

"You all right?" Matt asked her.

Dani nodded. "Hand and foot both went to sleep. It's an occupational hazard."

"I guess it is. You hold the poses so well. If you ever need a break early, you know you can ask for one."

"I know. It's all good though."

She saw Adam pointing the camera at her, and in a moment of defiance against the rules of shooting the show, she smiled and waved at him. Adam took that as his cue to stop recording.

"Are you all done?" he asked.

Dani looked at Matt, who said, "I'll see you Tuesday."

"Good," Adam said. "Let's get to the studio. I want to get your thoughts on the class while they're still fresh." And almost as an afterthought, he added, "You remember George Blanchard, our executive producer?"

Dani smiled at George and said, "Yes. How are you?"

"Doing great."

Adam turned and started toward the Radio and Television Building at a quick pace, and Dani fell in behind him, leaving George to either keep up or get lost on campus.

23

Dani

"It was different than day-to-day life. Normally, when I'm out, I'm moving, walking from one place to another. But in the class, I had to be still, up on that pedestal where everyone could see me, on display."

"Did you like that?" Adam asked.

Normally, Adam didn't ask many questions during these stool sessions and just let her talk about whatever she was thinking or feeling. Perhaps he felt the need to ask questions today because George was in the room, kind of like showing off for the boss. Cliff had stowed his camera and left. Mandy was still there in case Dani needed any hair or make up adjustment.

"I didn't dislike it," Dani replied. "Normally though, if I don't like the way someone looks at me, I just move along. Posing for the art class with everyone passing by and stopping or whatever they're doing, that wasn't an option. But I felt safe. I was up on the pedestal, and Matt was in charge of the whole thing. So I was fine."

As much as Dani tried not to, she found herself looking at George as she said the part about not liking how someone looked at her. George seemed not to notice this as his stance and expression never changed.

"But I love modeling for the art students. I'll probably keep doing it whenever I can, even after I leave CVU."

"You certainly hold a pose well," Adam said.

"Thank you." Dani talked more about the artwork done by the students and art in general. She kept hoping George would get bored and leave, but he stayed right where he was the entire time.

After what seemed to her like at least an hour, Adam called an end to the stool session. Dani stood and stretched before taking the towel off the stool and folding it into a small square.

"It's kind of cruel to take someone who just did a forty-minute pose on a stool and make her sit on another stool for an hour," she told Adam with a laugh.

"It's all for art," Adam replied, checking the playback on his camera.

"It's amazing that you're so comfortable like this," George said.

"You should have seen me ten months ago."

"Yeah, I read your book. Adam loaned me his copy. You're a brave young woman."

Dani grabbed her Kindle case from the table near the studio door.

"Have you given any thought to what you'll do after you're done here?"

"The plan has always been to go to law school somewhere."

"Pfftt," George said with a waving gesture, "so many more opportunities have opened up for you. You've got a look and a personality, and with this show, you'll have a name that people will recognize. You could go into television or even movies."

"I'll think about it. Let's see how this show does first."

George slipped a card out of his shirt pocket and pressed it into Dani's hand. "You call me whenever you like. I'll come to campus if I have to, and we can talk about your future over lunch or something."

"Thanks." Dani unzipped the corner of her Kindle case and slipped the card and the towel she had sat on inside before removing her phone. She saw that she had two missed calls and one voice mail from a local Palm Desert number.

Dani rarely got calls from local numbers here. Most of the people who called her were calling from back home in Texas. She had planned on making her escape from the taping by claiming to have a paper to write, but curiosity got the better of her. Clicking on the voicemail, she was surprised to hear Dr. Slater's voice. Even though Dani and Michael were both in one of Dr. Slater's classes, a class that had already met three times with Adam there recording a rather uneventful session just that past Monday, Dani hadn't talked directly with Dr. Slater in a few weeks.

"Hi Dani, this is Dr. Slater. I apologize for calling you on your personal cell, but I got some news that I wanted to share. At tomorrow morning's Board of Regents meeting, they will be taking up a resolution banning public nudity on campus. It seems that while nude women are tolerable to the powers that be, nude men are not. This is, of course, entirely predictable, but I didn't expect them to move this quickly. I thought you might want to know and to address the Board yourself since you did so admirably there this past June."

"Oh shit," Dani said when the message ended.

"What?"

She realized that Adam had probably never heard her utter a curse word.

"Listen to this."

She switched her phone to speaker, turned the volume up to maximum, and replayed the message. When it finished, everyone was silent for a moment.

"They can't do that, can they?" Mandy said.

Adam shrugged. "They can do whatever they want. They're the Board of Regents."

"But we have too much money tied up in this thing," George said.

"Maybe we should address the Board tomorrow too," Adam said.

Dani turned and walked from one end of the studio to the other. She had addressed the Board before during a disciplinary hearing regarding Dr. Slater, and it had been one of the most nerve-wracking things she had ever done, mainly because she had done so nude to make a statement that mere words couldn't have made.

"Do you have enough for a full season?" George asked Adam.

"I could cut together a full season just from Dani's stool sessions. But more is always better, of course."

"We should tell Michael," Dani said. "Unless Dr. Slater called him too."

George looked at Adam. "I told you no one wants to see a naked dude."

Adam ignored George and kept looking at Dani.

"I mean, he told me the first time he left his dorm naked that he did it because of me, to experience what I felt. If the Board is taking this up now because of him, they should hear his side of it."

"I agree," Adam said. "I'll call him." He pulled his cell phone out of his pocket and hit a few buttons.

"I was hoping for more than one season," Mandy said with a sigh.

Dani heard Adam talking into his phone but not well enough to tell what he was saying. Mandy was putting her things away, and George was just staring at her as he strained to hear what Adam said.

"We could find another setting," George said to no one in particular. "I mean, she doesn't have to be a student here."

Adam lowered his phone, clicking it off. "The whole point of the show was to follow a girl who had stopped wearing clothes throughout her day-to-day life. Where and under what other conditions can she do that? If she's wearing clothes when the cameras aren't rolling, then the whole thing becomes something else."

"If season one is a hit, they are going to demand a season two."

Even though Dani was more affected by the future of the show than they were, all she wanted to do was get away and be alone.

"I have to go write a paper," she said.

Adam touched her elbow and asked, "Are you okay?"

"I'll be fine. Talk to you later."

Once she got out of the RATV building and out into the sunshine, she stopped and took a deep breath. The late January sun on her shoulders gave her a sense of warmth even as the cool breeze caressed her whole body. She had never felt such things from the sun and the breeze before Dr. Slater's nudity project. How dare they try to take these things away from her! No, she couldn't have a defeatist attitude toward this. She would fight it. They would all fight it: Adam, Michael, Dr. Slater, and herself. Dr. Slater had suggested that she address the Board, and that's what she would do.

Once she got back to her dorm room, she had gotten herself so worked up that she couldn't sit down. After pacing the room several times, she had to talk to someone. Picking up her phone, she called Samantha who answered on the first ring. Samantha was the only person back home who knew what this experience had meant to her, so she made a good listener as Dani talked about what would happen if it was taken away from her. They talked for twenty minutes about the nudity project, what Dani should say in the hearing, and what she would do if nudity was banned while she looked at the lone outfit in her closet, next to her overcoat, the yellow dress she had worn on the flight from Dallas Fort Worth to Palm Springs and taken off in the airport parking lot because she couldn't stand to wear clothes a minute longer than she had to. After those twenty minutes, she and Samantha finally started talking about things and people at home in Texas, and Dani finally felt the stress and anxiety begin to ease a bit. They were just about to say bye to each other and end the call when someone knocked on the door to Dani's dorm room.

"I gotta go," she told Samantha.

"Okay. Call me tomorrow after that thing."

"I will."

Dani ended the call and opened her door, expecting to see anyone but the person standing there.

"Mr. Blanchard?" she said, unable to bring herself to call him George.

She closed the door just a bit and looked at him through the crack. He was sweating a bit from, she assumed, the walk over here.

"Hi Dani. I, uh, I got an offer for you. You like being naked here, right? And we all need this show. Some of us more than others. So if you want to go to dinner or something, I can make sure that this ban they want to implement goes away."

"Goes away?"

"Yeah."

"And how are you going to do that?"

George grinned. "Money in the right pockets can make anything go away."

Dani took a deep breath. "Mr. Blanchard, I want nothing more than to keep living my life the way I've been living it these last ten months. But I am not going to sleep with you to make sure that happens."

"Whoa, who said anything about sleeping together? I just said dinner." He shrugged looking up and down the hallway before continuing in a quieter voice. "I could help you with a career beyond this little reality show, you know."

"Like I said, I'm not looking for a career in movies or TV."

"Adam said he had enough for a full season. If that season airs on Netflix, and it will, I'll make back my investment. But you and Adam need more than just one season to really make something out of this. I would suggest you take this offer."

Dani looked around her room for anything she might use as a weapon, should it come to it. There was an ironing board and an iron that she had never used in the closet. They had come with the room. She could be in the closet in two quick steps and could swing the iron around into any intruder's head, if she had to.

"No thank you," she said, looking back at George. "I have a bit more self-respect than to sell myself for a shot at fame and fortune."

George sighed, straightened his dress shirt, and said, "Suit yourself. It was nice knowing you. Speaking of selling your body, I'm sure a lot of people will enjoy beating off to your TV show over the years."

He walked away while she was still too dumbfounded to come up with a worthy response. Instead, she slammed her door, and it was only then that she realized she was shaking. She looked out her window, wishing that it faced the direction of Adam's production trailer, wondering if George would go there or just head back to Hollywood or wherever he came from. Dani really wanted to talk to Adam, but she didn't want to face him if George was with him.

She sat in her desk chair and did a few deep breathing exercises to calm herself. Surely, George wouldn't go back to Adam after making such an ass of himself with her. Once she was sufficiently calm, she would get up and see if Adam had made it back to the motorhome behind the dorm. All she had to do was go down the stairs and out the door, and she would be there. She was just about to stand when there was another knock at the door.

Dani had visions of George, come back to get what he really wanted. Well, he wasn't going to get it. She retrieved the iron from the closet and held it in her right hand in such a way that she could swing it with its sharp point first when she threw the door open. Adam stood in the hallway. He looked at her face, down at the iron in her hand, and then back to her face.

"You know, the show would gain quite a bit of publicity if the main financier had his brains bashed in by the star. But I'm not sure it's the kind of publicity we'd want."

Dani sighed and put the iron back in its place in the closet. Adam stepped inside her room, but he left the door open.

"How did you know that was meant for George?" she asked.

"I saw George stalking away as I was walking back. It didn't take a rocket scientist."

Dani took a deep breath. "I don't have to tell you what happened."

"Not if you don't want to." Adam sat down in the desk chair that Dani had just vacated.

"Are you upset with me?"

Adam shook his head. "With you? No."

Dani sat down on the side of her bed. "Well, I'm sorry anyway."

"I should be the one apologizing to you. I knew something like that would come from George. He's got that reputation. That's just the

Hollywood system. You have to make deals with devils to get anywhere."

They sat there a moment, both of them silent, until Dani said, "What do we do now?"

Adam shrugged. "I'll shoot the hearing tomorrow and whatever happens afterward."

Dani didn't have anything to say in response. After another moment, Adam stood up, and Dani rose with him. She walked him toward her open door. He turned to her and said, "I'm proud of you. I mean, I'm proud to know you."

Without thought or planning, Dani rose on her tiptoes and kissed Adam on the mouth. It was quick, more like a peck than a kiss.

"Thank you," she said.

Adam appeared to swallow with some difficulty. "You're welcome," he said with a forced smile before walking away toward the elevators.

24

Michael

Michael felt strange sitting naked in a chair while Mandy blow-dried his hair and applied stage makeup to his face. It was going to be even stranger walking into a university Board of Regents meeting where people were dressed in suits and ties and him wearing nothing but a pair of sandals. At least Dani would be with him, wearing the same thing. They were in the Radio and Television building since it was closer to the Administration Building than the production's motorhome was.

They left as if marching into battle, Adam leading the way, followed by Dani and Michael, with Mandy and Clifford, the second cameraman, and three production assistants trailing behind them. Once they got to the room, Dani and Michael both signed up at a computer terminal to testify before the Board against the proposed ban on public nudity, where a placard next to the monitor specified that each witness would have only two minutes to speak, and then found seats on the front row. Adam, Clifford, and the two production assistants found seats at different locations, with Mandy sitting in the seat on the other side of Dani. Michael could see the camera unobtrusively between Adam's legs pointed straight at Dani and him, the viewfinder facing up at him. Clifford, he knew, was doing the same thing from a different angle.

Michael had been up past two AM the night before trying to write out what he would say to the Board. He had never been a big fan of public speaking, and now he was about to address a governing body of his university stark naked with multiple cameras recording him. He had almost decided to just not show up. Even now, the exit door looked enticing.

But he couldn't leave and disappoint Dani or Dr. Slater or Adam, although he thought that this hearing was probably a lost cause for them. Once a Board like this takes up something, they usually follow through on it, especially with something so out of the norm like going naked in public. He unzipped his Kindle case and took out a pen and the sheet of paper with his typed "speech". He knew he couldn't get through it all in two minutes, so he was going to have to make some cuts and adjustments. Reading it at what he hoped was his normal speaking speed and timing it with his phone, Michael came up with three and a half minutes. He'd either have to speak so rapidly that he would lessen the impact of what he was saying, or he would have to cut as much as a third of it. After crossing out a couple of sentences and eliminating some adjectives and adverbs in several more, he read through it again, coming up with two minutes and twenty seconds. That was good enough, he decided. They could just throw him out when he went over time.

The Board members filed into the room in one line and took their seats all at once, almost like a coordinated attack. As those Board members walked in, the seats behind Michael and Dani began filling up as well. Dani turned and was about to say something to the person sitting behind Michael, but before she could get a word out, the chairman called the meeting to order. He had the secretary call the roll and announced that all members were present and that a quorum was achieved. It was all very formal, which had Michael wishing he had stayed in bed longer as the minutes from their last meeting were approved. At least they had voted to dispense with the reading of those minutes. The chairman then announced that this was a special meeting of the Board of Regents to address an ongoing situation on the campus of Coachella Valley University, specifically the ongoing nudity of certain members of the student body as sanctioned and encouraged by a certain member of the faculty.

Michael glanced around at the room, seeing several faces he knew, including the manager of the Bistro and the preacher who had conducted the Sunday service he and Dani had attended. But he did not see Dr. Slater. He looked over at Dani who looked back at him and shrugged her shoulders.

The meeting continued with the chairperson announcing that they would start with several invited witnesses and then move to those who had come on their own and signed up to testify. Apparently, the invited witnesses were under no time limit whatsoever as the first person called was Lawrence Bach, the manager of the Bistro. He gave a fifteen-minute description on the encounter he'd had with Michael and how sales were down and customer complaints were up since naked people had been dining at the Bistro. Michael would have loved to ask some cross examination questions, especially since he knew he was one of the "naked people" in question, but he figured doing so from his seat would get him ejected from the meeting. The second invited witness was the new chair of the sociology department who talked about what a rogue Dr. Slater was, how her methods and research were out of the mainstream, never mentioning the journal articles Dr. Slater had told Michael she had already published.

The Board then called two pastors from the local Palm Desert community, a Catholic priest and a Methodist minister, who both gave mini-sermons on how public nudity led to pornography addiction and about the passage in Romans chapter 14 on how one shouldn't cause a brother to stumble which was somehow what nude people in public were doing to everyone else.

There were statements from two Board members, both of them negative toward public nudity, and then they called for the testimony of those who had signed up to speak. Even though Michael had signed up after Dani, he still felt relief at not being called first. That honor belonged to the university's Christian chaplain, Donald Haddon. The tall minister sat at the table and spoke clearly and forcefully into the microphone, stating his name and his position at the university.

"I am new to CVU, having just started in my position within the last month. Knowing that this university was where Ms. Keaton was attending nude, was being allowed to attend nude, had a large impact on my decision to seek and to accept the position here. In fact, I took less money here than another offer I had at a church in San Bernardino. I did that because I saw and heard what Danielle Keaton was doing. I think she's doing it for the right reasons. The Bible says that we are all made in the image of God. It's right there in the very first chapter of the very first book. Doesn't it stand to reason then that covering our bodies, and insisting that everyone else cover their bodies, is actually covering the image of God?"

Donald Haddon turned to the other two ministers and looked directly at them.

"You brought up Romans Chapter Fourteen about not causing your brother to stumble. What if the constant insistence on covering the human body, covering the image of God, is what sexualizes it, perverts it, and is what actually promotes pornography, leading people to it? What if this insistence on covering is what is causing your brother to stumble? I've said it before, and I'll say it again, we have an epidemic of pornography in the country."

He turned back toward the Board.

"Being an employee of the university, I was able to contact the IT department here, and they told me that the number of hits of pornographic sites by devices using CVU's Wi-Fi dropped nine percent this past December when compared with December one year ago."

"Your time is up," the chair of the meeting said, and Michael could see the little shining red light on the desk in front of Donald Haddon.

"That nine percent becomes even more significant when you realize that the number of students enrolled here increased by almost five percent in that same interval," Haddon said, ignoring the red light. "If the nudity of Miss Keaton and others on campus has had any effect, it has been in the reverse of what the other ministers who have testified here today would tell you. And if it is the reverse of what they would tell you, then this new ordinance or whatever you're calling it should be rejected. Thank you."

Haddon glanced over at Dani and Michael as he got up. The chairman sighed as he looked at his notes.

"Next up is Matt Roth."

The person behind Michael, the one Dani had begun to speak to, stood up and walked over to the chair behind the lectern. He looked to be in his thirties with sandy brown hair and wore a polo shirt and blue jeans.

"Yes, my name is Matt Roth. I'm the chair of the drawing and painting program for the art department here at CVU. I teach figure drawing, among other classes, and figure drawing uses nude models. It is essential that artists see and draw the human body in its undraped state. Even if they never draw nudes again, they need to know what's under the clothes as they draw and paint how those clothes conform onto the body. The way I'm reading this new ordinance, it leaves the use of nude models in class in an ambiguous state. The proposal prohibits nudity in any area generally accessible by students or staff. Does that include classrooms? If so, that would affect our figure drawing classes."

"It does not affect traditional figure drawing classes," the chairman said.

"But that wording is not there. Your saying that this ordinance doesn't affect traditional figure drawing classes doesn't mean a thing when campus police or lawyers read and interpret what this actually says."

"Perhaps an amendment is needed," the chairman said.

"Or perhaps this whole thing needs to be scrapped," Matt answered. "We have a very strong sense of freedom on campus. Intellectual freedom, artistic freedom, freedom of expression. If that freedom can be taken away simply because a few people don't like that it is being exercised, then we were never free to begin with. And that will affect everything at this university going forward."

"Thank you, Mr. Roth."

Michael saw that the red light was on. The art teacher got up and walked back to his seat behind Dani.

With a sigh that told everyone in the room that he would rather not call the next name, the chairman said, "Danielle Keaton."

"Good luck," Michael whispered as she rose from her seat. She grabbed her towel from the gallery seat and dropped it so smoothly and quickly into the seat behind the microphone before she sat on it that Michael suspected that he may have been the only person to notice.

"Good morning," Dani said in a cheerful voice. "It's nice to see you again."

The chairman gave her a forced smile and said, "Likewise."

"The last time I was here, I was arguing against any sanctions against Dr. Slater. Even though I was thrust into her project, I had grown to love the freedom that being like this has given me. And I'm not talking about the physical freedom of not wearing clothes, although that's part of it. I'm talking about the freedom from society's arbitrary rules and expectations that say we have to cover certain body parts or that we should be ashamed of them if they are seen by others. In all of the modern world people are forced to wear clothes whenever they step out into public, whether they want to or not. Except here. Coachella Valley University was a little oasis in the desert where a person could be free to be simply human, without any additives. I've been on a pretty fast track since I got here, taking classes in the summer, so my graduation is looming sooner than it otherwise would be. I've given a lot of thought to what life after this extraordinary freedom at CVU will be like, and, to be honest, it's something I look to with sadness. That sadness is even more profound when I contemplate the removal of this freedom, that future students would not have the option of experiencing the freedom that I have.

"In today's world, everyone is always touting minority rights. African Americans, Latinos, lesbians and gays and whatever other letters get included in that. But the smallest minority is the individual. And if we deny the individual a right just because others are quote, offended, where does that end? If I say that I think abortion is murder, someone will be offended. Do we prohibit people from saying that abortion is murder then? And how do you do that when the First Amendment guarantees each of us the freedom of speech?"

"But the Constitution doesn't guarantee anyone the right to run around naked," the chairman said.

"Maybe it should," Dani answered. "It does guarantee the right to life and liberty. The only limits on that are, or should be, when your actions infringe on the right to life and liberty of others. Merely not liking, or being offended by, the mere appearance of a person, not even their actions but just their appearance, is not sufficient reason to force that person to change his or her appearance."

"Thank you," the chairman said, and Michael saw that the red light was on.

"I'd also like to reiterate what Matt said, that if you take away someone's freedom just for exercising that freedom, then we were never free in the first place."

"Thank you Miss Keaton."

Dani seemed to think about saying something else but didn't. She got up and walked back to her seat. Michael's name was called, and he got up slowly, taking his towel with him but leaving his binder in his chair. His handwritten speech was in his hand. He spread the towel out flat on the witness chair and sat down. The microphone in front of him waited.

"Um, my name is Michael Cooley." He took a look down at his notes but had trouble making out his own letters. "I'm against this proposal. Obviously." A few people in the gallery laughed.

Most of what he had written was similar to what Dani had said, and he didn't think he could get it all out in the time limit anyway. So he decided to just wing it.

"I went out a few times last semester without clothes. I had seen Dani doing it, of course, and I wanted to know what it felt like to be so —" He thought for a moment. "It's hard to come up with just one word to describe it if you've never experienced it. Free, open, exposed, natural, pure, vulnerable —"

Michael looked up to see if any of the Board members were listening to him. Three of them were looking down at papers on their desks, but the others had all their attention directed at him.

"You really wouldn't know unless you tried it yourself. But then, you have all your trappings, this image you have to project to people here at the university and other places. You all wear masks, and you can't allow yourselves to go without them because of what everyone else will think. I suppose it's like a prison. And you want to stick everyone else in that same prison with you. It's really sad that you can't allow people who might be a little different to be their true authentic selves."

The light on the box in front of him moved from green to yellow. Michael wished he could say something profound, so thought provoking and so eye opening that it would make everyone on the Board look at things through different eyes. But nothing came to him. After a silent few seconds in which the yellow light moved to red, he said, "Thank you," got up, and went back to his seat in the gallery.

"Well, I sucked," he whispered to Dani.

"You did great."

"Seeing no more sign ups to testify, I'm going to adjourn the Board into executive session to discuss wording and amendments. And then lunch. We will meet back here at one o'clock for a reading and a vote."

The Board members all got up and started heading to another room behind the dais. Dani sighed.

"What's the matter?" Michael asked.

"Dr. Slater. She didn't show up."

25

Adam

When Adam checked his cell phone, he saw that George had tried calling him three times during the Board of Regents meeting. Talking to George was the last thing he wanted to do, especially after their last conversation about Dani's "cooperation", so he sent him a text, "Board will reconvene at 1:00 to vote." Adam was both surprised and pleased that no one had forced him and Clifford to stop recording the meeting, although he had kept most of his camera covered under his jacket. Between the two angles they had gotten and the video from the official university cameras that he knew Sylvia would give them, he should be able to cut together a compelling episode from this. Unfortunately, it might be the last episode.

Adam motioned for Clifford to meet him over where Dani and Michael were just getting up. Dani marched toward the exit door with Michael close behind. Adam had to rush to meet her there before they left the room.

"Where are you going?" Adam asked Dani.

"Dr. Slater's office."

"Why?"

Adam, lugging his camera equipment, jogged to keep up with her as she made her way toward the building's exit.

"To find out why she didn't show up for this hearing," Dani said as she stalked through the corridor. "You'd think this would be important to her since she's the one that started the whole thing."

"Whoa, slow down," Adam begged.

He had to resist the urge to grab her arm. Thankfully, she stopped and turned to look at him.

"You're angry," he said, feeling like he was stating the obvious.

"Yeah. She abandoned us."

"And you want to confront her about it?"

Dani sighed. "I don't know. I don't know what to do anymore. I mean, this whole thing is so ludicrous. Look at me. How did this running around naked all the time become so important to me?"

Adam looked to Michael who stared at the floor at Dani's feet. Mandy was following at a distance, in case she was needed to do a touch up for a shot, and Clifford had just caught up with her.

"Because you owned it," Adam said. "You owned it, and it became a part of you and brought you attention and fame and money."

"No, I would feel the same way even without you or the show or the book or the money. I'd still want to be free."

"Because you owned it."

"Yeah."

"So, if you want to talk to Dr. Slater, let's shoot it for the show."

Dani's shoulders seemed to fall, but she said, "OK," and started walking again, although at a normal speed.

"Hold up," Adam said as motioned Clifford to set up ahead of them and as he got his own camera ready to start recording.

Dani waited until Adam gave her the go ahead, and they all started walking with Clifford somewhere far ahead and Dani and Michael in front of Adam and Mandy.

"How about some conversation?" Adam called.

Dani glanced back at him with what Adam could only describe as a dirty look. Thankfully, Michael chipped in.

"What are you going to say to her?"

"That depends on what she says to us."

That was, apparently, all the conversation Adam was going to get out of them as they both continued walking in silence. There was only so much walking he could put into the show anyway, so he paused recording and lowered his camera. He moved off the concrete path so he wouldn't have to worry about removing himself from the shots Clifford was getting.

He turned his camera back on when they entered Carlisle Hall, having passed Clifford, and took shots of them going up the stairs and into the Sociology Department office. The receptionist smirked at the two naked people but then flashed a smile when she saw Adam with the camera.

"Is Dr. Slater in?" Dani asked.

"She is, but she asked to not be disturbed."

"I don't care about that."

Dani padded right past the receptionist with Michael at her heels and Adam following behind them. The receptionist started to get up, but Dani was already at the closed door to Dr. Slater's office, opening it without knocking and barging in.

By the time Adam caught up with everyone, Dr. Slater had already looked up from her laptop screen.

"Yes, I should have been expecting you," she said.

"Did you forget about the meeting that you called and told us about?"

Dani asked.
"No, I didn't forget."
"Then why didn't you come and say something to try to stop this stupid ordinance?"
Dr. Slater sighed. "Because this is still a scientific study. You may not officially be in it anymore, but Mr. Cooley is. And as the conductor of the scientific study, I can't interfere with the natural progression."
"What you're saying is you abandoned us." Dani looked at Michael, who shrugged. "You abandoned me."
"No, if I had abandoned you, I wouldn't have given you advance warning about the new proposal and just let it go through."
"You really thought we could make a difference?"
"You made a difference before."
"If they called a special meeting with a new ordinance already drafted, then you had to know that they already had every intention of passing it, no matter what anyone says."
"Well, did they pass it?"
"Not yet," Dani admitted.
"Why not?"
"Because the art teacher said the current wording might affect his ability to have nude models for figure drawing."
Dr. Slater's eyebrows rose. "So the testimony can affect the Board's vote."
"They didn't vote yet," Dani said. "They went into executive session to redraft the resolution."
"Amend it," Michael added.
"Whatever," Dani said, and Adam knew she wasn't in the mood for jokes. "They're still going to pass it."
"And you think I could have convinced them otherwise?"
Dani sighed, and her shoulders slumped. "I don't know."
Dr. Slater looked at Dani and Michael with a forced smile that Adam thought conveyed sympathy. "Please sit down."
Michael dug into his binder to find his towel, and by the time he did, Dani was already sitting across from Dr. Slater. Adam kept his camera pointed at all three of them.
"What am I supposed to do when they pass this thing?" Dani asked. "I only have one outfit here. Everything else I own is over a thousand miles away."
Dr. Slater looked toward Adam and his camera. "I'm sure you have enough money from your book and your TV show to get four or five changes of clothes. You shouldn't need more than that." She looked back to Dani. "You just don't want to wear them."
"I don't want to be forced to wear them. No."
Dr. Slater leaned back in her chair and smiled. "You've come a long way since that first day back in March."
"I guess so."
In the silence that followed, Michael finally found his voice. "If they

pass this thing, you don't expect me to keep doing this, right?"

"Of course not. I can't require you to do anything that is against the law, misguided as that law may be."

Michael sighed. "OK, good. I don't need an arrest record."

Dr. Slater laughed at this. "Actually, I have to be honest. I knew you wouldn't be nearly as welcome a sight on campus as Miss Keaton here. So much so that I didn't think the semester would end before something like this happened. I am rather stunned by how quickly they moved on it though. We're not even out of January yet."

"So that's it then?" Dani asked. "The experiment is over?"

Dr. Slater shrugged. "Maybe. Maybe not. We'll have to see what responses they have when certain things happen."

Dani leaned forward. "What things?"

"I couldn't say right now. We still don't how things will proceed."

Dani sat back again with a sad expression on her face, and for a moment, Adam thought she was going to cry. He felt an urge to try to comfort her somehow, to give her a hug and tell her that everything was going to be all right. But he was the guy behind the camera, supposedly a neutral observer of whatever the characters in his show were doing.

"I had been dreading the time I had to leave CVU and go out into the rest of the world," Dani said. "I guess I don't have to dread that anymore. Instead, I can dread tomorrow and get it over with."

"Do you want to go back to the Board meeting when they vote?" Michael asked her.

Dani shook her head. "No. I want to enjoy being outside for the rest of the day."

She got up and walked out of Dr. Slater's office. Adam stepped back to let her out and panned his camera to record her departure.

26

Dani

Dani spent the last afternoon that she could legally be nude in public on campus walking two laps around the perimeter of the university. Thankfully, she had been alone. Michael had, she assumed, gone back to his dorm, and Adam had not followed her out of Dr. Slater's office. She read about the results of the Board of Regents vote from an email she read on her phone that had been sent to all students, staff, and faculty explaining the new rule. The vote was 5 to 2 in favor of a new ordinance banning nudity in public places on campus but leaving professors the authority to allow it in their classrooms. Dani supposed she could go nude in Dr. Slater's class if she wanted to, but outside of nude modeling for the art classes, who was going to go to the trouble of wearing clothes to any class and then taking them off once they got there, even if the professor allowed it? The email said that the new ordinance went into effect at midnight tonight. After that, violators would be given five minutes to get dressed. If they refused, they would receive a citation for disorderly conduct.

It just seemed so unfair that something that had been normal on campus for almost a year would now draw a criminal charge and a fine. Dani thought of Andrew Martinez, the supposed inspiration for Dr. Slater's sociology study, and how he must have felt when both the city of Berkeley and the University of California at Berkeley both made public nudity illegal as a direct response to him. The freedom to be one's natural self had been stolen.

After her two laps, she walked through the middle of the campus, along the edge of the Commons. Everyone seemed to look at her with pity, and a few people commented how what the Board of Regents had done wasn't right. Dani smiled and nodded at the comments but didn't say anything beyond a simple thank you. She wondered what the authorities in Berkeley would have done in the early nineties if the person going nude in public had not been Andrew Martinez but a young, attractive girl. Would they still have banned public nudity then? Dr. Slater's position seemed to be that they wouldn't. Maybe that was the point of this experiment all along.

She wandered until she found herself outside the Radio and Television Building just before sundown. Shivering as the temperature dropped with the setting sun, she stepped inside and made her way to the studio they used for the stool sessions. As she had expected, Adam was there sitting at a sound mixing board with a camera set up and pointed at the stool in the middle of the room.

"I was hoping you'd come," he said.

Dani looked around but didn't see anyone else.

"Mandy and Clifford went home," Adam said. "I know you have a rule about not being alone indoors with a man, so if you want to do this tomorrow…"

"It's fine," she said. "To be honest, it meant the world to me that you have always tried to adhere to that."

Dani stood there a moment, wanting but also not wanting to say more, before removing her towel from her Kindle binder, setting that binder on the table behind the camera, and taking her place on the stool.

"I did go back to the meeting and got footage of the final reading and the vote," Adam said.

"Did anyone else testify?"

"No. They didn't call anyone."

"Was Dr. Slater there?"

Adam shook his head. "I didn't see her."

Dani shrugged. "Well, let's get on with this."

Adam turned the camera on and said, "Action."

Dani took a deep breath and started talking. "When this whole thing started, I was scared and frightened and embarrassed all the time. We're all taught that our bodies should be covered at almost all times, so carrying on with my daily life while never wearing clothes took some getting used to. But I did get used to it. I got so used to it that it became part of my identity here and it made me dread the day I had to leave here and go out into the rest of the world where I would be expected to wear clothes. But leaving here and putting on clothes would have been my choice. That choice was stolen today by a bigoted and misguided Board of Regents who listened to the complaints of just a few people about merely seeing a penis, a body part that half of the population possesses. This little island of freedom from one of society's most inexplicable rules, that we have to always cover certain parts of our natural bodies, was ruined by these narrow-minded people who wield more power than they should ever have been trusted with.

"I'm angry and sad and…. I don't know. When the nudity project first started, I imagined that I would feel relief when it ended, that I could put clothes on again. But relief is not among the things I feel. I've worn clothes on my trips home, and let me tell you, when you experience not only the freedom of not wearing them but the freedom from caring about people seeing your body in its natural state, you really don't want to wear them again unless it's only for protection from cold or rain. I know most people won't believe me, but most people have never experienced what I have here at Coachella Valley. To see that taken away for no good reason is infuriating."

Dani paused and looked at Adam. "Is that too much?"

"Too much what?"

"Emotion."

"No. Raw emotion, especially right now, is good. People will want to see how you feel."

Dani nodded and looked back to the camera. She sat there in silence, trying to think of something else to say, but nothing came to her. Anything else she might bring up would just dilute what she had already said, so she decided to leave it at that. Adam seemed surprised when she stood up from the stool and folded her towel.

"OK," he said.

Dani heard her own voice as Adam watched the playback on his camera's screen. She was afraid that he would want to do a reshoot, but she could neither recapture the words or the emotions. It was like getting them out on camera had exhausted her, and there was nothing left. But Adam looked up from the camera screen and said, "Perfect."

"Perfect?" Dani said.

"Yeah. You put something out there that's raw and real. It's perfect for the show."

Dani nodded. She supposed that she should get going. It would be dark outside, and she felt drained.

"Do you want me to walk you back to the dorm?" Adam asked.

Dani, of course, very much wanted that. Her face must have betrayed that desire because Adam was quick to add, "I have to go back to the trailer anyway."

Dani waited just inside the studio door as Adam shut down the electronics and the lights.

"All right," he said, turning off the last light switch and opening the door for Dani.

They walked through the hallway and out into the cool evening together. Why did it have to be so cold on her last night of freedom?

"I have to tell you," Adam said after they had walked about a quarter of the way back to Dani's dorm. "I have enjoyed every minute of working with you on this show."

"I've enjoyed it too. I wish there was some way we could keep it going."

"I'm mulling over a couple of ideas."

"Really? Like what?"

Adam shrugged. "I'm still thinking of them."

Dani gave him a disappointed look.

"I'm just not ready to face not seeing you every day," Adam admitted.

"So there's got to be something I can do with this show to keep it going."

"I don't think I'm interesting enough for a whole series if I'm wearing clothes like everyone else. I mean, there's no hook. A show has to have a hook, right?"

Adam sighed. "Yeah."

They walked a bit in silence.

"I will want to shoot you wearing clothes on campus for the first time," Adam said.

"I still only have the yellow dress."

"And I can get some footage of you out shopping for clothes."

"So that will all be tomorrow. What then?"

"What do you mean?"

"I mean that tomorrow will probably be the last day of shooting. What else will there be to shoot after that?'

Adam stopped walking, so Dani stopped, turned, and looked at him.

"Nothing," he said. "There will just be a lot of post-production."

A cool gust almost caused Dani to shiver, but she willed herself to stay still. "So I won't see you much after tomorrow."

"Not as often, no." After a pause, Adam said, "But I'd like to keep seeing you in some capacity."

"I'd like that."

As cold as Dani was, she longed for Adam to take her in a warm embrace, but she knew that he would maintain his professionalism and not do anything that would even hint at trying to take advantage of her. It would, therefore, be up to her to make the first move. Putting her hands on Adam's shoulders, she pulled him to her and kissed him on the mouth. She felt his hands on the middle of her back, but he didn't pull her into him like she wanted. Ending the kiss, she looked him in the eye.

"I've been wanting to do that for a while," she said.

"I'm glad you did."

"You sure?"

Adam smiled. "Yeah. It's just, you're vulnerable, and I'm.... Well.... I don't know. You know?"

It had become plain to Dani during their interactions with George that Adam saw himself as a protector, even though Dani didn't need protection. She thought Adam realized this as well and was having trouble articulating what he was feeling. Hopefully, that would change tomorrow when she was fully dressed. If so, at least something good might come from the new ordinance.

"I think so," she replied.

Dani took his hand, and they continued walking toward her dorm.

"Of course, I would have been busy editing and other stuff," Adam said, "even if this hadn't happened."

"I know."

As they neared the dorm building, they turned so that Dani could go in the back entrance and Adam could go to the production trailer. They stopped near the threshold of the dorm entrance.

"Thank you," Dani said to him. "For everything."

"No, thank you. You have been amazing. If I can cut this right, this show could actually give me a career, even if it is only one season."

They both stood looking at each other. Dani wanted him to kiss her; she didn't want to have to take the lead again.

"Text me when you wake up," Adam said. "Mandy and I will come up and shoot you getting dressed and heading out to shop for more clothes."

Dani nodded and tried to say okay but got choked up on the word. Adam leaned down and kissed her. When he started to pull away, Dani stayed with him, rising into her toes to prolong the kiss. When she couldn't raise herself any higher, the kiss ended, but Adam had a smile on his face.

"Good night, Dani," he said.

"Good night, Adam."

27

Michael

After leaving Dr. Slater's office, Michael went back to his dorm. He'd had doubts about being able to continue the constant nudity even when he had signed Dr. Slater's contract. As a new resident assistant, he longed to be able to perform his duties without the sneers and whispers that he kept seeing and hearing. When Dr. Slater said that he would no longer be required to be nude if the ordinance passed, he wished he could go back and change his testimony to be in favor of the proposal. Dani and Adam were so against it and so upset that it might pass that he didn't want to be around them and either rain on their parade or try to put up a good front as they continued to talk about how awful the ordinance was.

It was not lost on him that when Dani was the only full-time nudist on campus, everyone seemed fine with it, even putting up with the occasional naked excursion from others like himself. But when Michael completely gave up clothes, at the behest of Dr. Slater, he experienced nothing but rejection. He had gone on his early excursions because he had wanted to feel what Dani felt, but he now realized that, being male when she was female, he could never experience what she did, not when people perceived the two sexes so differently. He had heard people say that Dani was brave, that she was fighting for freedom and for body image, that she should be admired for making herself so vulnerable. Michael had been asked to leave the Bistro, had endured criticism from people in his dorm, and now, after just a couple of weeks, had seen the rules changed to prevent him from doing what Dani had been doing for almost a year.

Michael thought about going back to the Board meeting to see the vote take place, but he didn't want to go back by himself naked, and he didn't want to get dressed until he was officially released from Dr. Slater's study, which wouldn't happen until the Board passed the proposal. He took one of the back entrances into the dorm building and climbed the stairs to his floor, something he had made a habit of lately. When he got to his room, without being seen by anyone, he fished his car key out of his desk drawer and took the same stairwell back down and outside. He popped the back of his Prius and took out his black suitcase. It had wheels, and he rolled it behind him back into the dorm. He pushed in the handle and carried it up the stairs rather than taking the elevator. It was light since it only had one set of clothes, the ones he had worn to drive here from home.

When he got back to his room with the suitcase, he felt a sudden need to call his mother. The nudity on campus may end today, but it would still keep going for him when the show aired on Netflix. Michael figured he would be in at least three episodes. He thought of the scenarios that could play out and didn't like any of them. His mother could find the show on Netflix and start watching it on her own. She'd expressed nothing but disdain for Naked Dani, but surely she would watch a show that was filmed at a school where her son attended. How would she react when she saw him naked on her TV screen? Would she scream or cry? Or would she close up in shock and refuse to speak to him or anyone else. Or maybe that disdain for Dani would keep her from watching the show herself until she got a call from one of her friends who had watched it.

"I saw your son naked as a jaybird on Netflix," the friend would say. And again, would she scream or cry or curl up in shock?

The only solution was to tell her ahead of time. The shock of hearing it from him weeks or months ahead of the show's airing would be much less than the shock of seeing him without any prior warning about it. Michael took his phone from his Kindle case and pulled up his mother's contact page. He had no idea how he would even broach the subject with her, but he had to tell her. And, he thought, it would be much better for him to tell her over the phone than in person. Taking a deep breath, he hit the dial button.

"Hey Mikey," she said, answering after two rings.

"Hey Mom, how's it going?"

"It's good. Are you calling to tell me that you are coming home for the weekend?"

"Uhhh, no. Not really."

"Awww, I wish you would, at least one weekend this semester."

"There will be spring break Mom."

"That's two months away though."

"It'll be here before you know it."

"You're probably right. I'm glad you called though. It's usually me calling you."

Michael wanted to tell her that since she called way too often, he had to balance by not calling much himself, but he restrained himself. "Yeah, well, there's something I need to tell you."

"All right."

Michael took a deep breath, tried to speak, and then stopped. How to even begin?

"What it is sweetie?" his mother asked.

"Um. Well, you remember Dani Keaton."

"The naked girl?"

"Yeah."

"Don't tell me you're dating her?"

She was always pushing him to get a girlfriend, so why would she assume he was dating Dani just because he brought up her name. "No, I'm not dating her."

"Good. You want to stay away from girls like that."

"She's actually really nice."

"And how would you know that?"

It was obvious from her TV appearances that she was nice, but his mother was just blind to that. "I've been sort of working with her."

"Doing what?"

"Well. There's this TV producer who is shooting a reality show about her."

He stopped talking and let the sentence hang there.

"And you are working for this producer?" she finally asked.

"Sort of. I'm in the show."

"You're in the show? With her?"

"Yeah."

"And why would this producer have put you in the show with her, out of all the students on campus?"

"Because I'm..." Michael stopped, afraid of his mother's reaction even over the phone.

"Because you're what?"

"I'm part of the same study she did last semester."

"The same study? What does that mean?"

He took another deep breath. She was going to make him say the obvious. "Don't be mad. But I've been living naked the last couple of weeks."

Michael closed his eyes and waited for an outburst or a gasp or something. But his mother was dead silent.

"Mom?" he ventured, but she remained quiet.

Finally, she let out a sigh.

"I thought I raised you better. What would your father say now?"

"He's not here."

"I wish he were."

"We've all wished that Mom. And if he were, our lives would be so different from what they are now."

"Are you saying you wouldn't have done this if your father was here?"

"No, that's not what I'm saying. And it's not as bad as you think it is."

"You're going to be gallivanting around naked on Netflix, and that's not as bad as I think?"

"No, it's not. First of all, it's for science. And second of all, Dani and I actually went to church together. When was the last time you went to church?"

"Church? Naked? Was it a cult? Was everyone else naked too?"

"No Mom, it was a non-denominational Christian service here on campus, and Dani and I were the only naked people there. But you should have heard the sermon. He talked about things in the Bible that I had never heard before."

"You were always such a good kid. Never drank, never did drugs, never got into trouble."

She was talking more to herself than to him now. He wanted to tell her he was still a good kid, that there was nothing wrong with being naked, that, until midnight tonight, it was legal.

"It's over though," he said, interrupting her.

"What's over?"

"The study or experiment or whatever. The university is outlawing nudity on campus as of tonight." He didn't know that for sure, but he was fairly certain that the ordinance was going to pass.

"I'm glad someone has finally come to their senses at that college."

"That means the TV show is over too."

"Good. What am I going to tell everyone when they see you on Netflix? That my son, the boy I raised, is doing nudie shows. How do I explain that?"

"The same way I am, that there's nothing wrong with the human body. That we were created in God's image. That's what the preacher said."

"I'm ashamed of you."

Michael felt like hanging up on her. But he couldn't do that. Instead, he just remained silent on the line. His mother was silent as well.

The silence was interrupted by a knock on the door.

"Mom, I have to go. Someone's at the door."

She didn't say anything.

"Mom?"

Continued silence.

"I have to go. Bye."

He disconnected, set the phone on his desk, and opened the door to see Debbie standing in the hallway.

"Everything okay?" she asked, looking at him with her customary elevator eyes.

Michael shrugged. "I was just talking to my mom."

The grin on her face was replaced by a more serious expression. "Oh. How did that go?"

"Not great. I told her about the nudity experiment, and she told me that she was ashamed of me."

"Oh. I'm sorry."

Michael shrugged. "I had to tell her eventually since I'm going to be in that show."

He realized he hadn't invited her in, so he stepped back and motioned for her to enter. When she did, her eyes lit on the suitcase on the floor next to his bed.

"You going somewhere?"

He looked over at the suitcase and shook his head. "No. I figured it was time to bring it up from the car."

"What for?"

Michael motioned for Debbie to close the door. When she did, he said, "The Board of Regents is about to ban public nudity on campus."

"Who?"

"The Board of Regents."

"Can they do that?"

"Yeah, they can do that. They're kind of like the city council for the university. If the university was a city."

Debbie gave Michael a distressed look and sat down on the side of his bed. "So what does that mean?"

Michael looked at his suitcase. "It means I'll be wearing clothes most of the time like everyone else."

"But I like you like this."

"I know. But I can't get myself an arrest record."

Michael sat down at his desk, turning the chair to face Debbie. She looked back at him with a serious expression.

"I like looking at you," she said. "And I like showing you off."

"Why?"

Debbie shrugged. "I don't know."

Michael sat looking at her, trying to forget the conversation with his mother and wanting to say something to Debbie but not sure how it would be received. When she continued to sit in silence, he finally gathered his courage. Whatever she said couldn't be as bad as the conversation with his mother.

"What am I to you? What are we to each other?"

Debbie shrugged.

"I like you," Michael continued. "I like you a lot. You being the ex of my roommate — former roommate — and best friend has kept me from seeing that. Or expressing it. Of course, my best friend hasn't spoken to me in a while. I don't know if it's because I'm doing this experiment or if it's because of you. But if we were to have a relationship or just go out on a few dates, I'd want to be like a regular couple and not have it based on some weird fetish like you wanting me to be naked all the time."

"I like you too," Debbie said in a quiet voice.

"And you'll like me when I'm dressed?"

"I've always liked you. Even when I was with Dave."

"Did that have anything to do with the breakup?"

Debbie shook her head. "No, I don't think so. We just weren't going the same direction."

Michael waited for more, but Debbie remained silent. He finally nodded. "OK."

Debbie smiled and then laughed. "Such a serious conversation while you're naked."

"Well, I'm always naked, at least for the time being."

"The first time I saw you out on campus naked, I was amazed at how brave you could be. It takes a lot to make yourself so vulnerable. I know I could never do it. And not because of my father and his campaign. I just couldn't be so raw. So I've admired you from the start of this."

"It has been tough do this around other guys. They feel threatened, I guess."

"Well, most of them know they don't look as good naked as you do, and they probably know it."

Michael smiled.

"You're so cute when you blush."

"I'm not blushing," Michael said, even though he knew that he was.

Debbie stood up and grabbed Michael's desk chair by the arm and wheeled him close.

"Yes, you are," she said.

Before he could protest, she planted her mouth on his, kissing him long and hard. Michael surrendered to it, enjoying the feel of her lips, thinking that he had never been wanted like this before. When Debbie broke the kiss, she backed away slowly, looking into Michael's eyes and exhaling slowly.

"Wow," she said.

Then she looked down at Michael's lap, and her eyes widened.

"I guess we better stop now before that demands attention. We're not quite to that point yet."

Michael, embarrassed, crossed his legs, trying to hide his erection. Debbie laughed.

"You don't have to hide it from me. It's flattering, actually."

"Well, I don't think you should see it unless, you know, we're actually doing something about it."

Debbie laughed again. "We'll get there eventually."

Michael got up and grabbed a towel hanging from a hook on his closet and put it in his lap when he sat back down. "I hope so."

"Me too." She leaned in and kissed him again, short and sweet this time.

"You had dinner yet?" Debbie asked him.

"Not yet."

Michael took a quick check of his email on his phone and saw a new one from the University administration. He felt nothing but relief as he skimmed it.

"I'm free," he said to Debbie after he looked up from his phone.

"What?"

"I'm free of this experiment. The Board voted to ban public nudity, so I can get dressed. Hell, I have to get dressed if I don't want to get cited."

"And you're happy about it?" Debbie asked as Michael threw his suitcase onto his bed beside her and zipped it open.

"I'm ecstatic. Do you know what it was like having to deal with guys in the dorm while I had to be naked?"

"They didn't appreciate it the way I do?"

"No, not hardly."

Debbie looked into the suitcase and said, "I thought you had clothes in there."

Michael pulled out the pair of jeans he had worn for the drive out here and started stepping into them.

"I only brought one set since I was supposed to have been naked the whole semester."

"So what are you going to do?"

"Buy some new clothes, I guess. Either that or go home and get more." But he didn't want to go home and see his mother any time soon.

He pulled the pants up, taking care to not get his pubic hair caught in the zipper, and grabbed the San Diego Chargers t-shirt from the suitcase. Debbie watched him finish dressing in silence. Clothes felt strange and foreign while also feeling distantly familiar. Once he had his socks and shoes on, he stood up and pretended to walk a catwalk for Debbie, modeling his new look.

"Nice," she said. "But it doesn't look like the real you."

"Maybe I don't want to share the real me with *everyone* anymore."

"As long as you share it with me as often as possible."

Michael smiled at her. "Okay."

He opened the door to his room.

"What do we want to do tonight?" Debbie asked.

"I have a car. We could go into to town, have dinner and see a movie."

"Sounds good to me."

He took her hand as they walked into the hall and toward the elevator.

28

Adam

Saturday's shoot was sad and lackluster. Adam and Mandy arrived at the door to Dani's room at 8:30 AM as had been arranged by text earlier that morning. She had already showered and styled her own hair, although Mandy did make a few adjustments with a brush and some hairspray. Dani wanted to go without any makeup just so viewers of the show would better see how sad she was, but Mandy wouldn't have it. Adam told her to use a minimal amount.

They started with a shot of Dani walking the hall from the showers back to her room. She carried a towel slung over her shoulder and carried her bag of shower items but was otherwise naked. She had splashed water over her head in the bathroom to make her hair look at least a little damp. Once back in her room, she did what she had never done during the production; she turned and began talking directly to Adam and the camera, with Mandy right behind him, wanting to stay out of the shot.

"So yesterday was the last day I could be nude in a public place. Technically, I shouldn't have walked from the shower back to my room without being wrapped in a towel since the dorm corridors are considered public areas. But if nobody saw me, there's nothing wrong with it, right? And if anyone did see me, it's not like they haven't seen me this way every single day for almost a year. This whole thing is frustrating and doesn't make any sense. Why can't I be free to be myself just as I've been doing for month after month?"

Dani sighed and looked away from the camera and toward her closet.

"So now I have to cover up my body, a body that was created in the image of Almighty God, and put on a disguise, all because a bunch of old stogies want to lord their power over us and remove any semblance of true freedom."

She stepped over and opened her closet door. Adam was able to get a great shot of the yellow dress Dani had worn on the plane ride back to Coachella after the Christmas break. Her winter coat was pushed to the side, so it looked like the yellow dress was the only thing there. After a sigh, Dani took the dress off its hanger and unzipped it. She stepped into it one foot at a time and lifted it up to her shoulders. She put her arms in and zipped up that side zipper.

"And here I am," she said, "the social conformist."

She slipped her feet into the same pair of flats she had worn many times and grabbed her hand purse.

"I guess I don't need this," she said, removing her little black towel from the bag and dropping it onto her bed.

Dani pulled at her collar as if she was trying to lift the dress off her shoulders. Adam felt like he should turn the camera off, but he also thought that these first few moments back in clothes were important to get on video.

"Since I'm now forced — I mean required — to wear clothes now, and since this is the only thing I have with me to wear, I'll be going to the store to get a few more casual outfits."

Dani let go of her collar and walked out of the dorm room.

"Cut!" Adam said, expecting Dani to turn around and come back.

But she kept walking all the way to the back stairwell.

"Dani?" Adam called.

Mandy brushed past him, saying, "I'll get her."

Adam was frozen. He wanted to go after her as well, but he didn't want to leave her dorm room open. And he didn't know if she'd had her room key in her purse. Thankfully, Mandy persuaded Dani to come back up to the corridor just outside the stairwell.

"Do you have your key?" Adam asked.

"Yeah."

He closed the door and then tried to reopen it to make sure it locked. Dani stood with her arms crossed and tapping her foot.

"Why are you in such a hurry?" Adam asked, raising his camera and hitting record.

"I want to get away from campus. Wearing this here just feels wrong."

As Dani turned and pulled the stairwell door open again, Mandy looked at Adam and shrugged. They both followed her, Adam with his camera paused and lowered. When they got to the bottom, Adam told Dani to wait in the stairwell while he went outside to get a shot.

"There's nobody here to see you," he said when Dani started to protest.

Adam hurried out the doors, knowing that Dani wasn't likely to stay there very long. He had barely gotten his camera up on his shoulder and switched to record mode before she burst out the door. Thankfully, Mandy had stayed inside to let him get the shot. Once Dani passed out of camera range, Adam turned off the camera and gave up. He might get a few shots of her at whatever store they went to, looking for new clothes, but he didn't think that Dani's demeanor would make for a complete segment.

Mandy caught up with him in the parking lot, and they both caught up with Dani at the car she had been using.

"Do I get to keep the car?" she asked from her place behind the wheel with the door open, waiting on them.

"I don't know. It belongs to the university, so you should ask Sylvia."

Dani sighed and started the engine.

"There's a Kohl's and a Ross about two miles away," Mandy said, looking at her phone.

"I'm just going to Walmart," Dani replied.

"The cost of the clothes can go on the production budget," Adam told her.

Dani shook her head. "If I'm going to be thrown back into my old life, I want to go somewhere familiar. And I haven't been to a Walmart in months."

"All right. I'll follow you in the Vette. Mandy, you want to ride with me?"

"Sure."

Adam figured he had enough footage of the big Crown Victoria on the streets that he could splice something in if he really wanted to.

The shoot at Walmart was short and uneventful. Since he didn't have a production assistant other than Mandy, he only shot Dani with no one in the background. And since she was fully clothed, she didn't draw any attention from any other shoppers. He got shots of her taking clothes into the fitting room and of her walking out of the store carrying three plastic bags full of her new outfits and getting back into the car.

When they got back to campus, Adam and Mandy followed her up to her dorm room. By then, Dani's melancholy had spread to Adam. He wanted to get her in the studio for a stool session and started to tell her that when he realized that it would probably be their last one. He wondered when he would see her again after today. There would be a premiere party of some kind when the show dropped on Netflix. But other than that, when would they see each other, with him in LA and her here in Palm Desert? Adam had known that he would miss seeing Dani every day after the show wrapped, but now that he had reached this point with the end of principal photography upon him, he was on the verge of devastation. His thoughts were preoccupied with ways in which he could keep seeing Dani on a somewhat regular basis if not daily when he should be concentrating on editing the hours and hours of video he had shot into coherent episodes.

"You want to walk over to the Radio and TV Building?" Adam asked.

Dani, still in the yellow dress, shrugged. "I guess."

Adam carried his camera in a backpack. He kept his hands on the straps as they walked. The desire to take Dani in his arms was so much stronger than it had ever been. Was that because she was clothed now and seemed less vulnerable, less in need of protection? The thought was ridiculous. Dani never seemed to need any protection. But why did this urge to jump her bones come up now and not before?

Dani walked to his left with Mandy ahead of them so that she couldn't see anything that might happen between them, and he took his left hand off the backpack strap, hoping Dani would take it, hoping that the kiss they had shared the night before meant something as special to her as he was thinking it meant to him. Dani didn't seem to notice his hand close to hers though, and he realized that she was still grieving the loss of something that had been so important to her over the last two months and that he should just back off. All of this uncertainty, trying to read another person's romantic interests which can be a mystery even with someone you think you know well, was why he didn't date much. He was also a workaholic.

When they got into the studio, Dani surprised him as he was setting up the camera by unzipping the dress and letting it fall to the floor. Adam watched her take one of her little black towels from her purse, spread it out on the stool, and sit on it. He only realized that he had stopped what he had been doing when Dani looked at him with one eyebrow raised, and he jumped back to work. Mandy stepped between them to touch up Dani's makeup, and Adam finished setting up the camera. Once Mandy was satisfied that Dani looked as good as possible, she stepped away. Dani adjusted herself on the stool and then nodded at Adam.

"And action," he said.

29

Dani

Dani was at a loss for words for just a moment. Adam stood behind the camera on its tripod, waiting. She knew that he could edit out any pauses or delays, so he was usually patient with her.

"Today was the first day I had to wear clothes out on campus. I started to say that it was the first day I had to wear clothes on campus since the beginning of Dr. Slater's experiment, but that's not really true. I could have gone without clothes before that, but I, like everyone else, chose to wear them. It had never even occurred to me before then to not wear clothes. It was unthinkable. Until Dr. Slater came along. Going without clothes everywhere I went was crazy at first, and doing it for Dr. Slater's little experiment was the hardest thing I've ever had to do. I felt like a freak, constantly embarrassed, shunned by people I used to hang out with, and generally regarded as something I am not.

"But as time went on, I was embraced by other people, seen as someone who was bravely embracing freedom. Every day there was some kind of new discovery I made about myself. When the experiment ended and I went home, I discovered that clothes really aren't that comfortable in a hot Texas summer. I came back to campus early and took the opportunity to continue living free from clothes for as long as I could. And I was afforded this freedom by the powers that be. But that same freedom was not allowed when someone else took it up. And since they couldn't tell him to cover up without telling everyone to, they told everyone to. Which seems fundamentally unfair."

Dani stopped for a moment. She wanted to say something profound and meaningful in what was likely to be her very last stool session for the show, but she felt like she was just rambling. Thinking of Dr. Slater's opening speech to her the day she was first called into her office, Dani started to speak again.

"When I was first recruited for the experiment, Dr. Slater talked about a guy named Andrew Martinez. He was known as the Berkeley naked guy. He started going to classes nude there back in the early 1990s. He wasn't hurting anyone, just doing his thing. And he became a minor celebrity for a while. But the people in charge didn't like it. Or they got tired of hearing from the people who didn't like it. I don't know. But it didn't take long for them to outlaw public nudity, and it didn't take long for Andrew to be arrested, which just seems so wrong, to change the law and arrest someone for doing what he had already been doing for months. It's amazing how little freedom we actually have in this supposed land of the free. Because if someone doesn't like what you're doing, they can work to stop you from doing it, even if it doesn't harm or cost them in any way. Andrew was arrested, and from that point on, he suffered some emotional and mental issues. He took his own life in a jail cell in 2006.

"The question I have is, did he go naked on campus because of his issues, or were those issues caused by the denial of his right to be a natural human being?" Dani shrugged. "I didn't know him, so I can't say. I was only ten when he died, but thinking about him still makes me sad because I can identify with him so much. I think I gained a lot more acceptance than he did simply because I'm a female and am somehow perceived as less of a threat than a nude male. People may scoff at that opinion, but it seems to have been proven by the Board of Regents here who have banned nudity on campus just as soon as a male began appearing nude in public regularly.

"And now, this whole experience seems to be at an end, and I'm feeling the loss. Yes, I've lost the freedom and the comfort of being in just my own skin, but that brought with it a lot of attention that I wouldn't have otherwise received. Like this show. I've developed relationships with the production crew that I hate to see end." She couldn't help but look right at Adam as she spoke. "But I don't see how the show can go on if I'm wearing clothes just like everyone else. My life was never this interesting before I stopped wearing clothes. Not interesting enough to keep shooting a reality series. So if that means this is the end of this, it means that the people I have seen and worked with every day will no longer be here with me every day."

Dani stopped, the knot in her throat telling her that tears were forthcoming. She didn't want to start blubbering on camera, but she was unable to hold them back completely.

"Taping the show was the only reason they were here, in Palm Desert. If there's no show, how often will I get to see him? Them, I mean."

She felt a tear roll down her cheek, ending at the corner of her mouth, salty and warm.

"When will I see you again after today?" she asked Adam.

He shrugged. "I don't know. A few days maybe." He paused. "I'll make sure it won't be long."

Dani nodded and smiled through her tears.

"Now that you're among the clothed, maybe you can come to LA."

"That would be nice," Dani said. "I've never been to LA."

Adam adjusted something on the camera, probably pausing it or turning it off altogether. He looked over toward Mandy who was sitting in the back corner looking at her phone and stepped close to Dani.

"You know, I was hesitant about dating anyone I was working with," he said. "But if the show is really over, which it seems to be, then I was wondering if you'd like to go out. Like on an official date."

"Yes," Dani said without a hint of hesitation.

Adam sighed with relief which made Dani laugh.

"Did you think I would say no?"

"Well, I didn't know. I'm good at reading people in general but not so good with dating interest when it involves me."

Dani slid off the stool and stepped into Adam so that he had no choice but to put his arms around her. He kissed her, and she kissed him back.

"Mmmm," Dani said when he pulled away.

"Nice. But you had better put your dress on before my hands go somewhere you aren't ready for them to go yet."

Dani couldn't help but smile. "That's one of the reasons I said yes. You are a proper gentleman."

"Humph. I don't feel like a gentleman."

Dani put her hand on his chest. "You are." She gazed into his eyes, and he gazed back.

"You are one in a trillion," he said.

Dani smiled at him, probably blushing but she didn't care, before crouching down to pick her yellow dress up off the floor where she had let it fall.

Later, as they walked hand in hand back toward her dorm and the production trailer, she said, "When are we going to do this date?"

"How about a week from tomorrow? I can drive out here in the morning and take you back into town, and we can just make a whole day of it."

"Sounds good. What are we going to do?"

"I have a few things in mind. You like movies, right?"

"Yeah."

"There's a place in Burbank I'd like to show you."

"What is it?"

"I'm not going to tell you ahead of time. It would spoil the surprise."

They stopped at the back entrance to the dorm which was near the trailer.

"You seem happier than you were a few hours ago," Adam said.

"Acceptance is one of the last stages of grief."

"Oh really? You didn't experience any distractions from what you're grieving?"

Dani laughed. "There may have been a little something to distract me."

"A *little* something?"

Dani just smiled at him for a moment. "You're leaving now, aren't

you?"
Adam sighed. "Yeah. I'll be editing video all week. And then some."
"All week?"
Adam nodded. "It takes longer to cut episodes together than to shoot them. You have to watch all the takes, decide which one to use and then how to splice them together, and to get it right, you have to watch it so many times. Very time consuming."
"But you'll really come back next Saturday?"
"Absolutely."
"OK." She looked toward the door to the dorm and then back at Adam. "Well, I guess this is it. I hope the editing goes well."
"Yeah, me too. My career is riding on it. On you."
Dani laughed and shrugged at the same time. "No pressure."
Adam laughed too. "The pressure is on me to make you and all of this entertaining."
"I know."
They both stood looking at each other. Dani looked toward the production trailer and then at her dorm room. "Which one of us is going to leave first?"
"Not me."
She stepped close and kissed him again.
"All right," she said when they broke away, "it's up to me to do the dirty work."
She walked to the door, opened it, and stepped inside. She looked back before she closed it. Adam was still standing where he had been.
"Bye," she said.
"See you later."
"You better."
He smiled.
"Now go get to work," she said before turning and walking inside.

30

Michael

Michael ignored three calls from his mother over the weekend before, on Sunday evening, he finally answered her fourth attempt.

"Hello," he said.

"Mikey, how are you?"

He had hoped she would apologize for saying that she was ashamed of him, but when she didn't start off with that, he figured that he wasn't going to get anything close to it.

"I'm fine."

"I've been thinking about this whole Netflix thing. Are you sure you're going to be on the show? Can't you convince the producer to cut your scenes out."

"I'm like the co-star of a couple of very important episodes. I don't think he can cut around me."

"Well, maybe we can get a lawyer to convince him."

"I don't want a lawyer to convince him. I want to be in the show. One of those episodes will be profound, I think."

"You're okay with the entire world seeing you naked? I just can't believe it."

"It's not so bad."

She then went on a rant about decency and how the world was going to hell, which Michael found funny since they had never been church goers the entire time he was growing up.

"I still love you," she told him, "but I am deeply disappointed."

"Well, maybe you'll get over it one day."

Five minutes after Michael had ended the call, he realized that he hadn't told her that he loved her back. He did still love her, but he couldn't help but be angry and frustrated with her, and he doubted that she would ever come around.

Monday, the first day of classes after the nudity ordinance, was a relief to Michael. Going to class with clothes on was a return to some semblance of normalcy. He still felt a bit strange walking into his sociology class fully clothed for the first time, especially when Dr. Slater looked up from the lectern and saw him. He smiled at her as he took his seat. She was the only professor he had who was always in the room before any of the students arrived. Every other instructor he'd had always breezed into the classroom or lecture hall a minute or less before the official class start time as if they needed to make a big entrance. Michael had assumed that Dr. Slater was always early to this class because her two big experiments, Dani and himself, were students, but perhaps she just enjoyed watching students interact as they walked from the outside and into the controlled environment of the classroom. She was, after all, a sociologist.

As soon as he sat down, Dani walked in wearing a plain white blouse and what looked to be gray gym shorts. It was obvious to anyone who saw her that she wore no bra. Why this seemed more provocative than the complete nudity she had displayed for ten months was a mystery to Michael. She looked toward Dr. Slater, and something passed between them, although Michael couldn't tell what. Dani ambled toward her seat next to Michael. They'd always sat together during the previous class sessions when they had been the only two naked students in the room.

"Hi," Michael said.

"Hey." She unzipped her Kindle case, pulled out one of her little black towels, and set it in her seat.

"What are you doing?" Michael asked as she pulled her shirt off.

"They said the professors can allow nudity in their classrooms, right? This is Dr. Slater's class."

She pushed down her shorts, stepped out of them, and folded them into her shirt and stored them in the book holder under her seat. As soon as she sat down, Michael looked up and saw Adam walk into the room with his camera on his shoulder.

"What is he doing here?" Michael asked.

Dani had been looking at her phone and hadn't seen him come in until Michael said something.

"I don't know."

She jumped up and rushed to him. Michael, feeling invested in the reality show since he was in several episodes, followed her. He could tell that Dani wanted to hug or kiss Adam, but the camera on his shoulder was in the way.

"This is a surprise. What are you doing here?" she asked instead.

"Not sure yet. Sylvia called and said that I absolutely had to be here."

Dani leaned in and kissed Adam's cheek. He smiled at her.

"I thought you had to be dressed now."

"Not in Dr. Slater's class I don't."

"I have made it known that anyone can be nude in any of my classes," Dr. Slater said. She looked straight at Adam. "Mr. Munch, I'm glad you're here."

"Thank you," he said with some hesitancy in his voice.

"If you want to stand in this corner, I'll get the class started. You'll want to shoot the beginning of it with reactions from the students, especially these two."

"All right." Adam looked at Dani and shrugged before retreating to the corner Dr. Slater had indicated.

Dani looked like she wanted to follow Adam for a second, then said to Dr. Slater, "What is going on?"

"You'll find out. Let's get started, shall we."

With that, Dr. Slater turned and walked back to the lectern at the front of the class. Dani stood where she was as Michael slinked back toward his seat.

"Dani, come on," he whispered to her.

Michael could see the genuine perplexity in her face when she turned toward him. He looked at Dr. Slater at the lectern who looked ready to burst if she didn't get the class started.

"All right," Dr. Slater said as soon as Michael and Dani were seated. "Let's get started, shall we." She walked out from behind the lectern and stood in front of it. "You should all be getting an email from the university this morning, if you haven't received it already, informing you of the results of last night's emergency meeting of the university Board of Regents."

In Michael's peripheral vision, he saw Dani checking her cell phone.

"This email," Dr. Slater continued, "is to inform everyone that the recent ordinance against public nudity has been rescinded."

There were some scattered murmurs among the students. Michael could see Dani scrolling through the list of emails in her inbox.

Michael shot his hand up.

"Mr. Cooley?"

"What does that mean, they rescinded it? Does that mean it's no longer in effect?"

"That is correct."

Dani was looking up at Dr. Slater now. Michael could detect tears in her eyes that seemed about to fall.

"Why?" she asked.

"Why what?" Dr. Slater said.

"Why did they pass the ordinance only to rescind it two days later?"

"The email didn't say. But why do people do anything?"

"Because it suits their self-interests," one student said from the back of the room.

"Yes, it does. Or, in this case, their perceptions of their self-interests." Dr. Slater looked right at Dani, seemingly talking just to her. "They passed the ordinance because, I'm sure, the minority of people against public nudity were louder and more insistent than those who are ambivalent or in favor of it. That minority convinced the Board that the university would be hurt in some way, either through academic reputation or financially. And the Board was convinced of this in spite of the rising numbers of new students and applications."

"Is that why they rescinded it?" Dani asked. "Did they come to their senses?"

"Unfortunately, no. They were shown the error of their way through other means."

"What other means?" Dani had her legs tucked under her, between herself and the chair, so she was almost standing.

"Financial," Dr. Slater replied. "They were informed that if the nudity ban were enforced, the university would lose its largest endowment along with the UHD camera security system, which is only on loan to the university."

"What endowment?"

"The one established by Evan Marley, the founder and chairman of the board of the Tech Warehouse chain of retail stores."

"And why would this Evan Marley withdraw the endowment."

"Because he's a big supporter of my research. And he's also my father."

Dani did stand at this point, and Michael heard the murmurs of shock from some of the other students in the room.

"So your father was the anonymous donor you told me about that first day in your office last March?"

"Yes. I'm always hesitant to bring his name up and give anyone the impression that I'm living off my father's fortune."

"But isn't that what you're doing if he's the main source of funding for your research."

"The funding is only a small part of it. The infrastructure supplied by the university is the most important thing."

"And you just used your father's fortune to make sure that infrastructure remains in place," Dani said.

Dr. Slater was silent for a moment and then nodded her head. "Yes, I did." She shrugged. "It had to be done."

"But why did you let them pass the ordinance in the first place?"

"It was part of the research, to see if they would go through with it. I always knew they would eventually. I hypothesized that they would tolerate a nude female but would act when a nude male was introduced, just as the board had in Berkeley in 1992. And I was right." Dr. Slater looked at Dani. "You don't seem happy."

"I am happy. I just— Going through the Board hearing and the vote and having to wear clothes over the weekend, that was rough."

"I apologize, but it had to happen this way."

Dani nodded, reached down and grabbed her rolled up t-shirt and gym shorts, walked to the door of the room, and threw them into the trash can there. Adam kept his camera on Dani the entire time.

Michael sat in his seat, afraid to look at Dr. Slater as Dani made her way back to her seat. Would she expect him to ditch his clothes too? After all, he had signed up to be naked for the entire semester.

"Mr. Munch, the rest of the class will be a regularly scheduled lecture. You're welcome to stay, or you can duck out now."

Adam lowered the camera, and Michael saw him exchange a look and a couple of mouthed words to Dani before leaving the room. Michael relaxed as Dr. Slater went further and further into her lecture. He didn't mind being naked here or out on campus, but he dreaded having to be naked in his dorm while also serving as his floor's RA, and he hoped Dr. Slater would release him from this. He was going to talk to her about it after class, after the rest of the students had left. The only problem with that was Debbie was supposed to meet him here after class so they could have lunch together.

Dr. Slater ended her lecture right on time, as if she had planned for the delay at the beginning. Dani jumped up and headed straight for the door of the class, probably looking for Adam. Michael remained in his seat until all the other students had left. Dr. Slater was still packing her things into a leather satchel. As he finally stood up, Debbie bounded into the room.

"There you are," she said.

Dr. Slater looked up at Debbie's greeting and saw that Michael was still in the room.

"Mr. Cooley. You have a question?"

He looked at Debbie and gave her a wave before turning back to Dr. Slater.

"Yes ma'am, I do."

He approached her desk hoping that Debbie would remain by the door to the classroom. She didn't.

"I was wondering about my part in your research."

Dr. Slater continued packing her things and said, "You signed a contract agreeing to remain nude for the rest of the semester."

"Yeah, but you said that was rendered void by the new ordinance."

"Which has just been rescinded."

Michael sighed. "Yeah, that's what I thought."

Dr. Slater clicked her satchel closed and gave Michael her full attention. "Your participation in this study has already proven invaluable, and for that, I thank you. I know that you haven't received anywhere close to the same reception that Miss Keaton has. I'm not going to hold you to the contract, if you want to back out."

"Can't you amend it?" Debbie asked.

"What?" Michael looked at her.

Debbie looked at Michael, rubbing his arm. "You like going naked. I know you do. And I love it that you do."

"But I'm the RA on my floor, and it's just— I can't do it while I'm working. The guys won't respect me or come to me with problems if I'm always naked there."

Dr. Slater smiled. "If you want to remain dressed while performing your duties as Resident Assistant, you may do so. As long as you remain nude everywhere outside your dorm for the rest of the semester,

I will consider your contract fulfilled."

"I'll make sure he stays naked." Debbie gave Michael a mischievous grin as she said this.

"I'd still get the sociology credit hours?"

"Yes."

Michael nodded. "OK."

"Thank you," Dr. Slater said as she picked up her satchel and started for the door.

They watched her leave, and Michael turned to Debbie.

"Thanks, I guess."

She kissed him and said, "You're welcome. Now take them off."

"Let's wait until we get back to the room. I don't want to have to carry them around."

Debbie agreed although she acted like she didn't want to. "But we'll stop at your room before we eat. I want a nice view with my lunch."

31

Five Years Later

The large smiling naked man made his way through the throng of people undressing next to their bicycles toward one particular couple he had spotted from a distance.

"You're Naked Dani. Dani Keaton, I mean," he said when he reached them.

The woman, as naked as he was and looking to be about five months pregnant, was stuffing her folded clothes into the backpack her companion was wearing. She looked at the naked man as she zipped the backpack closed, saw the microphone in his hand and the man with the camera behind him.

"I am," she said. "Or I was. It's Danielle Munch now."

"That's right. You married your show producer."

The man with the backpack turned to face them.

"I'm Adam," he said.

"Great to meet you."

They both started to extend hands to shake and then seemed to remember the pandemic of the last two years and withdrew those hands.

"I'm Tim, and we are shooting footage of the World Naked Bike Ride for Clothes Free TV."

"We've seen that before online. I guess that's why you look familiar."

"Yeah, we did a lot of stories about you and your reality show a few years ago. I just wish we could have had you on our show."

Dani smiled and blushed as she shrugged. "Life was so strange and busy back then.

"Yeah, I bet. I would be ecstatic if I could get a quick interview with you now though."

Dani and Adam looked at each other. Adam seemed to shrug as Dani nodded.

"Sure," she said.

"Awesome!"

Tim took a clipboard from the cameraman.

"That's Corky with the camera. He's not just the cameraman; he's also the director and producer."

Corky waved to them but kept his gaze on the camera's viewfinder.

"This is a standard release so that we can use the video on the show," Tim said.

Dani took the clipboard and read through the release before taking the pen from the top of the clipboard and signing her name. Tim noticed Adam walk his bicycle several yards away.

"You don't want to be in the shot?"

"I'm more comfortable behind the camera," Adam replied.

Tim shrugged. "All right." He took the clipboard back from Dani and put it on top of the camera case that Corky had set on the ground beside him.

Dani turned toward the camera, leaned her head back and shook her head so her hair would move freely. "How do I look?"

"You look great," Corky replied as Tim took his spot to the left of Dani. Corky held three fingers up and used them to count down.

Tim waited a full second after Corky's fist closed and then began.

"Hey, it's me; it's him; it's T - I - M, and you will never believe who I just happened to run into here at the Los Angeles World Naked Bike Ride. It's Naked Dani from Coachella Valley University and the TV show *The Girl Who Stopped Wearing Clothes*. Dani, how are you?"

"I'm doing great Tim. How are you?"

"How could I not be great at such a big naked event? Is this your first World Naked Bike Ride?"

"Yes, it is. I've been wanting to do it for a while, but the pandemic kind of altered our plans the last two years."

"It is good to be back, and the event here looks bigger than ever."

"Yeah, it's amazing."

"Of course, you're no stranger to public nudity, having famously gone naked your last two years of college. How do you feel about that experience now when you look back on it?"

Dani took a few seconds to think about it. "You know, I wouldn't change anything about it. It was such a special time, and it taught me so many things about myself. And, I think, it caused a lot of people to take a different view on our bodies."

"You wrote a book and starred in your reality show while you were there at CVU. Why did the show end after only two seasons?"

"There are a lot of reasons for that. Our main financial backer was caught up in the whole Harvey Weinstein Me Too movement and wound up leaving the industry altogether. And viewership for that second season dropped quite a bit."

"I thought the second season was great. It was even funnier than the first season."

"Thank you. You know, I saw a quote once that said something like 'Nudity quickly becomes unremarkable when generally practiced.' I think that applies to the second season of our show. We weren't going for comedy *per se*; we were just showing what being naked in a contemporary society was like. So in way, the drop in viewership proved that quote and the message that we were trying to get out, that our naked bodies really are natural and shouldn't be that big of a deal."

Tim nodded his head. "That's certainly a positive spin on it."

"Well, I've always tried to be a positive person."

"So you graduated from CVU?"

"I did."

"And were you naked at your graduation?"

"Not quite. I did wear the cap and gown. But nothing underneath."

"And how was that?

Dani took a deep breath. "It was both sad and happy. It was a big milestone. Graduating from college. But at the same time, it was the end of a freedom that I knew I would never get to experience again, the ability to live my life clothes free all the time."

"Well, we here at ClothesFree were always envious of you during that time."

"Yeah. After that, I went off to law school. I finished that degree last year. Now, I'm working for an entertainment legal firm and loving it."

"They don't let you work nude in the office, do they?"

"No, I wish. I do get to work from home a lot, and I'm naked then. Especially now, with the baby coming. Being pregnant in the summer, it's so much more comfortable to be naked."

"I'll bet. And your husband now was your show's producer?"

"Yes, Adam and I got married in 2019 while I was in law school."

"And this is your first child?"

"Yes, it is."

"Do you know what it is yet?"

"It's a boy."

"Awesome! Congratulations. I have to ask. How long did it take you to get comfortable wearing clothes again after you left CVU?"

Dani smiled and shook her head. "I don't think I ever got comfortable wearing clothes. Why do you think I'm here at the World Naked Bike Ride? It's a chance to be outside in comfort."

"Well, as a fan of yours since 2016, it has been a thrill talking to you for ClothesFree TV. Thank you so much for being on."

"Thank you for having me Tim."

The two of them looked at Corky who lowered the camera and looked at a few things on the viewfinder while listening to the headphones he had on. "Got it," he said.

"Awesome." Tim turned back to Dani. "Again, thank you."

"No problem. Enjoy the ride."

Dani walked her bike over to Adam, and the two of them disappeared into the crowd of naked people.

Acknowledgements

Sadly, Danielle Keaton and Coachella Valley University are both fictional. I have no idea how Netflix selects its programming in the real world, but in that fantasy world where CVU exists and Dani and Michael are able to live their lives without clothes there, Netflix selects its programming as described in these pages.

I'd like to thank author R Wellvyne for the editing job he did. His suggestions helped make this a better book. Check out his erotic novels and stories at www.mailgirlenterprises.com.

I'd also like to thank Eden Phil of AchingforEden.com for taking an early look at the theology presented in the sermon described in Chapter 20.

Huge thanks to my wife and family for putting up with me as I worked on this manuscript.

Most of all, I want to thank the readers. I promised a sequel to *The "Volunteer"* a long time ago. For those who hung around, here it is, finally. I hope you all feel that the return to Dani's world was worth the wait. Whether you do or not, thank you for reading.

Printed in Great Britain
by Amazon